Falling

Ellie Lynn

Opening Doors Publishing

Contents

Chapter 1	1
Chapter 2	15
Chapter 3	27
Chapter 4	34
Chapter 5	49
Chapter 6	65
Chapter 7	77
Chapter 8	83
Chapter 9	93
Chapter 10	97
Chapter 11	105
Chapter 12	111
Chapter 13	125
Chapter 14	133
Chapter 15	145
Chapter 16	151
Chapter 17	155
Chapter 18	169
Chapter 19	185
Chapter 20	189
Chapter 21	197
Chapter 22	211
Chapter 23	219
Chapter 24	227
Chapter 25	253
About the Author	265

Copyright © 2023 by Charity/Long
All rights reserved, including the right to reproduce
this book or portions thereof in any form whatsoever.

Opening Doors Publishing

www.ellielynn.com

ISBN: 979-8-9882609-0-5

This work is dedicated to my beautiful kids, friends, and family. Thank you for always supporting my dream.
And a special thank you to those who have served in our Armed Forces. May your sacrifice for our freedoms never be forgotten.

Chapter One

Maggie

April 12, 1946

You know that feeling when you miss a step on the stairs? That catch in your breath, that quickening of your heart. A second feels like an eternity as you imagine that lost step continuing forever. I had been standing on top of a cliff, gazing out at the beautiful landscape. I was secure, safe, my feet fully grounded in the reddish earth beneath them. Then everything changed. My feet kicked air, trying to find purchase and my arms flailed in the wind as if they might somehow find something to grab onto. As if, maybe, I could suddenly learn how to fly.

I am falling to my death. I'm surrounded by jagged cliffs, majestic trees, the blue of the sky, and the song of birds. I don't notice any of it. I don't even know if I am screaming. Do people scream as they fall to their death? All I can do is stare in horror above me. As I fall, I feel as though I am not breathing. I am frozen in shock, waiting for the end to come. It doesn't. At least not yet.

Time, it seems, is relative when one is about to die. As I am falling mere seconds seem as if they are a lifetime. A lifetime that I can suddenly and vividly remember. Does time stop for all people who are about to die, or just those who know they are? As I watch the face of the man above, simply staring at my demise, I notice a calmness in his eyes. How can they be so calm? How can he be so calm after having just pushed me off the cliff?

It was a rainy day on April 12, 1946, in Okmulgee, Oklahoma. I was twenty but lately I felt much older. I felt tired and worn out. The kind of tiredness that sleep did little to relieve. This was to be expected though, as the long war was finally over, and everyone was still reeling from the realities of how humanity had fallen so far. I imagine most everyone felt tired. People were broken. Everyone had suffered too much, and many were still recovering from the Depression and the previous war, the one that was supposed to end all wars.

Ellie Lynn

It seemed as though everyone at least deserved a longer break between the two.

People walked in the streets and shopped, neighbors greeted each other, lovers married and started families. Life just seemed to continue. I often wondered though if this was a cover. An act to mask the turmoil that surely gripped so many. Mothers grieved in private for their lost sons, secret beaus never came home, and returned soldiers pretended that all was well. The ones that were visibly broken, those who simply couldn't hide the trauma they had faced, endured the avoidance of eye contact on the streets or the occasional shaking of head or tongue clicking of sympathy, usually by older women. Women who had been here before. Women who'd seen this unraveling in their own loved ones.

I was lucky that I didn't have a family member fighting, besides a couple of distant cousins that I barely knew. My mom and I didn't wait with anxiety creeping up our backs and an all-consuming fear that we would receive a killed in action letter or that a chaplain would show up at our door.

Our neighbor hadn't been so lucky. I'll never forget the day I came home from an afternoon walk to hear those anguished wails coming from his house. Mom was over there trying to comfort him. Not long after, it happened again. Both of his sons were killed in action.

The war changed all our lives. Women took over men's work positions. On top of helping my mother mend and make clothing, I worked at the Glennan General Hospital filing paperwork three times a week. Glennan General Hospital was used as a medical facility for prisoners of war. I had gotten the position thanks to my Aunt Harry who had worked as a nurse there alongside the German POW doctors. This was a lower and less favorable assignment as most nurses in the Nurse Corps signed up to help American soldiers. Our soldiers.

Harry, despite being a brilliant nurse, requested an assignment to be closer to home. Closer to her husband, my uncle Liam. This posi-

Falling

tion was usually reserved for colored nurses, but since few colored nurses were allowed into the Nurse Corps, they also sent white nurses to work at the POW medical centers. Harry didn't care who she treated; a human was a human.

After the war, it's as if we removed a blindfold and we could now see human nature more clearly. Humans we learned could be driven to unimaginable depravity. Hunger, desperation, anger, and a sense of entitlement created monsters out of everyday people. And even those that didn't become monsters outright often turned a blind eye, which is its own kind of monstrosity.

It made me wonder if, under the same circumstances, I would be any better. Would my own sense of humanity prevail even if it meant my death, or worse, the death of my loved ones? It was a question no one really wanted to ask of themselves. With these thoughts and questions running through my mind, it was no wonder I felt so tired.

By late morning the rain turned to drizzle as I walked into Pete's Grocery to pick up some flour for baking with mom. Mom made the most amazing Irish soda bread that instantly reminded me of my childhood. Nothing smelled better on a chilly, rainy day, than freshly baked bread. It was also something that, with just a few ingredients, could easily be made; making it a cheap meal when paired with a simple stew. It was a meal I grew up on.

I felt cold and slightly damp from the rain and my brown shortly cropped hair curled wildly as it did on rainy days. I didn't look my best, although I remembered to put on some pink lipstick before leaving the house. Rain was no excuse for not trying to look presentable. At least that is what my mom said to me that morning. According to her, one must always look presentable. She thought a woman held power in her looks and could use it to her advantage. I suppose she was right, even though I would never tell her that. Instead, I ran back upstairs to my bedroom in an annoyed huff, slid the lipstick across my lips, ran my hands through my curls to untangle them, and pinched my cheeks to make them rosy. This was all the effort I would give it.

Ellie Lynn

I walked to the back section of the store for the flour, barely giving the few other shoppers a glance. My footsteps echoed in the quiet store, making a rhythmic clicking noise. My stockings felt damp and uncomfortable. I would most definitely take them off as soon as I arrived back home. I couldn't wait to put on my warm worn-out slippers with little faded rose blooms speckled all over them. They were a gift from my mom for my seventeenth birthday.

I picked up the heavy bag and had that tingly feeling of being watched. I turned to see a man staring at me. He looked at me intently with a serious expression as if studying me, trying to decide if he knew me or not. Or if he wanted to. Looking at him, I knew we never met before as I would have most definitely remembered him. He was one of the most handsome men I'd ever seen, with his dark hair combed back away from his forehead, brown eyes, and a tall, thin build. Something about him made me want to catch my breath.

I gave him a slight smile and nod and started walking towards the front of the grocer to check out. I tried to ignore the slight quickening of my pulse. Despite Okmulgee being a growing city, Pete's grocery was a small grocer on the outskirts of the busier part of town with its regular customers. Seeing someone new, and especially someone like him, felt exciting, although it had been a bit rude of him to stare at me like that.

"Excuse me, Miss," he said quietly behind me.

I jumped a little in surprise as I hadn't heard him walk up behind me. He was like a cat. Did that make me the mouse? I stopped and turned.

His eyes were still intent, but also held a hint of mischief in them.

"I noticed you and although this may be quite bold of me, I can't let you leave Pete's without at least knowing your name."

I stood stunned for a moment, unable to speak. This handsome man had not only talked to me, but wanted my name. My mom always said I was pretty, but when I looked in the mirror, I saw a plain

Falling

face with a splatter of freckles, brown hair that frizzed in humidity, and hazel eyes. Grateful that mom pestered me to put on lipstick, I wish I had taken more time with my hair. Although truth be told, it probably wouldn't have mattered given the dampness outside.

I answered with a nervous smile, "Margaret, Margaret Byrne. And you are?" I arched my left eyebrow feeling bold as well.

"Margaret." He said in a whispered breath, more for himself than in conversation with me. "It's nice to meet you. I'm George Harkins."

He extended his hand out and his smile **was** just heavenly. My knees felt a little weak. That always seemed like a silly cliché. Knees actu-ally going weak from a man's attention. But indeed, they did. I shook his hand and then stood there for a moment, waiting for him to say more, but he didn't. He just smiled at me.

"Well," I let out a bit of a nervous laugh, "It was nice to meet you, Mr. Harkins. Good day."

I turned and walked to the check out. He chuckled and followed me. I pretended to ignore him, even though I felt his presence standing a couple of feet away. My breath caught in my throat. The cashier rang up my purchase.

As I started to hand over the 25 cents for the flour, he stepped up next to me.

"Please allow me. Can you ring up my can of peaches as well, ma'am?" He said to the cashier a heavyset woman in her fifties or so who smelled slightly of peppermint, as he placed the can on the counter.

He grinned and winked at me. This man was a charmer.

"That is very nice of you, Mr. Harkins, although unnecessary. I can pay for my flour."

"It's George, and please, allow me, since you obliged me with your name. I would have been quite broken-hearted without it, and then have to scour the town in search of it. So, you have saved me a lot of time and a lot of work. The least I can do is buy you a bag of flour." He laid his hand across his heart in feigned distress, his brown eyes looked mischievous and beautiful.

I laughed at the ridiculousness of it all. He was indeed one of those dangerous men who women fall victim to all the time.

The cashier cleared her throat and I turned toward her. She obviously did not approve or appreciate George's charm. She had a job to do and wanted to get on with it.

I gave a slight laugh again as I agreed to let George pay for my flour. After he paid, George grabbed both the flour and peaches and walked towards the door. I felt frozen in my place. I wasn't quite sure what to do. I hadn't even thanked him yet and now he walked away with my flour.

He paused at the door, turned his head my way. "Are you coming?"

It was a simple question, maybe even a challenge, but I knew if I followed this man, my life would never be the same. It was something I felt deep within my soul.

Looking at him standing by the door, wearing a smile on his face, his brown eyes alight, I think I fell in love with him right then and there. It wasn't really a choice. I had to follow him. I suppose this was the beginning to my end. I followed him out the door into the blasted drizzle, which to my dismay hadn't stopped.

"Thank you, Mr... uh... George. Have a nice day." Then I reached for my flour, but he held it out of my reach.

"Will you get a cup of coffee with me? We can walk down to the diner. It's not far and I have an umbrella in my truck I can grab" George said.

"I'm supposed to get this flour back to my mom..."

"Just a quick cup, then you can deliver the flour post haste. I promise, on my reputation of being a gentleman, that your dear mother will probably not notice the extra time being gone. And if she does, I'm sure she won't mind, being that it's for a worthy cause." He said with a twinkle in his eye.

Falling

"Mr. Harkins, first, as I've just met you I'm quite certain I haven't heard of any such reputation in favor of you being a gentleman or not." I said in a haughty voice. "Second, what worthy cause would possibly require my having a cup of coffee with you? And lastly, you really don't know my mother. She fancies herself as a real Jane Marple."

He laughed. I believe he enjoyed our banter as did I. "Well Margaret, first off I believe I asked you to call me George, secondly, I'm sort of new in town and therefore I'm not surprised that you have yet to hear of my reputation but I'm sure you will. Which brings me to my next point. Isn't it considered a charitable and worthy cause to befriend newcomers? To help show them around and introduce them to others. It's the hospitable thing to do. Thirdly, we are getting soaked through in this rain so drying off a bit while enjoying a cup of coffee would be the sensible thing to do. While doing so, you can tell me who this Jane Marple is."

Then the man smiled. He bested me, and he knew it. I was secretly glad. He walked over to his truck and grabbed a black umbrella, then opened it, and held out his arm for me to take. I only paused a moment before linking my arm with his. We walked down the sidewalk and I felt the heat radiating off of his body next to me. A tingle of excitement raced up my spine. I had never walked down a sidewalk with a man before, uncle and school mates not included. This was romantic. He smelled slightly of hay and gasoline which was a surprisingly sweet combination. His smell seemed to envelope me and made want to lean in closer. I felt protected and beautiful walking with him.

The time it took to walk the block to the cafe seemed to pass in a blur. Before I knew it, we were there, and George was pulling down the umbrella and opening the door for me to walk in. George shook out the umbrella, sending little beads of water flying, before following me inside. We were met with that amazing mixed aroma of bacon and coffee. It made me breathe in a little deeper the moment we walked through the door. Corner's Cafe was a nice place with beige

Ellie Lynn

walls adorned with pictures of the town, and past and present important people in Okmulgee.

There were bright green curtains that looked clean yet slightly tattered, covering the windows. Shiny wooden tables scattered about, as well as a large bar sitting in front of the kitchen that seemed to greet you the moment you walked in. This is where most people liked to sit. My aunt and uncle brought me here several times when I was a child for breakfast as a treat. We always sat at the bar. It made me feel grown up sitting in the tall chairs.

George and I walked to a small table in the corner. Looking around at the mostly empty chairs all I could hear were the few patrons clanking forks against their dishes as they quietly talked. A rush of relief ran through me as I wouldn't want to sit with this man, this stranger, in a busy room. Privacy seemed important. Isn't it always that way, though, when you are trying to get to know someone you have an interest in? Asking and answering personal questions, flirting, smiling, showing in subtle and not-so-subtle ways you want to know more about them.

I played this game twice before, although they were boys and I just a girl. I instinctively knew this would be different. George was not a boy, and I didn't believe he saw me as a young girl. He held himself with a confidence, though, that belied his youthful appearance. As if he had life figured out and the years of experience to back it up. Yes, this was different. George was a man, and I was a woman.

Trying to back up his claim of being a gentleman, George pulled out a chair for me to sit before sitting across from me. No sooner had we sat down when a young waitress walked up to the table and asked us what we would like to order. I recognized her. Betty and I were once school mates. She being one of the popular girls and I a wallflower made sure we weren't friends. Once, she smiled and said hi to me as she asked Anna Beth to a small girl's sleepover at her house. The invitation not extended to me, my best friend Anna Beth, thanked her but declined the most sought-after invitation among the girls in our grade.

Falling

As soon as Betty left, Anna Beth turned to me and said, "The nerve of her! I wouldn't go without you." To which I replied she could if she wanted to, and it wouldn't hurt my feelings. We ended up having our own sleepover, just the two of us. I truly loved Anna Beth at that moment.

George ordered two coffees and then asked if I wanted to order anything else. After giving my negative reply, Betty glanced at me before turning around to leave. I saw the brief instance of recognition before she turned away. No greeting or acknowledgement of it, of course, but a small smile. It was better than looking straight through me as she used to in school. At twenty, it felt silly how that simple smile felt good. I shouldn't have cared.

"Do you know her... the waitress?" George asked.

"Sort of, we went to school together. Although we weren't friends. She was friendly with Anna Beth, who is my best friend in the entire world. But I didn't fit in with that group and..." I paused and gave a small, uncomfortable cough. I realized my rambling at the uncomfortable topic almost too late. It wouldn't have been with anyone else, but I wanted him to see the best of me. I didn't want to point out my shyness in school. Jane Marple became the perfect change of topic.

"Anyway, you asked who Jane Marple is." At his small nod, I continued. "She's a detective of sorts. A fictional one, anyway. My mom loves Agatha Christie's crime novels and Miss Marple is a character who is a smart, shrewd, elderly spinster. She is simply brilliant at solving crimes."

"Do you read these novels as well, then? Do you enjoy a good crime story?" George asked. I guess he picked up on my enthusiasm as I talked about Miss Marple.

"I admit, I do like to read them as well. I'm not as obsessed with them as my mom is, but I do enjoy them." I replied with a small laugh, as if he'd gotten me to admit something that embarrassed me. I wasn't, not really. It was just a personal and private hobby of my mom's and mine.

Ellie Lynn

"What about you George? Do you enjoy reading?" I asked.

"I read a little. I enjoy reading articles in Reader's Digest, the paper, you know that type of stuff. I mostly enjoy reading up on politics and current news topics. Now I'll admit I'm not much of a book reader." He pulled out a cigarette and a match. Before lighting it, he asked me if I minded if he smoked.

"Of course not." I replied.

Then I watched him light the cigarette between his lips, inhale deeply, and then turn his head to the side to blow the smoke away from me. He then leaned forward and narrowed his gaze as if studying me. I felt a little excitement as I waited for him to say something.

"Why Miss Byrne, you and I have discovered our first thing in common." He leaned back in his chair, wearing an adorable lopsided grin.

"Is that so, pray tell me sir what we have in common because I'm having trouble following you. All we've discovered is that I like to read books and you don't." I chuckled as my chin rested on my fist. I stared back at him intently.

"Well, you see, you like to read about crimes and me, well, I like to solve them. I'm a police officer here in Okmulgee." He winked almost triumphantly.

"Really? How interesting and exciting that must be. Have you been a police officer long? You said you were new here." His announcement surprised me. All the police officers I met always seemed a little hard, distant, and well, I guess authoritative. Which of course was probably how they were supposed to be. George, though, seemed so warm and approachable.

"Well, I must confess I'm not that new. I've lived here full time and worked at the police department for the past six months, but I used to visit here every summer growing up. I stayed with my aunt and uncle at their small farm, just on the outskirts of town. They both passed away about a year ago, a couple of months apart. They left me their farm and after coming home from the war, I knew here is where

Falling

I wanted to make my home." He said the word *home* as if it carried a weight to it.

He had been a soldier in the war! This shouldn't have surprised me as so many young men who were whole and capable fought in the war. My mind buzzed with questions I knew I wouldn't ask. At least not now. This explained him seeming older than he looked. A lot of boys left for the war, but only men came back.

"I'm glad you made it home safe." I said quietly and sincerely.

"Me too." He replied quietly as well. Then gifted me with one of his devastating smiles again right after taking another inhale of his cigarette.

Just then, Betty came back to the table with two mugs of coffee, a miniature pot of creamer, and a small bowl with sugar cubes. She deposited them on the table and then just as quickly turned around and walked away as my mumbled thank you followed her.

We poured cream in our coffee and spooned in sugar cubes. I noticed he took three cubes to my two. The clanks of our spoons against the cups as we stirred almost seemed comical. Or maybe it was the situation, the newness, the unfamiliar territory that made me want to giggle. More out of nervousness than any actual humor.

"So, Officer George, tell me more about yourself" I felt my cheeks redden a bit. Did I just ask such a bold question? My courage surprised me as did the calmness in my voice. I felt a little embarrassed at the way I said *Officer George*. As I deepened my voice to tease him I didn't know if we were acquainted enough yet for that.

George, thankfully, didn't seem to take any offense. In fact, he chuckled softly and seemed to enjoy my teasing. Then his voice became serious. "Of course. First off, I'm a terrible dancer. I also smoke a little too much. I've been told I sometimes snore, but only when I'm exhausted. I tend to make bad jokes during inappropriate times, and I really dislike custard. I know most people like it, but I find it disgusting." He paused for a moment with his eyes looking up as in real thought before continuing. "I'm also a terrible farmer, so I'm not currently growing or raising anything on my small farm. I don't really know the difference between a salad fork and a dessert fork, and I don't care for fancy dinners, anyway. I am, however, adequate at playing the guitar."

I stared at him open-mouthed for a second before my eyes watered as the deep rumbles of laughter escaped from my chest. Was this man delightful or crazy? I couldn't quite say, but the hilarity of it didn't escape me as well as the surprise.

When I finished laughing, he continued. "I always find it best to get all the terrible qualities out on the table to begin with. Then you can focus on all the good."

He said this so matter-of-factly, and I wondered if this same scenario played out before with other young women. If so, how many of them made some excuse and quietly left the room? I certainly would not.

"And what about you, Margaret ...Margaret...it sounds so formal. Do you by any chance have a nickname?"

"My aunt and uncle and well pretty much everyone but my mom has always called me Maggie."

"Maggie, I like it. So, Maggie, besides the fact that you read crime novels, have a best friend named Anna Beth, you don't mind small walks in the rain, and you bake bread with your mother, tell me something about yourself."

It suddenly struck me that I had absolutely nothing to say. What was I supposed to say about myself after he gave me his long list of bad habits and things he wasn't particularly good at? Do I blurt out about my frizzy hair, my nail-biting habit, my inability to be the perfectly docile female with no opinions whatsoever? Listing my bad qualities could go on for a while, and even if I took the time, I didn't want to divulge them. I suddenly realized I wanted him to like me.

I glanced down at my half-finished cup of coffee and knew at some point I needed to get the flour delivered back to mom. I'm sure she sat waiting for me.

I took a deep breath. "To be honest, George, I'm not sure what to say. The last few years have changed things so much that I barely

Falling

recognize the world we live in anymore, never mind recognizing myself. I guess I'm still figuring it out. I know that must sound crazy." Pausing, I closed my eyes in a sort of long blink as I thought about my next words.

"What I know is I enjoy having a cup of coffee with a handsome man, I enjoy baking with my mom and my aunt, I love going for walks on a cool autumn day when the leaves are falling, and I love to curl up with a good book before bed with some warm vanilla milk. I guess what I love and appreciate now is these simple things." My voice took on a nostalgic tone, and I felt bared, and he would either like what he heard or not.

"So, you find me handsome?" George said after studying me for a moment.

"Uh, yes." My cheeks flamed with embarrassment.

George didn't seem to notice as he reached for one of my hands with his. His hand felt large, warm, and calloused against mine. "Well, I'm glad, because I think you are the most beautiful woman I have ever seen."

Chapter Two

Maggie
April 1946

George and I talked a little longer in the cafe, then he walked me back to his truck. He tried insisting on driving me home but of course I refused. I didn't want mom to see me getting out of a strange man's truck.

Reluctantly George agreed if I promised to see him again on a real date. I gave him my address and a promise to see him the following night for supper. I could feel him watching me as I walked away with his umbrella propped above me to ward off the light drizzle that still insistently came down.

He insisted and I agreed. Having his umbrella ensured he would call on me, even if to just retrieve the thing. At least that was my hopeful reasoning.

When I walked through the front door of the small home mom and I shared, it became obvious mom was annoyed on how long I took. It made her worry. Mom loved schedules, and we were now late in starting the bread. I told her I met someone. That we made plans to go on a date. I told her he was beautiful and funny and smart, and that time simply ran away from us. Mom paused and narrowed her brown eyes at me as she tossed her long brown hair back from her shoulder.

"Now everything makes sense. You're late because of a man. I hope he's a gentleman and not some scoundrel. There are a lot of them out there, you know?" Then, with a sigh and a quick hug, she continued with a much softer tone. "I am happy you met someone, Margaret. I'll look forward to meeting him. Now why don't you run off to see Anna Beth as I know you are dying to and I'll make the bread. Please make sure you are back by six so we can eat together."

"Of course, mom." I said, planting a small kiss on her cheek before turning back out the door and walking the eight houses down to Anna Beth's. She was the one person who I told everything to, who I trusted with any and everything.

Ellie Lynn

"Oh my God, he really said that?" Anna Beth said with her hand slightly over her open mouth. Her blue eyes looked dreamy as I recounted everything that transpired at the Cafe. "Not that I doubt it or anything, it's just so terribly romantic."

"He did. He really did, and I think he meant it. Me, beautiful." I said the word beautiful in a sigh, as if in a dream. No one called me beautiful before in my life and I never expected it. Anna Beth is the beautiful one, not me.

"Well, it's about time someone recognized it." Anna Beth said as she grasped my hand in hers and kissed the knuckles. Then she flung herself onto her back. We both were laying on her bed facing each other. I propped my head up against my hand as I recounted all George and me talked about. She laughed when I told her about George listing off his undesirable traits. She agreed on the custard as she didn't really care for it either and in her opinion, this counted as an extra point in his favor.

"Promise me Maggie, that when you two marry I get to be your maid of honor." Anna Beth said, still using her dream like voice.

"Now that's a little premature. But we are seeing each other tomorrow night." My voice sounded like a squeal.

Anna Beth raised her perfectly arched eyebrows, "How did your mom take the news of you being late because you were having coffee with a *man*?"

"As you'd expect." I rolled my eyes as I proceeded to tell her the rest of what happened an hour before.

A little while after my emotions became wistful and sad. "Oh Anna, what am I going to do when you are all married and moved away next month. You know everything is going to change." I said, looking at her now. We were best friends since age five. She moved into the big house down the street from me. Anna Beth always dressed up in pretty little dresses with lace and shiny black shoes. She's a blonde haired beauty with bright blue eyes and when we first met, she reminded me of a porcelain doll.

Despite urging from mom for an entire month, I refused to walk

Falling

down to her house where she always sat playing in her yard. Then one day I did. I took a deep breath and asked her if she would be my friend. Her eyes lit up like a midday sky and we have been best friends ever since. I can always count on her to be there for me through everything, as I her. We were more like sisters than friends.

"I know, but I won't be that far away. Just a couple of towns out, not even a day's drive. Plus, you can always come and visit me and Hank. You can stay in the spare bedroom, and it will be almost like old times." Then she took a deep breath and with a shaky voice, continued. "I have to admit, I'm nervous about it all. I mean, I'm going to be married! Can you believe it? I don't even remember living anywhere else but here. In this bed, in this bedroom, with you down the street. To think, I'll have my very own home. Hank will be done with medical school soon and I'll be a doctor's wife. It's kind of scary but also exciting."

"You are going to make Hank the best wife. I hope he knows how lucky he is." Then with a sly smile like only best friends give I continued, "At least soon, you will get to have your wedding night and finally know what all the hype is about."

Anna Beth turned bright red and gave a nervous laugh. "Well, about that." Then she pursed her lips together with a guilty look.

"You didn't! When? Why didn't you tell me?"

"It happened a couple of nights ago. I figured why not since we are so close to getting married and well, Hank really wanted to." Then with a small smile and a brief pause, she continued, "It was nice."

"Nice? Really? Your curtains are nice. Last week's church service was nice..."

"Okay, okay. Maybe nice is the wrong word." Anna Beth admitted, while holding her hand out in a defensive gesture. I sat up and tucked my legs under me. Anna Beth did the same. "It was exciting, new, a little painful, and a little awkward. At least for the first time. But afterwards I felt different. I felt full, loved, and closer to Hank than I ever have to anyone before. I felt like a woman afterward."

Ellie Lynn

Anna Beth's already red cheeks deepened in color. She looked at me with pleading eyes not to laugh, or lecture, or question. I didn't and wouldn't, of course. I imagine it's a very personal feeling when you first have relations with a man. How she felt may not be how I will feel when the time comes. I could only speculate at this, of course, but I was secretly anxious of the experience.

"I'm happy for you Anna Banana." I said quietly, using the nickname I gifted her with when we were ten. It sounded so clever and funny at that age. She was Anna Banana, and I was Maggie Magpie. And we always would be.

I left Anna Beth's house at 5:45 pm with enough time to walk back home before supper. As I skipped down the sidewalk, I couldn't help but feel strangely melancholy and happy at the same time. I guess it was all the changes that were taking place. Change always reminded me I only had so much control over life.

Two weeks later, as I pinned an annoying curl back from my face, I couldn't help but smile. Tonight, I sat getting ready for another date with George, and I was so excited I could barely stand it. I looked good tonight too. My hair shone in waves just past my chin, my eyes sparkled, and my red lipstick was bright and even across my smiling lips. My freckles weren't even bothering me as much as usual as they seemed to hide some with my smile and, of course, the light coating of powder I applied. I turned as I heard a small knock on my door and then my mom entered right after. Walking up to me, she had a bright smile on her face as well.

My mom Aileen was a robust woman who, despite her years, was still beautiful. Mom pulled her long brown hair back in her usual neat bun and her green eyes sparkled. She had a wide grin, a loud laugh, and she always seemed to smell like the roses she liked to grow in her garden. She was also a well-liked and matronly lady of the town.

Falling

"You look so pretty, Margaret! George is going to have his heart aflutter. Where is he taking you tonight?"

So far we went dancing, to the movies, and even a small dinner party at one of his co-workers' house.

"I'm not sure. He said he had somewhere special to take me. Oh mom, George is so wonderful! He's exciting and mysterious and he looks at me like no one ever has before. Plus, he looks so handsome in his police uniform."

My cheeks turned red. I hadn't meant to say all that out loud. Especially the part about his police uniform. Mom didn't like the idea I was dating a police officer. Especially one who also fought in the war. She worried he could have "issues". I wasn't sure what she meant about that, but this was the first time I'd experienced more than two dates with someone. Lately I've noticed that I've formed some strings of attachment.

"Now Margaret, you have fun, but remember you don't know him very well. He's a nice enough fella, handsome to boot, but I don't want to see you get your heart broken." Mom said in a cajoling voice.

"It's just a date, mom. It's not like we are running off to the wedding chapel." I said before turning back to the mirror to double check everything was in place.

In the two weeks since meeting George, I felt like I knew him already. I learned he served in the Army and obviously fought in the war. He didn't have much in the way of family, At least since his aunt and uncle passed. They were the only people he'd ever been close to. I knew it was in his personality to protect, which is why he became a police officer after the war. Instinctively I knew this, as I always had this sense of feeling protected and safe around him. He made me feel things I never felt before. I felt special and beautiful. In my young mind, this was about all I needed to know. Mom held this deep-rooted distrust of men in general. I understood why, at least to an extent, but I wouldn't let her distrust influence my happiness.

As I was dabbing on a small amount of perfume to my wrists, there was a knock at the front door. My heart skipped a beat and

Ellie Lynn

mom turned away to head downstairs to answer it. Once she left, I closed my eyes and took a deep breath, reminding myself he would never like a girl giggling and fawning all over him as I felt like doing. I needed to be smooth, charming, and sophisticated. Or at least try to be. His interest in me honestly amazed me. Opening my eyes, I took one last look in the mirror, smoothed a few wayward curls down again, grabbed my shawl, and walked downstairs.

George stood in the doorway with mom. He wore gray pants, a wool sweater with a checkered collar sticking out, and his dark hair combed back. My heart skipped a beat. He looked so handsome. I felt like a young girl of thirteen nervously descending the stairs to go to her first dance. Two pairs of eyes were on me, and I prayed I wouldn't trip. I looked from George to mom; she was holding a bouquet of daisies in her outstretched hand. Her face looked pinched and I knew it was because she was terribly allergic to them. I knew they would be thrown out the moment we left. On top of being allergic to them, she also considered them a weed flower when compared to her treasured roses. I suppressed a smile at the look on her face.

"Look how sweet Margaret, George brought me flowers. Now isn't that the nicest gesture." Mom said as she smiled tightly and then gave off a loud sneeze. Mom's sneezes were anything but soft and delicate. Her sneezes seemed to come up through her feet and almost doubled her over. They were ear piercing loud as well. They always embarrassed me when I was younger, especially if she sneezed in church. Considering her spring and summer allergies, this happened often, and I was sure the people sitting in the church pews were used to it despite the few heads that would turn our way.

"Oh, excuse me! Must be some dust in the air. Well, you two have fun tonight. I'm going to put these daisies in some... water."

Mom rushed out of the room as she spoke. I looked at George and he looked back at me with an amused look on his face. Then he held out his arm for me to grab.

"Shall we be going?" he asked as I wrapped my arm through his.

I smiled up at him. "Of course, where are we going?"

Falling

"Oh, you will see, it's a surprise." Then after a small chuckle, "Your mom's allergic to daisies, isn't she?"

"Terribly so." I replied. Then we both looked at each other and laughed.

As we got settled in the vehicle, George looked over at me for a moment. I felt a little embarrassed as he looked me over in his quiet and intense way. Then he cleared his throat before saying, "You look beautiful." He then looked straight ahead and pulled away from the curb to head down the street.

"Thank you, so do you." I said softly, before realizing I implied he looked beautiful as well.

As we drove, my eyes kept looking over at him. I think I could have stared at him all night. He talked most of the way. Mostly about his home, the weather, and our last date at the dance hall. I answered and talked as well, but I was mostly interested in watching him. Watching as he talked, as his mouth moved, and the expressions he made. The way he smoked his cigarette and flicked the ashes out through the gap in the window. He said I looked beautiful tonight. He was stunning.

The sky turned dark outside as we continued to drive. It seemed as if we were going nowhere. Finally, George pulled the vehicle over and we were... nowhere. Literally. Looking around, I saw nothing but fields with only a scattering of trees here and there looking like darker blobs in the darkening horizon.

"George, are we lost?" I asked, a little hesitantly. It confused me why we were here instead of a fancy restaurant, or a dance, or the movies again. Some normal date place with food. I was also starving!

George chuckled. "No, Maggie, we aren't lost. We are right where we need to be." He then walked to the back, opened the door, and began shuffling for things. He brought out a lantern, a couple of blankets, and a basket. "Have you ever had a picnic in the dark?" He asked, and then before I could answer, he continued. "If you trust me, I promise you will have fun."

"Okay, I trust you." Still feeling a little hesitant. To be honest, I

Ellie Lynn

was a little disappointed. I dressed for a night on the town and had been eager to be out and about with George. I loved how being on his arm made me feel. This night was not starting as I imagined.

George laid out the blanket in a patch of dried weeds on the side of the little dirt road. He lit the lantern, illuminating the green and yellow blanket. I walked over, feeling a little overdressed in my dark blue dress and heels, and sat down awkwardly on the blanket, tucking the ends of my skirt under my legs. George chuckled; I must have looked ridiculous. Now I wondered if he really thought I looked beautiful, or if he simply sized up my inappropriate attire for what he planned. Well, he should have said what we would be doing. I would have worn trousers, a warm shirt, and practical shoes I thought a little annoyed.

George sat next to me and opened the basket. A wonderful smell of chicken wafted up from it, making me wonder how I hadn't smelled it during the drive. I guess I had centered my focus on him.

"I have some chicken, some bread, cheese, and a bottle of wine for us tonight. I wasn't sure what kind of wine you prefer, but I got some kind of white wine. The clerk said its popular with the ladies, so I hope it's good." He said with a grin and sort of feigned worried look. It was dark, but not dark enough with the light from the lantern that I couldn't make out his expressions. I couldn't help but giggle a little. He looked young and boyish.

"I'm sure it will be perfect." I replied.

We ate in silence for a little while. The chicken was wonderful, the bread a little crusty but thankfully the wine was sweet to wash it down with. The wine made me feel relaxed and warm. When we finished, George packed up the basket and put it away. It was completely dark at this point, the distance all around looked inky black. The warm light from the hissing lantern illuminated the blanket as a few bugs swarmed around it, attracted to its light. It was almost too dark. As if the darkness closed in all around you. I had to take a couple of deep breaths to ward off any claustrophobia. I waited patiently as George returned to the blanket, sat next to me, and then

Falling

put out the light in the lantern. Suddenly, everything around us was in total darkness. I felt a little nervous as the darkness was instantly everything.

"Are you cold?" George asked quietly from beside me. I turned to him even though I couldn't see him, and I was sure he couldn't see me, but I could feel his warmth though and feel his breath.

"A little. Thank you." I said, as George laid the second blanket over my shoulders. I felt thankful because the light shawl I had brought was barely keeping the chill at bay.

"Do you still trust me, Maggie?" George asked. I nodded, which he must have noticed despite the darkness, because he continued. "Then lie back with me. Don't worry, I'll keep you safe and warm."

I laid back against the soft blanket and could feel George lay down next to me. His scent seemed to envelope me as I wiggled closer to him, drawn to his warmth. After getting settled, we simply looked up. Being out in the middle of nowhere with no light around on a clear, cloudless night created the most beautiful thing I ever saw. The sky was speckled with what seemed like millions of bright stars. Suddenly, the dark night seemed illuminated by their beauty. I no longer felt claustrophobic, but instead, I felt like a small speck in the universe. I had never seen the sky look so amazing before, so peaceful and majestic. In retrospect, I don't believe I've ever taken the time to look. It also felt incredibly intimate laying on the blanket next to George under a sky full of stars. It felt like we were the only two people in the world.

"What do you think?" George asked beside me. His breath felt warm against my cheek and smelled sweet, like the wine we drunk. He was lying right next to me, and I could feel his heat radiating off him, warming me even more. Much more than the wool wrapped around me.

"It's wonderful George. I've never seen the sky look so beautiful… with so many stars." I turned my head to look at him. My eyes adjusted to the darkness some, and I saw him looking at me already.

"I agree, absolutely beautiful." He said, his eyes never leaving my face. I became even warmer in that instant. It was the two of us laying under the most brilliant blanket of stars I had ever seen and this man next to me thought I was beautiful. I started to believe that maybe to him I was beautiful. He looked back up to the sky and then I followed.

"When I was in Europe, there were a few times I could look up on a night sky such as this one and the horrors of the day would fade away. No matter what happens on this earth, no matter the evil or good, love or hate, the stars will still stay constant. They will still shine." He paused for a long moment then he continued, "I remember I used to look at the stars and imagine myself at home, lying on a blanket with a beautiful girl and everything would be right in the world. It's even better than I imagined. You're more than I could have dreamed of Maggie."

My heart felt stuck in my throat. I didn't know if I wanted to cheer for his words, comfort him for his past pain, or just tell him he could have me for as long as he wanted. Instead, I did something I never thought I would be brave enough to do. I asked him to kiss me.

I could see George smile in the moonlight as he leaned in closer and raised one hand to my cheek. Then he pressed his lips gently against mine. The kiss started out gentle and sweet but quickly turned hungry as our lips melded together and our tongues tasted one another. I couldn't seem to get enough of his kiss, but all too soon his mouth left mine, and he placed small kisses on the side of my mouth, my cheeks, my neck.

Then he tucked me into his side, my head supported by his shoulder, and we once again gazed out at the heavens. This was the most amazing and romantic night I ever experienced. More than I could ever imagine, and much more than what I expected it to be.

Chapter Three

George
February 2, 1942

My hand shook lightly as I held my enlistment papers. I sat on my bed, watching the shadows of leaves dance across the wall. I could hear my mother weeping in the next room, and I wanted to go to her but thought it would be best to give her a little time. My mother had a tendency towards melodrama, so it wasn't that unusual sitting on my bed while listening to her cry between our thin walls.

We lived in a small house outside of Albuquerque, New Mexico. The faded green paint outside was so sun-bleached it looked to be a dirty white color. There were areas where paint all but faded away, giving it a much lived in look. On the street we lived on, our house looked like any other, except for our freshly painted white as a cloud door which clashed terribly with the rest of the house. It stood out like a single tooth in a gaping and decaying mouth.

The neighborhood houses were all so close together that they looked almost attached. One faded sun-bleached house seemed to run into the next. I wish I could say that looking at my house, where I lived all my life, felt like home, but it didn't.

Years before, as a young boy of six, I spent hours outside playing with my friends Billy and Jacob. They lived in other faded houses down the street. We started a club where the three of us were so far the only members. We spent one hot June day going over our rules, initiations (if we ever recruited new members), and of course the options of where our club meetings were to be held. We spent quite a bit of time arguing over what our club's name would be. The Tiger Boys so far reigned in as the contender. I walked home to try to sneak a couple of cookies my mother baked that morning to take back to my friends.

When I walked in, I saw my mother curled up in the corner of our small living room. Her face towards the wall corner, I could see her shoulders silently shaking. She cried, even though little noise came from where she sat. I slowly walked towards her to touch her shoulder. She turned her head to look at me with a red rimmed blank stare.

At the age of six, I didn't understand what happened, and it

Ellie Lynn

scared me. I told her everything would be okay, and I sat next to her until my father came home. By that time, the sky darkened, and I continued to sit with my mom. I later learned the doctors called her condition a mental breakdown. I didn't understand except that it meant I would be sent away for a while. My father packed me into the car and drove me to Okmulgee, Oklahoma, to visit my Aunt and Uncle Clemmons at their farm for the rest of the summer.

This became my true home. To give my still fragile mother a break, I lived there every summer as well as most winter breaks. There I could relax and be myself. I learned to fish, plow land, stargaze, and most importantly it's where I felt truly loved.

Looking down at my papers clutched in my hand, I reread everything on it for probably the tenth time. Leaving tomorrow for training made me feel a little nervous. Although, truth be told, not as nervous as telling my father about my decision. Last week when I brought up enlisting at the supper table, my father's arm snaked out as he quickly backhanded me. I finished my pork chop with a small trickle of blood at the edge of my bottom lip. It made it difficult to chew the dry meat.

I decided then that I wouldn't bring it up again until I enlisted for real. Early this morning after father left for work at the factory, I quietly and solemnly walked down the dirt road leading into town. The child in me a couple of months ago would have kicked rocks while whistling a tune. This morning I walked down the street a man. Despite what my father thought, I knew exactly what I was doing. I could die, but after the attack on Pearl Harbor I couldn't sit around and do nothing. No one would mistake me for being a coward. I felt deep within me that enlisting was the right thing to do. When I reached Main Street, I walked to the recruiting office, opened the door, and accepted my fate. I waited in the line with other nervous young men, passed my physical, exams, and signed my name on the line. I was now in the US Army and I couldn't take it back.

I sat anxiously in my small room waiting for the front door to open, hearing my father's heavy footsteps as he walked in. Mother's crying in the next room helped to increase my nervousness. Mother's

Falling

tears would irritate my father and his punishment would probably be harsh. After getting home from the recruiting office about an hour ago, my mother met me at the door. Her eyes met mine accusingly as I stepped into the house. I didn't say a thing; she seemed to already know.

"You're my only son Georgie, how could you? What will your father say? He forbade you to enlist and you know this." She said accusingly. Always your father this, your father that. This decision was about me.

"Mother, I had to do it. I'm sorry but..."

I didn't have a chance to even finish what I was about to say before she ran down the hallway and slammed the door to her room, ending any other conversation with me. At least for now. Instead of this being about me, my decision, my sacrifice, she would turn it into something about her or about my father. It's what she always did.

Sitting on my small bed, I can't help but feel time is simply being wasted in crying. I would leave in the morning, and God only knew if I would ever return. Fourteen hours and twenty-seven minutes, to be exact. I knew those hours would not be spent pleasantly.

Almost ready to get up and try to reason with my mother, I heard the front door open and close. I could smell the faint hint of cigarette smoke that always seemed to follow my father around. Probably because he rarely was seen without a cigarette dangling between his whiskered lips.

I closed my eyes and took a deep breath to steady my nerves. I stood up and walked to the door, ready to get it over with. I walked out into the hallway with my papers gripped in my hand. Walking straight up to him I held the papers up, not saying a word. I didn't think I needed to. My steely eyes bared into his, showing I was not afraid, despite my trembling stomach. Behind me I heard my mother open her door and step out into the hallway. My father looked from the paper to me, and then to my mom standing several feet behind me. Her angelic face probably looked red from crying, something my

Ellie Lynn

father couldn't bear. I stood firmly in front of him, defiant and strong. I waited for the blow.

His pupils dilated and his skin took on a reddish ruddy look which contrasted with his dark oil slicked hair and thick mustache. The muscles contracted in his jaw as he gritted his teeth. I don't think I've ever seen him so angry. I waited. My ears seemed to buzz in anticipation, and the silence in the room was deafening.

If my mother still cried, I couldn't hear it. My arm ached as I waited for my father's fist, but it never came. He didn't hit me as I expected him to. I struggled to understand as I slowly lowered my arm with the enlistment papers clutched in my hand.

"So that's the way it's going to be, is it?" He asked before turning around and walking out of the house. The front door quietly shut behind him. With a whoosh, I let out a held breath that I didn't even realize I held. I slowly turned around to see my mother looking just as dumbfounded as I felt. Then her eyes locked with mine and she ran back into her room with a cry. Her door slammed shut.

I slowly walked back into my room to sit at the chair by my desk. I heard the clock on my desk tick rhythmically. Thirteen hours and fifty-two seconds left. Next to my clock stood a framed picture of my aunt and uncle. Picking up a piece of paper and pencil, I wrote them a letter telling them of my decision. I knew they would be supportive and write to me. Oh, how I wish I was there right now instead of here. I wish they were telling me goodbye tomorrow instead of my parents.

I've never seen my father so angry. His anger seemed beyond his usual display of temper. A part of me feared a little that I would be disowned for going against his wishes in joining the Army. But then again, I never felt like his son to begin with.

My father never talked about his service. I asked him once to tell me about the war since we were learning about it in school, but he smacked me upside the back of the head instead. He told me to never bring it up again. A couple of years later mother asked me to fetch her a new needle off her nightstand. She sat diligently

Falling

working on another needlepoint of Jesus to go with her many others.

I walked into the bedroom and found my father standing in front of the full-length mirror by the window. He wore his uniform from the first world war. I stopped where I stood and stared. I couldn't take my eyes off him, and I couldn't just walk away. My twelve-year-old self stood simply fascinated. His eyes seemed distant and never actually met mine in the mirror. Coming to my senses, I started to turn around and leave when he finally spoke.

"Do you know what the hardest part about war is, son?"

For a moment, I felt shocked into silence. I didn't know if this was a trick, if I would feel the sting of his fist when he came to his senses. My skin prickled and my forehead broke out in a cold sweat. I knew, though, that I couldn't stand there like a jackass. I had to give him an answer. My mind quickly thought of all the possibilities. The killing, the food, the cold, the blood... and before I could answer, he continued.

"Not dying."

He gave this answer with a faraway and haunted look. His gaze never met mine. Even now, all these years later, I don't quite understand what he meant about that, and I never dared to ask him. I wish I could. At the time, my mind had burned with questions. What did that even mean? Who wishes for death? Isn't the point of war to kill the bad guys and then go home to a better and safer place?

I always wanted to ask these questions and even now I wish I could sit down at the table and have an actual conversation with him on it. Afterwards, in my imaginings, my father would embrace me and tell me how proud he was. Mother would cook in the kitchen, wanting to make sure my last meal at home would be special. I wished for this so badly. At the farm, it would be reality. My aunt and uncle would make sure I felt loved on my last night home.

Instead, mom stayed in her room the rest of the night. My father came back late and went straight to bed. I tiptoed into the kitchen for a piece of stale bread, unable to stand the rumblings of my stomach

Ellie Lynn

any longer. There would be no special supper for me tonight. The next morning, I stepped out of my room ready to leave only to find my mother standing in the hallway at my door. Her blonde hair hung in tangles around her pretty face. Her blue eyes were red rimmed from crying all night. She looked as fragile as her mind, as if at any moment she could shatter apart and fall to the ground. Instead, she held up a brown paper bag and gave me a faint smile.

"I thought you would be hungry. There is some bread and an apple in there for breakfast that you can eat on the way. And Georgie," she hesitated before continuing, "stay safe, my son." Then she patted my cheek, as if I were five. Her hand felt cool. I didn't expect the usual farewell that most would expect from a mother so it was okay. I knew our relationship wasn't like that.

I gave her a quick hug and kiss on the cheek. Then I grabbed the paper bag, thankful for the food, and left. My father never emerged from the bedroom. Walking out into the early morning sun, I felt a renewed determination and sense of rightness. Maybe even a little excited for the adventure.

Chapter Four

Maggie
June - July, 1946

"Maggie, just follow me I won't let you fall." George smiled as he tried to lead me out by the opening from the second story of his barn.

Being afraid of heights, even though his barn wasn't that high, I felt slightly breathless as I looked down from where I stood. George made a clicking noise with his tongue as if to say I was being silly before sitting on the edge of the opening.

The night felt warm, and the sky started to darken as the sunset approached. The air felt thick and smelled faintly of car oil and old hay. It smelt just the way George did the first day we met. Thinking of this made me smile.

George used the barn as a place to work on his 1933 Lancaster, a car left to him, along with the small farm from his aunt and uncle. This explained the musky but sweet smell. In the two months since seeing George, we became inseparable and my plans revolved around when I could see George next.

"I'm sure I can see the sunset from where I'm at George, besides dangling my feet from two stories up doesn't sound too appealing." My breath caught as I cautiously peered over.

George sat on the edge, swinging his legs slightly as the light breeze ruffled his dark hair. He looked very handsome sitting there in his dark gray trousers, boots, suspenders, and gray shirt. He looked so young and carefree, despite the subtle intenseness that seemed to linger around him that he tried to cover up with humor and lightness.

"Come on, Maggie." He held his hand out to me. "I won't bite. Well, maybe a little." He gave me a mischievous grin, as if we shared a secret joke. I laughed and reached my hand out to grasp his. He gave a slight tug for me to sit next to him. As my legs dangled, despite my fear we held hands and I felt safe.

We sat there as the blue in the sky turned slightly pink with hints of purple. Then the colors changed to deep oranges and reds as the sun slowly crept from the earth. It was breathtaking. One of those times when God makes His presence known and you feel overwhelmed with the beauty. George had a way of making me see and realize all the

Falling

beautiful things around me. I wasn't sure if being in love played a role in it like seeing everything for the first time through someone else's eyes. I turned to look at George to find him already looking at me. I could tell he wanted to say something but wasn't sure how.

"What is it?"

"We should marry." He said in a breathy voice.

It wasn't a question, more of a statement of what should happen next. I didn't care, as all I ever wanted was him. My heart soared, and as I started to say something, he smiled and kissed me. I would do anything for one of his kisses.

I sighed and wrapped my arms around his neck as he deepened the kiss. We laid on the floor of hay. His body on mine felt heavy and comforting at the same time. I felt safe, and I felt loved. It was as if I waited my whole twenty years for this one moment.

I broke away from the kiss. "I'm guessing that was your way of asking me to marry you. Don't you want to know my answer, George?"

"Your kisses are all the answer I need." He hungrily kissed my mouth again.

George unbuttoned the bodice of my cotton printed dress as he spread kisses over my chest and collarbone. My heart felt as if it would burst. I never experienced these feelings and sensations before. I felt a little nervous, but I loved him, and we planned to marry so I figured it didn't matter that we continued. My mom would have a fit if she knew. I didn't care. George's hand went under my dress and ran up my knee to my thigh. I felt a small hesitation at the unknown as he touched me.

"George," I said on a gasp, "I need to hear you say it."

He continued as if I said nothing. I pulled back from him. "George, if we are to marry and... do this, I need to hear you tell me you love me." I assumed he did since he wanted to marry me, but suddenly it became very important for me to hear it.

George laid both hands on my cheeks, cradling my head. His

Ellie Lynn

calluses felt rough against my soft cheeks. "I love you, Maggie." He said quietly with all seriousness.

"I love you too." I whispered.

There were no other words between us as he bared my skin to the cool breeze and the tickling hay. Right there, in his barn, lighted by the moon and stars, we made love.

Later I laid nestled to his side as he lightly hummed a song. I felt the vibrations coming from his chest as my fingers lightly ran up and down his skin. Anna Beth was right. I felt different. I felt a closeness and connection to George I never felt with anyone before.

"What is that song you're humming?" I asked. "It sounds familiar. I think I've heard it before." George smiled and before I knew it, he was above me, supported by his elbow, with one hand around my waist. He sang words to the song *This is the Army Mr. Jones*.

I laughed as he sang to me. The song was funny, and George's eyes sparkled in the darkness with good humor. His song choice surprised me though as innocent and fun as it sounded. George fought in the war, and he didn't like to talk about it. At times I felt guilty after trying to ask him about his life in the war, as if I was doing something wrong or breaking some unspoken rule. Yet, I yearned to know more about him. Anything, even if it was something horrible, like the war. His experiences were still a part of him. When he finished, he kissed me.

"Was it terrible George," I asked as he kissed down my neck. "The war?"

George lifted his head to look at me. "Of course it was sweetie, wars are always terrible." The sparkle from his eyes disappeared, even if his smile was still there. We were both silent, as if we were both battling with what to say next.

I spoke first. "I know war is terrible in general, but I want to know how it was for you. Where you went, what you saw. You never mention it and I want you to know you can. I'll always listen George."

George looked at me incredulously. "You want to know what I

Falling

did there, what I saw?" He said in a calm voice, although the undertones showed his anger. "I killed men Margaret, and I saw death." No one seems to understand what that does to a human and most don't care.

"George, I'm sorry, that's not what I meant. I don't wish to make you angry..." I hesitated, trying to pick my words carefully before deciding to proceed.

"That is all, Margaret. It's time everyone moves on. Now, no more talk about the war. I know you are curious, but you don't understand. I don't want to talk about it." George said before I had a chance to say anything else. It was probably for the best. I wish I said nothing to begin with. It felt like I ruined the moment.

"I should get you home before your mom worries." George continued as he stood up and brushed away the clinging pieces of straw. I continued to lie in the hay for a moment, watching him in the moonlight. Then I buttoned and straighten my clothes. He was right, mom would surely be pacing.

"I love you, George." I said, as I watched him light a lantern with a match from his pocket. He turned to me, smiled, and told me to be careful where I stepped so I didn't fall. His carefree expression was back, as if I said nothing. As if I hadn't mentioned the war.

About a month later, in the small little church my family attended for years, we married. My mom could barely contain her tears of frustration when we told her of our plans to marry the month before. She didn't care for George much, despite his humor and relaxed demeanor. This was one of his traits that I loved so much. He was always joking around and made light of everything. My mom didn't like this. She said she didn't trust a man who fought in the war and yet could still be joyful. I guess she imagined the darkness of war

Ellie Lynn

would blacken a soul so much that there could never be light. Foolish thinking if you asked me.

She insisted I didn't know George well enough to marry him. Marriage was a forever commitment. Swearing in a church to love, honor, and obey a man in front of God and witnesses should never be taken lightly. I felt thankful she didn't know, or suspect George and I already made love. She couldn't understand that George and I loved each other.

In my bitterness over her dislike of George, I thought she didn't want us to be happy. The Lord knows she wasn't in her marriage. Bless my father's departed soul, but he did little to make my mom happy. She always pretended to be in front of me, but when I was a child, and my father would leave the house, she would cry when she thought no one was looking. At times I saw bruises around her neck before she covered them up with her pretty floral scarf. Her excuses of falling were lies she told. She felt shame for the abuse and worried what others would think.

I remember hiding under the bed or out behind the hedges when the yelling began. Despite my hands clasped over my ears, I still heard the unmistakable sound of skin being bruised, a lip splitting, a dish shattering, and wood splintering. I tried bringing it up to her after my father's death but she refused to talk with me for a week afterwards. She loved him once, and that was the only memory she would allow herself to have. I swore to myself I would never have that type of marriage. George couldn't be more different from my father. Kind and caring, he wanted to take care of me. My father drowned himself in alcohol and would become short tempered and violent. George didn't have a drinking problem and rarely drank alcohol at all. I would not end up like my mother.

The morning of the wedding I woke up in my childhood bed to find my mom sitting in a chair next to me. She sat awake looking at me as I cleared the sleep from my eyes. Blinking, I turned on my side to look at her, smiling slightly I knew why she was there. She felt worried about me. As a young child, my mom would sometimes crawl

Falling

into bed with me or sleep in the chair next to it if I was sick or upset. This morning I felt neither, she sat there for herself. For her own worries and reasons that the deep creases running across her forehead gave away.

"Morning baby. I'm sorry if I woke you, especially on such an important day." Mom said quietly as she covered a yawn. She was still in her nightdress with a faded pink terry-cloth robe loosely tied at her waist. She looked so familiar and comforting to me.

"You're fine mom. What are you doing in that chair? I hope you didn't sleep there all night." I asked, truly concerned. I hated that she worried so.

"No, I came here about an hour ago." She said, then looked up at the ceiling and closed her eyes. "I can't believe this is the last time you will stay in this room. That you will have your own home and responsibilities. A husband." The last she whispered, and it sounded strained.

"Mom, everything is going to be okay. Why are you so worried? Why do you dislike George so much? And please don't tell me you don't because I can tell you do." I sat up against my elbows. I told myself I didn't need her approval, but I wanted it so badly.

"It's not that I don't like him..." mom held up her hand against me starting to protest. "It's that I do. I like him, he's charming, he's likeable, he seems so carefree. But this is happening so quickly, Margaret. You do not know him very well. When people first meet, they always show their very best side. It's not until later that you see the not so good side as well. We all have one. It's a matter of liking or loving the person still knowing both sides."

Mom took a deep breath, as if preparing herself for what she was about to say next. "I thought I knew your father when we first met. I liked him a lot too." She whispered as a tear dropped down her cheek. "I loved him so much. He was my everything at one time. Before I had you of course."

I sat there, stunned. I waited with my breath held, knowing she was going to reveal something important. Sitting up I leaned further

Ellie Lynn

against the wood carved headboard in anticipation. I barely felt the wood pressing uncomfortably into my back. It didn't matter. My hands gripped the surrounding sheets.

"Margaret, do you know how your father and I met?" she asked. I shook my head because I honestly didn't. Conversations about my parents and their relationship wasn't ever discussed. I waited with baited breath for her to begin the story.

"It was a hot July day. You know one of those days where the back of your shirt clings as you feel the sweat running down. I remember thinking how a dip in the pond a mile up the street would feel heavenly, but I couldn't go. Your uncle Liam was sick with a fever and a nasty cough, and I worried for him. What a day to have a fever. Between your grandma and me, all we could do was try to keep him cool with wet cloths on his head. That night, I remember crying myself to sleep thinking he would die."

"The next day, the Lord must have heard all our prayers because his fever broke, and he felt better. That afternoon I snuck to one of our neighbor's farms who grew some of the best apples around. I walked down the dusty road while the hot sun seemed to scorch me. Mr. Brown was a mean old man who would have blistered my hide if he caught me, but I wanted a couple of those apples to give to Liam. They were his favorite, so crisp and sweet. I climbed one of the trees quickly after making sure no one was watching and picked a couple apples to put in the pockets of my trousers."

"I was normally great at climbing trees, but with the heat and being tired I ended up losing my footing on the way down. I fell pretty hard. I scraped my leg up against the rough bark and was lucky I didn't break it. As I got up and brushed myself off, I heard a voice asking if I was okay. I turned around to see the most handsome boy I had ever seen. He looked concerned as his eyes looked me up and down." Mom paused at this, deep in thought, and gave a slight chuckle before continuing.

"He must have thought me a clumsy fool, but he was as sweet to me as one of those juicy apples. He was Mr. Brown's nephew, visiting

Falling

for the summer. You never met your pa's uncle because he passed away before you were born. Anyway, your pa helped me sit on a grassy patch under the tree and we talked for a while before he helped me walk home. My leg hurt, but I barely noticed the pain because he became my focus." Mom smiled as she spoke of the memory.

She talked as she did when she told stories of growing up. The stories that were important to her, cherished memories of times that helped to shape her. Lessons she learned over time. Some passed on to me. I could have heard a pin drop as closely as I listened. I didn't want to miss a thing. I wanted to soak it all up hoping to have a better understanding of my parents, of my pa.

"We spent the rest of the summer together. We fished, talked, and we went for long walks together. I remember walking with him down the dusty road at that magical time, you know, right before the sun sets. I can still smell the Mother-of-the-Evening flowers growing along our path and the calluses on his palm as he held my hand. We seemed to talk about everything; our dreams, what we wished we could do, and how our lives could be together."

"I was seventeen, and he was nineteen. I think I fell in love with him the first time I laid eyes on him, and it only grew the more time we spent together. He seemed in love with me as well." The last she said with almost a question, as if she was just now wondering if it was so. After a moment, she continued, "We married a couple of months after meeting, and everything was wonderful for a while. Soon I became pregnant with you and so excited. I couldn't wait to be a mom. Your pa was overjoyed as well." Smiling, Mom stared across the room in thought for a moment. I could see how happy the memory made her. I smiled as well.

"Oh, he used to fawn all over me right before having you. He treated me like the most delicate piece of china. It was quite endearing. Next thing we knew, you were with us. Our lives seemed to change overnight. We were young, and it was a big change... parenthood." Mom's voice changed. "Your pa became a little restless and

Ellie Lynn

started to drink. Most nights he would go straight to his friend Benny's place after his shift at the factory instead of coming home. For a while he lied about what he was doing, but I could smell it on him. I admit I became a little resentful of it. I was on him a lot about his drinking. We seemed to argue constantly and over time, the drinking became worse."

"Then one night, after an evening of drinking, your pa broke his leg in a freak accident. The factory fired him, and we relied on your grandma and grandpa's help to even buy food. Being a man and supporting your family is an important expectation of a husband. Your pa started having fewer days sober and when he drank, he became a different man. He... he became abusive. I resented his drinking, and he resented feeling trapped with me. At least that's what I think. I don't know. We talked of so many plans together and he had so many dreams for his life. I have often wondered if he blamed me for taking away those dreams. We were so caught up in the whirlwind that is love that we didn't realize we weren't meant for each other."

I sat there, not knowing how to feel. It's hard not to feel hurt knowing your parents quit loving each other after you were born. I couldn't help but feel sad and a little angry. I always knew how their story ended, but never how it began. A few months of them being happy didn't exactly erase years of misery.

Mom sat silent for a minute before she continued. "Things don't always turn out like you imagine, Margaret. I didn't know your pa long before we married. I knew he wore a friendly smile, was funny, and that he practically dripped with charm. I didn't get the fairy tale ending you dream about as a little girl." I could tell this was very difficult for her to say. Mom then leaned forward to grab my hands.

"Margaret, I don't want you to make a mistake you can't change. I wish more than anything for you to be happy." Mom cried softly.

I climbed out of bed and reached to comfort her. The sun slanted in through the window and the room smelled like roses and early morning. I loved the familiar scent. I breathed in the scent of the

Falling

room and of my mother deeply. I suddenly realized that maybe she needed me to comfort her occasionally. I patted her back and stood to look down at her. "Don't worry, mom, I will be happy. You will see."

∽

Just before the small ceremony I stared at my reflection in the oval mirror hung up in the dressing room of the church. It wasn't a very well-lit room, but the small window behind me cast a ray of sunshine that seemed to help with my bridal glow. I felt nervous, but also excited. My simple dress looked beautiful in the mirror billowing down my hips to the floor with lace trim. My mom bought the material and made the dress herself. She gave it to me as a gift which surprised me since quality fabric was expensive and we didn't have a lot of money.

It was also scarce these days since the end of the war. My mom's talent made a perfect career since there seemed to be a shortage of clothing. People needed a talented seamstress. She could make about anything look new again. All my clothes growing up were made by her.

I ran one of my gloved hands over the front folds of the dress, pressing out any wrinkles. My hair looked neat and styled, and my cheeks were pink and rosy. I didn't wear a veil. I wanted nothing obstructing my view of George standing at the altar waiting for me. Plus, I always thought they looked a little old-fashioned. My mom seemed disappointed about my decision and thought every bride should wear one.

I couldn't wait for George to see me in my wedding attire. Just then I heard a soft knock on the door before mom walked in.

"Don't you look beautiful." She said with one of her famous grins.

"Thanks mom, I'm so nervous. Have you seen George yet?"

Mom pursed her lips slightly "I have, and I have to say he looks handsome. He cleans up pretty nice. I still can't believe his parents aren't coming for the wedding. Who doesn't go to their own child's wedding?"

"He's estranged from his parents. They barely talk so it's not surprising they aren't coming."

"Oh, Margaret, are you sure you want to do this? You're still so young and..." mom caught the last of what she was going to say on a small sob.

"Mom, I love George. Everything is going to be fine. I am going to be so happy. We're going to be so happy together." I said sternly before tearing up a bit myself.

"Alright my girl, no more tears for us. I'm going to believe you. George better make sure you are happy, you deserve it." She replied with a twinkle in her eye.

I gave her a hug. Not a delicate obligatory hug, but a hug as if to say I'm still your little girl. Mom chuckled as she patted my back. "Alright now, no more of this, you're going to wrinkle your dress. Besides, I have something for you."

I pulled back to look at her as she reached into her pocket to pull out a hairpin. I recognized it from my mother's jewelry box. It sparkled gold with green stones at the end in the shape of a flower. When I was a child, I used to love to sneak into my mother's bedroom and try on her few pieces of jewelry. The hairpin felt special to me, almost as if it called to me.

My Grandma Faye gave it to my mom on her wedding day. I held my grandma as a centerpiece in my life until four years ago when she fell down a set of stairs. She broke her hip, and later died from infection. The loss devastated me.

Grandma was a sweet but superstitious woman from Ireland. She knew nothing but hard times and always insisted that I didn't waste anything. She would say, "Maggie, finish your soup and don't even leave one pea. Such a waste that would be. There are starving children in the world who would love that soup." I learned to take less food on my plate when she was around. Better to get seconds than stuff myself. To this day, I feel guilty throwing away any food.

Falling

Holding the little gold and green pin that sparkled in the light brought a catch to my breath and a deep longing to have my grandma place the pin in my hair. I felt a small pang of guilt for the wish, but oh, how I missed her. Mom placed the pin in my hair, then ran her hand gently against a couple of wayward curls.

"I know it's green and not blue, but I think it will give you luck. She would have wanted you to have it today."

I gave mom a small smile and turned to look at my reflection in the mirror. This was the day I had dreamt about. The dressing room door opened again, and Anna Beth walked in.

"Oh Maggie, you look so beautiful! Are you ready?" Anna Beth wore a wide grin and still glowed from her own recent marital bliss.

I nodded, suddenly filled with too much emotion to speak. Plus, I hated to admit, that I also felt a pang of nervousness. My insides shook as leaves do in a breeze.

"Oh dear, Margaret, I almost forgot this." my mother exclaimed as she pulled out a penny. "Imagine the bad luck if we forgot it, you need all the luck you can get. Now let's get the shoe off."

Mom placed the penny inside my shoe before I stepped back into it. I could feel the penny on the sole of my foot, cool at first but warming up. It was uncomfortable, but also a welcome distraction. Now I stood ready with my shoulders squared in determination.

My uncle Liam walked me down the aisle. He's my mother's only brother, and I have always felt very close to him. Much closer to him than my own father. Quick to smile, intelligent, and kind, he always tried to look after mom and me. As a young girl in high socks and pigtails, he always snuck me a peppermint or a sweet stick when he came to visit. It didn't matter what time it was and if it would likely ruin my super. It was our little secret.

Uncle Liam married a feisty red-haired woman who everyone called Harry. Her actual name is Harriet. The last of seven girls, her father wanted a boy so badly that when she was born, her mom called her Harry as a jest. Much to her husband's annoyance, the name

Ellie Lynn

stuck. Uncle Liam and Harry never had children of their own, so they doted on me.

Walking down the aisle, I locked my eyes on George. He did indeed look handsome. George stood there in a nice brown suit which matched his brown eyes nicely. He smiled, waiting for me to join him. When we joined hands and said our vows, the pews spotted with a few friends and relatives, my heart bursting with joy, I knew this was God's plan. My love for George would withstand anything. After the long years of uncertainties during the war, the loneliness of worry, trying to keep the home front from failing, my future was finally ahead. I was excited to start this new chapter in my life.

Chapter Five

Maggie
September 23, 1946

Sometimes things don't go as you would imagine. Suspended in time during the most terrifying and abhorrent memories of my short life seemed to be a cruel joke. What is the point and why would I want to reminisce about such things knowing that I'm about to die? I'm confused and angry, wishing to hit the ground. I want to escape this death sentence, but I can't. It seems to have captured me completely. Why prolong my fear, my suffering, just to relive some memories? And yet they only continue.

"Margaret, what are you daydreaming about?" My mom said to me one cool morning as she kneaded dough next to Aunt Harry.

"Nothing really, Mom." I said, embarrassed they had caught me daydreaming instead of measuring sugar, like I should have been.

"What's wrong Margaret? Now, before you say anything, remember you can't fool me. I know my girl, and I know when something is bugging you."

I smiled at that. Either I wore all my feelings on my sleeve, or she had some sort of superpower because I couldn't hide anything from her. "I'm worried about George. He woke up from a terrible nightmare last night shouting out and drenched in sweat. One day he's going to hurt himself with his thrashing about." I sighed. "This was the third one this month, and he is so quiet and withdrawn afterwards. I want to help him, but I'm not sure how."

Married for two months now, and despite George working long hours at the police department, we were still in that honeymoon phase. We still craved every moment with each other, every touch, every kiss, and every embrace. I also started to realize recently that there was still a lot I needed to learn about my new husband.

Harry looked at me and gave a sympathetic smile before turning back to her work. When Harry wasn't working or off on one of her many charity projects, she usually joined us to bake. She wore a bright pink apron, which clashed terribly with her red hair slung over her shoulder in a thick braid.

Ellie Lynn

Mom pursed her lips together and clicked her tongue. "Well, he's bound to have nightmares, Margaret, what with being in the war. I cannot even imagine." Sighing, she brushed a loose strand of brown hair away from her face, leaving a white streak of flour across her forehead. "As his wife now, I suppose you will have to try to help him through it. Although I guess it could be worse. You know my friend Rose? Well, she told me that her husband's cousin came back from the war and had to be put in a hospital because he went crazy. The government is looking at doing surgery on him." She whispered the last part as if she was telling a secret.

"That's ridiculous mom. I've never heard of anyone having surgery to fix craziness." I chuckled at the absurdity of it. My mom loved hearing and reciting gossip while we baked.

"No, she's right Maggie. I've heard about it too. It's called a lobotomy. Apparently, some doctors think that if you go and mess things up in the front part of the brain, that will help with these poor men who suffer from combat fatigue. Seems to me these doctors are the ones who are crazy. Nothing good is going to come out of that I tell you." Harry looked at me with a serious expression.

I wasn't surprised Harry would know the name of the procedure. Being a nurse, she always liked to stay on top of new medical advancements. I always told her she should be a doctor, but she enjoyed being a nurse. She said that being a doctor, she wouldn't be able to get as close to her patients as she does now. To her, it was all about relationships and people.

"That's terrible. It doesn't seem right. I'm sure time to adjust is all these men need, not surgery. As for my George, these are just nightmares. I'm sure that he doesn't suffer from this combat fatigue. He's perfectly fine during the day." I reassured them, certain that time and having a supportive wife was really all he needed.

After a quiet moment, Harry spoke. "Maggie, have you tried to talk with him about his nightmares? I think it would help. Combat fatigue is a real thing, and a lot of men suffer from it. Having night-

Falling

mares is one of the symptoms. It's nothing to be ashamed of and it may help if he talks about it with someone."

"Yes, of course I have, but George insists it's part of the past and should stay there. He gets annoyed and sometimes angry when I mention it. I'm not sure what else I can do." I shook my head in frustration.

"There is a doctor that specializes with this type of stuff at the Vet's hospital that may be worth seeing. It could help." Harry shrugged.

"George doesn't want to talk to me about it. Do you really think he would talk to some head doctor?" I asked, a little flustered.

"It's pride." Mom said this in a matter-of-fact sort of way. "Margaret, men have so much damn pride it's coming out their ears!"

Harry and I looked at one another and busted out laughing.

Harry held her side with her flour dusted hands, "I've only seen Liam with hair coming out his ears Aileen, but I guess you never know, maybe someday I'll see pride coming out his ears like stalks of corn!"

"You know what I mean, Harry." Mom chided. She never enjoyed being the brunt of a joke and she never did quite understand Harry's quirky sense of humor... or taste, for that matter. "Men are too damn prideful. They would rather be covered in honey and sat on an anthill rather than ask for help. Lord knows Robert never would."

I wanted to tell her how George was nothing like my pa, but I didn't. The comparisons she continued to make felt frustrating and hurtful. Instead, we all continued our work. Harry began telling us about her charity work she'd been working on, along with a few other women from the church. They were helping with making food, blankets, and other needed items for some of the poorer families in the community. Some of these families had suffered severe hardships during the war.

Many farms not only lost loved ones but those people they depended on to help with the work on the farm. Some managed, and some didn't. One positive aspect of having had POW's around during

Ellie Lynn

the war was their ability to help with some of the work after they recovered from any injuries. Some families were grateful. Some were just angry.

"And the Westerly's, I could barely handle the stench when entering their home. I understand poor but I can't understand filth. Mrs. Beverly and I took them over a pot of stew and some apples for the children. The Lord knows they need it. I really worry for those children as they all are so thin and unkept looking. It's not their fault their parents are who they are. I keep telling Liam that we need to do something about it. I'd take those poor children in myself if I could, but he keeps telling me it's none of our business how they raise their kids. If you ask me, it should be someone's business."

Harry got all worked up, as she was prone to do when talking about something she felt passionate about, especially when it involved children. Harry did what she could about injustice, a champion of the weak, which is probably why she made such an amazing nurse. If anyone could change the world, it would be Harry. Even if it was through one person at a time.

"I've seen Mrs. Westerly a few times in town and frankly I don't think much of her at all. Every time I've seen her, she's flirting with one man or another. Last week, I saw her smoking a cigarette with Mr. Davis outside the cinema. You know Mrs. Davis is laid up in bed getting ready to have their fifth baby. The nerve, to be so open about it all. I don't know what Mr. Davis would even see in her. She smells. I do wish though that she took better care of her babies. I didn't realize things were as bad as all that." Mom pursed her lips.

The Westerly's lived in a small shabby house outside of town. Mr. Westerly lost a leg before the war in an accident at the farm he worked at. Because of it, he couldn't enlist to fight. Being an unhappy, grumbling man before the accident, he is now a belligerent drunk who's regularly thrown out of the local bar for drinking too much and harassing other patrons.

His wife's just about as unfriendly and always seems to have an unwashed smell hanging around her. When I first saw her, she looked

Falling

angry but given a closer look, you could sense a sadness about her. I once bought her daughter a watermelon liquorice stick while they were standing in line behind me at Pete's. Her daughter looked to be about four with stringy blonde hair and big brown eyes. Her face looked sullen and pale, and her blue dress had frays at the ends and elbows. I couldn't help but feel bad for her. Much more than I did her mom.

Mom and Harry gossiped a bit more as we continued working on the bread. When all the loaves finished baking, I kissed mom and Harry goodbye and took a loaf with me. George loved a good cinnamon raisin bread. I figured we could have it with supper with a heavy smear of butter.

Smiling, I drove along the dirt road, headed to our home. It wasn't too far from Mom's house, which was nice but still far enough to allow us our privacy. I enjoyed the window down and the wind blowing the curls around my head and the collar to my dark blue blouse. The sun felt warm and bright even on this fall day and the fields stretched out before me. I felt a bit of excitement about getting home, seeing George that evening. I hadn't seen him since sunup that morning and the sun now blazed high in the sky. He awoke quiet and seemed to be in a bit of a mood. I hoped he cheered up as the day passed since it was such a beautiful day. The cinnamon raisin bread couldn't hurt either.

Turning the corner, I saw our small farmhouse in sight. The small white house with the patio in front was partially shaded with big oak trees. The white paint looked a little faded and started chipping in areas. It needed a fresh coat of paint which George insisted he would do soon, but it felt like home already. I loved to sit out on the porch with George drinking sun tea while listening to our few chickens squawk. We would talk. Mostly about our hopes and dreams for our lives and the children we hoped to have. These were my favorite times.

I pulled our 1942 Ford pickup truck onto our dirt driveway and hopped out the front. The dust was settling around me as I saw

Ellie Lynn

George coming around from the back of the house. He wore a big grin on his face in greeting and wore his plain clothes instead of his uniform. It was unusual for him to be home at this hour. His hours were usually long at the police department.

"There's my beautiful wife. I've been waiting for you for the past half hour." He said as he walked towards me.

"Sorry George," I giggled as he grabbed me around the waist and swung me around in a circle, held tight against his chest. It was obvious his mood was much better. "Harry joined us to make bread today and you know how her and mom are when they get to talking…"

"Oh, I can imagine. I wonder what they said about me today." George gave me a half joking look. He then slid me down his body to land on my feet. I wrapped my arms around his neck to feel his silky, dark hair. His hand still at my back.

"Now George, they both think the world of you," I started to lie, but then laughed at his knowing grin. "Okay, well maybe not mom but you know how stubborn she is. She decided a long time ago that nobody was good enough for me. I disagree though since I found the perfect man." I said as I stood up on my tiptoes to plant a brief kiss on George's lips.

As I started pulling away, his arms tightened around my waist and he groaned and deepened the kiss. It felt as if we were the only two people alive standing in that driveway. I pulled away to ask why he was home so early.

"Do I need a reason to spend some extra time with my lovely wife? I simply asked the thieves and murderers of the town to not cause a ruckus this evening so that I could come home a little early. Besides, it dawned on me you and I have never been up to Terry's nook to go fishing before." His smile broadened and his eyes gleamed. Behind his smile, though, I sensed a slight uneasiness.

Terry's nook was a part of the Lower Salt Creek that was considered a prime fishing spot. It sadly gained the name ever since a five-year-old boy named Terry Jensen drowned there about fifteen years

Falling

earlier. I always found it a little unnerving people would nickname the area after him.

"George, it's already a quarter past three. Isn't it a little late in the day to go out fishing? Maybe we should stay inside." I said as my smile broadened mischievously. I started to reach up to kiss him again.

"As tempting as that sounds, Maggie, we are going fishing. The poles and tack are ready to go." No arguing the point with George as he gently pushed me away. We were going fishing.

I didn't like fishing. I went once with my pa when I was twelve on a hot summer day. He took me by insistence from mom to spend more time with me. Uncle Liam asked to take me a few times before, but pa never let him. He insisted it was a father's duty to teach their children to fish. It took my dad twelve years to do it.

On that particular day, we cast our lines into the dirty pond a few miles from our house while we talked of simple non-consequential things. Then I got the first bite. I didn't know what to do as my pa yelled instructions at me. Eventually the fish untangled himself from my line.

"Stupid girl, just like your mother." Pa said as he smacked the side of my head. Then he reached for his whiskey bottle and took a long swallow. We left about an hour or so and a half a bottle later. It was the last time we tried spending quality time together before he died.

"Maggie?" George said with a concerned look.

Realizing I'd been caught up in my memory, I smiled and nodded my head in agreement as George let me go to grab the fishing gear and a basket of refreshments he packed. He threw them in the back of the pickup truck as I took the loaf of cinnamon raisin bread into the house. After I changed into a pair of trousers, old shoes, and a faded gray blouse with little purple flowers on it, we set off for Terry's nook.

Once there, we walked through the tall grass to a small clearing partly shaded by a big tree. George carried the fishing gear, and I carried the small basket of refreshments. I didn't even know what it held as George packed it. A slight breeze rustled the leaves, and everything seemed to be alive around us. There is something about the changing fall colors that I have always loved. It's as if the trees give one last shout out of everything beautiful magical in the world before the leaves die and crumple to the ground. Leaving a sense of hope that everything would be okay, that there would be life once again.

We sat against a fallen branch close to the water, and cast our lines in. This was, of course, after I failed miserably the first two tries before George helped me. He stood behind me with both of his hands over mine, showing me the motions while whispering in my ear what I needed to do. So close that I could feel my back slightly touching his chest. He gave out a breathy, small laugh and walked away to tend to his pole. It amazed me how he could still cause my heart to miss a beat simply by standing close to me.

We sat in silence for a while, watching the sun glisten off the water. We were both caught in our own thoughts. I, of course, was thinking what an amazing romantic surprise this day turned out to be. I surprisingly enjoyed fishing with him. As for George, well, I couldn't guess what he was thinking.

"George, what brought on this surprise?"

He closed his eyes and for a moment I wasn't sure if he would answer, but then he did. "I needed to get away today, do something relaxing and fun. Something normal." He spoke almost hesitantly.

"Thank you for bringing me. I have to admit it is relaxing and I'm having fun." I said, although I wanted to say more. Such a generic response, but I didn't know how to put into words what else I wanted to say.

"You're my wife Maggie. Of course I'd bring you. I'll make you a fine fisherman... er... fisherwoman in no time." He said with a broad smile that didn't quite reach his eyes. Patience, Maggie, patience, I told myself.

Instead of saying more, I smiled and turned back towards the

Falling

water where my small bobber floated. George talked about his work that day, although I was sure I only got a version of the events. George talked little about the difficulties of his work, as much as he avoided talking about the war. I knew his work could be difficult, dangerous even, and I could only imagine some of the things he saw. I wondered if something made him want to leave work early. He'd never done this before and I wished that he knew I was strong enough to hear about it. Strong enough to be there for him.

I loved listening to him talk. It was soothing and made me imagine growing old together, sitting on our porch, and remembering our lives so filled with love. He grew quiet after a while, as did I. I told him a little about the gossip mamma and Harry shared and we chuckled together. But then we fell into comfortable silence once again.

I began to lightly hum one of my favorite songs, *How Deep Is the Ocean*. My mom, Harry, and I would sometimes listen to music while we baked if there wasn't any gossip to share. Whenever this song came on, my body relaxed, and my soul seemed to glow. Funny how a simple song can make you feel good.

"It's a perfect day to be here, George." I said as I broke from humming. "Just looking out over the water makes me feel relaxed. Especially since I am here with you." I looked towards him with a small smile. "It reminds me of playing in the mud puddles with Anna Beth when we were younger." I laughed, "The smell of mud, the breeze, the sound of the bugs."

"I can see you playing in the mud as a child, Maggie, but Anna Beth? No, I can't picture that or anything else involving getting her hands dirty."

I laughed because he, of course, was right. As my oldest friend, Anna Beth was the perfect picture of a blonde girl, blue eyes, and pretty dresses. Yet she tagged along on my tomboy adventures. "Well, I should say, when *I* played in mud puddles. Anna Beth mostly watched. And squirmed a bit, and groaned, and held her nose." I gave him an overly serious expression before we both laughed again.

Ellie Lynn

Then we were quiet once more. George tried to snag a bite on his line but soon lost it, so he reeled his line in to re-bait it. I had yet to have so much as a nibble, which I didn't mind at all. After putting another worm on his hook, George stood up and cast his line back in, then, after turning his reel a few times, he sat back down. After a few moments of sitting in silence with only the sound of the water lapping against the shore gently and an occasional chirp from a bird, something seemed to change. Nothing in the atmosphere but more of a feeling. The silence stretched, and the air seemed heavy. After years of living with an unpredictable father, I could sense change. As I wondered more about it, George quietly spoke up.

"Maggie, do you know what sitting here looking at the water reminds me of?" He asked. I shook my head as my grasp on my pole became tighter. Something instinctually told me this would be important.

"It reminds me of a young girl, probably six or seven floating in a small dirty pond." George said, his gaze staring out at the water. He seemed to be tense and hesitant. I couldn't breathe. I didn't dare to.

Then, after a brief pause, he continued, "I saw her while in Italy. War devastated her small town. Some buildings were burnt, some were crumbling, but everything seemed to be touched by those German bastards. Cold out and in the middle of winter, days of walking and feeling as if your feet would surely freeze solid, the sun finally poked out through the clouds. Everyone seemed to walk a little lighter with that small amount of warmth shining through." George paused again. This time a little longer. His eyes looked far away even though his face looked relaxed.

I sat there waiting for him to continue to talk, which seemed to take ages. I wanted so badly to reach out and touch his hand, his shoulder, something to tell him I'm here for you, I'm listening. But I didn't, I didn't dare to. I knew it would stop him from talking, and I desperately wanted to hear what he would say.

"I walked down a small slope behind a couple of crumbling buildings, one which looked to have been a small bookshop. There were

Falling

books scattered about, half burned and covered with mud. Behind it there were some large trees and what looked like a glimpse of water. Hoping it was not fully frozen over, I walked down to it to wash my face. I knew it would wake me up, since we'd had been traveling endlessly. That's when I saw her. She looked so out of place amongst the beauty of nature. It's... hard to explain, but it was like the pond and her were complete opposites. The pond and trees and light looked so peaceful, and yet she proved it all to be a sham. An illusion, the sight of her embodied the evidence of violence. The epitome of evil. She looked so small and innocent. She wore a purple wool coat and black shoes and stockings. Her blonde hair floating out around her, and you could see her little bluish hands lightly bobbing in and out of the water. A gunshot wound marred the back of her head. The dark blood stood out against the light color of her hair, drawing your eyes right to it." George said in an even voice. No cracks, no actual emotion, as if he was telling me a story.

"I stood there for a few moments and looked at her. The sun shone, almost illuminating her as it sparkled against the water and patches of ice. A few black birds flew from tree to tree, and the breeze swept lightly through some of the tall dead grass. Life carried on as this little girl floated. It's interesting how that happens you know."

George turned away from looking over the water to look at me. "I've often wondered about her, her name was, where her family was." He sighed and closed his eyes for a moment. He almost looked pained for a brief second, but when he opened his eyes again it was gone, and he turned back to the water.

"After a moment, I turned around and headed back to my men. I didn't say anything to anyone about her. There was no need, and it wasn't that unusual to come across dead civilians including children." George said as one side of his mouth slightly slanted up. "We all fought own private battles in things that we saw, and for some odd reason she haunted me." He then looked at me for a moment before hanging his head down and looking away. As if it embarrassed him for sharing the memory with me.

Ellie Lynn

We were both quiet once again. I sat in a state of shock, not knowing what to say. I could picture her floating in that cold water, but I knew that what I imagined would never compare with seeing something like that.

"Thank you for confiding in me about her George." I said in a quiet and unsure voice. He didn't turn towards me; he didn't even acknowledge he heard me. What I said felt inadequate, and I knew it, so I tried again. "I cannot even imagine how horrible seeing her like that would be. I guess the only solace is knowing she's in heaven and no longer in pain, no longer experiencing the horrors of war." I said this hoping it would be comforting. The minute he looked at me, I could tell it didn't. He trusted me this once, and I failed him.

"Oh, well, that's a good thing I guess, she hopefully being in heaven. That is if there is one. How God could allow all of that to happen is beyond me and seriously makes me doubt there is one." He said mockingly. "But you... let's look on the bright side of things. You have no idea because that is the pleasant way people like you see things. The reality Maggie is she laid there dead with a hole in her head as her icy blue body rotted in that pond. Nothing more. She should have been snuggled up to her mom, or playing hopscotch, or sleeping in her warm bed. But she wasn't. Another forgotten casualty of the war, that's it. War doesn't discriminate. Babies, children, women, the elderly, this unknown child... they all died!" George's eyes were cold and angry.

I didn't say another word as I tried to swallow the lump rising in my throat. Tears sprang to my eyes, and I tried to keep them from falling. George gave a loud sigh and turned back to the water. I felt a tear slip down my cheek; I didn't want it to, but then a second one followed. I turned away and wiped my face against my shoulder. I didn't want George to know I sat crying, and I tried to be as silent as I could be.

"Christ Maggie, I didn't mean to make you cry. Forget everything I said. I love that you try to see the good in things. I love that about you." George said as he tried to give an apologetic smile before

Falling

reeling his line in. "Better bring your line in Maggie, we should probably get going so you have enough time to start on supper. Besides, I'm done fishing anyway." He said as if nothing unusual happened. As if for the past few minutes, he didn't just open himself up long enough to slam shut against me.

I nodded my head in agreement and reeled in. I could see the bobber skipping along as it got closer to the shore. I imagined her blue hands bobbing along as well. The sun got lower on the horizon and George stood right that it was time to go. The easy-going day drifted away. I could feel the tension in the air so strong that it felt tangible. Things went wrong so quickly, but I could hardly put blame on anyone for it. My heart hurt for my husband because I knew more now than I ever did known that he was hurting inside. I wanted to help him, but I didn't know how.

Later that night I laid awake in bed listening to the wind howling outside, along with the even breaths from the man lying next to me. They were almost in tune to one another despite one being even and steady and the other being tremulous. I could feel George's heat even though we were not touching. The cool air chilled me in my slight cotton nightgown despite the brightly colored patched quilt pulled up to my chest. His warmth beckoned me to move closer. I didn't. Instead I watched the shadows from the waving branches move across the papered wall in front of me. The shadows gave the pink and yellow flowers on the wallpaper an eerie look as they seemed to dance.

I felt tired to my bones. When we came home, I quietly worked on making supper while George sat on our porch drinking whiskey. The thought of it now made my cheeks burn with anger. George didn't drink, he professed not too many times. He knew how much I

Ellie Lynn

hated it, so he sat on the porch by himself. In my mind, despite my anger, I tried to understand.

Later that night, George and I made love passionately after retiring to bed together. Our lovemaking held a need and urgency to it. We felt deep passion before, as our bodies moved together and we were drenched in sweat. This was different. There held a certain amount of pain surrounding the passion. Not physical, but emotional. I could feel his need and pain and I accepted his sharing of it, even if it was just in the way he made love to me.

Now, I couldn't sleep. I couldn't help but think about the day, about the past few months, and of course, about the war. I couldn't help but think of the child who floated in the water and how seeing her impacted George so much. And then I thought of all the unknown stories of brutality, innocence, and pain that George hadn't shared with me and that I could only imagine. I closed my eyes and whispered a prayer, "Dear Lord, please be with my husband and help him with the demons that he fights. Please, be with me as I try to be a comfort to George and please help me be a good wife to him."

Turning over onto my side, facing George, I watched as he slept. His face looked so relaxed and almost boyish. His brown hair mussed, and his long dark lashes rested gently closed. He was bare from the chest up and I could see the scar about two inches long and jagged under his left shoulder, its white indent standing out against his tanned skin. There were small scars scattered around his chest, one under a nipple, one on the side of his neck, and a couple along his ribs.

I of course, noticed these scars before. I curiously wondered about how he got them, although I never asked. I assumed some may be from the war, which is probably why I never broached the subject, knowing how he didn't like to talk about it. Now my imagination ran with stories of how he got the scars. Was the one under his shoulder from a bullet or a bayonet? I wasn't even sure what a scar from either would look like. Was the one on his neck from shrapnel or from some other incident that didn't have anything to do with the war.

Falling

Now the thought consumed me with wanting to know. George experienced much more than I imagined. I felt naïve. I heard stories of the war, read the newspaper articles, saw some of its effects and I certainly felt the anxiousness and worry while waiting for word of my neighbors, of our men... other people's men. Now one of those men is my entire life.

I closed my eyes, feeling the deep fatigue finally hit me. My emotions were in turmoil, but I sighed and pulled the quilt up a little higher to ward off my chill. George turned over to face me while laying his arm over my waist, and he pulled me in closer. I opened my eyes, expecting George to be awake and looking at me, but he slept on. His warmth seemed to seep through my body as it lulled me closer to sleep. We had a lifetime to figure things out, to heal, to talk, but for now I snuggled in closer and let his presence comfort me. Tomorrow would be a new day.

Chapter Six

Maggie
December 25, 1946

The wind rushed past my body while my heart beat frantically. I can suddenly relate to the floating girl. Nature doesn't seem to correlate with what event is taking place. Otherwise, the sky would be dark and cloudy, and the land be dust. Just as the sunlight glistened off the ice and water surrounding the little girl's lifeless body, the warm sun is shining brightly above my soon to be one. The wildflowers are bright and beautiful below me, and the birds continue to sing and chirp. I'm aware now of all this beauty surrounding me as he continues to watch me fall.

    Christmas morning arrived cold and miserable as I woke up sick. I quickly climbed out of our warm bed and ran to the bathroom before heaving my small amount of supper from the night before. It was still dark out, although I could see the beginnings of sunrise shining in through the window. I pulled back the curtains to allow a little moonlight to shine in our window at night. George slept better that way.

    I laid my forehead on the seat of the toilet as I willed the nausea and slight dizziness to go away. This happened to be the second morning in a row I woke up sick. Yesterday it seemed to last a good part of the morning, then again right after lunch. I ate very little on Christmas Eve, which was disappointing since I made a special supper of pork roast and potatoes with caramelized carrots on the side. This was George's and my first Christmas together and I wanted it to be special, especially since he got to spend Christmas at home instead of at work.

    I barely touched my food, but George acted so sweet to me about the whole thing. After eating his fill and complimenting me the entire time on how wonderful it tasted, he sent me up to bed and cleaned up the dishes from supper.

    With my forehead resting against the cold toilet seat, I smiled at the memory. Feeling like the nausea was gone, I stood up from where I crouched at on the cold bathroom floor and walked over to the sink.

Ellie Lynn

It was chilly in there and goosebumps covered my arms as I shivered. My bare feet against the cold tiles probably didn't help matters much either. I turned the water on, cupped my hands, and sucked in the water. The coldness slightly hurt my teeth as I swished the water around and then spit and then did it once again. The third drink I swallowed, and the water felt good going down my throat. When I looked up in the mirror, I saw George standing in the open doorway.

"You okay sweetheart?" He asked. His brown eyes showing his concern that I could even see in the darkened bathroom. His tone was soft and worried.

"Yeah, I hoped I would feel better today since it's Christmas." I said and then as an afterthought, "Merry Christmas George."

George chuckled, "Merry Christmas to you, wife." He then walked over to me and drew me into his arms. He felt warm and heavenly against my cold body. "Do you think you could be pregnant?" He asked softly into my hair. It was a whisper, and I felt his breath move the hairs on the top of my head. I noticed a slight excitement in his voice.

"I'm pretty sure I am. I'm sorry I didn't mention my suspicion before, but I decided to wait for the perfect time. And I wanted to get it confirmed by the doctor, and well... I guess I've just been a little scared." I said, finally telling the truth of the matter which made me feel a bit ashamed. I pulled just far enough away to look up at George. His eyes were twinkling, and he wore a small smile on his face. He reached up his callused hand to stroke my cheek.

"You are going to make a wonderful mother Maggie. There is nothing to fear." He said sincerely, which was possibly the sweetest thing he ever said to me. It instantly melted my heart and my eyes filled with tears.

"George..." I started to say as my words caught on a sob.

George's other hand reached up to cup my other cheek. "Maggie, everything is going to be okay. I couldn't be happier."

"I'm happy too." A couple of fat tears rolled down my cheeks.

I gave a small watery laugh as I reached up on tiptoes and kissed

Falling

him. He laughed as well as he wrapped his arms around my waist and lifted me up against him. I continued to place kisses on his lips, his cheeks, wherever I could. I was filled with so much joy in that moment that some of my fear washed away. We were going to have the perfect little family that we had talked about.

The next thing I knew, George put his arm under my knees and lifted me up as if I was a child. He carried me back to our bed and covered me with the quilt before climbing back in beside me. As soon as he did, I snuggled into his side as he lay on his back. Before long, I was warm and comfortable listening to George as he breathed. I could hear his heartbeat rhythmically thumping from where my head was laying.

"Maggie, do you think I will be a good father?" George asked.

I lifted my head up slightly to look at him. I could tell from his tone that he was unsure suddenly. George never acted unsure. I guessed it was because he had never been very close to either of his parents. Especially his father.

"Yes George, you will make an amazing father. You will be so patient and loving, and... fun." I smiled.

"Fun?" He laughed slightly. "Really, I'm not sure fun is the most important quality for a father."

"Well, I happen to think that it is, thank you very much." I teased as I laid my head back on his chest. "Being able to have fun with your children is very important. I can see you now showing our son how to fish, how to kick a ball, how to build things with his small wooden blocks...how to laugh." Smiling, I had no doubts that George would make a fine father. "I wish my father had been more fun."

"Instead of a drunk, you mean?" George said a bit sarcastically. "That is the one thing I will never be." George then kissed the top of my head apologetically. I didn't mind, it was true.

"Besides Maggie, what if it's actually teaching her how to fish, kick a ball, and how to build things?" George said with a forced seriousness. I couldn't help but smile, too. I could picture this scene as

Ellie Lynn

well. A beautiful little girl with dark curly hair and big brown eyes, like George.

I yawned, feeling tired suddenly. George placed another kiss on the top of my head and told me to sleep for a little while longer. We needed to be up in a few hours to go to mom's house for Christmas. A little more sleep would be good and as my eyes grew heavy, I heard George whisper, "I love you, Maggie." I smiled in return, too tired to answer back.

A few hours later we were on our way to mom's house. In my lap sat a warm cherry pie. I could smell its sweet tartness as it cooled against my thighs. We sat in comfortable silence for the trip. I watched through the small opening that I cleared of fog as snow covered houses passed us by. Within minutes I would wipe my hand across the glass again for a clearer view, since my breath seemed to fog it back up.

Feeling eager to get there as my mom made the best ham and sweet cinnamon yams and I anticipated the sweet tastes on my tongue. I was also excited to see my Uncle Liam, Aunt Harry, and my great Aunt Evie. Aunt Evie was my grandma Faye's younger sister. Funny and spirited, she reminded me of my grandma even though they were quite different in personalities.

I missed my grandma Faye dearly, and I soaked up anything that reminded me of her. Getting up in years, I never took for granted any time spent with Aunt Evie. As we pulled to a stop in front of the house, I felt the small butterflies in my stomach. I was a little nervous. I turned to George, and he seemed to read my anxiousness.

"Let's wait to tell everyone until after Christmas, okay?" He said, then he leaned over and placed a small kiss on my lips.

I nodded my head and opened the door to step out into the cold. The snow crunched beneath my boots as I walked to mom's front door, George just behind me. I stood there looking at the Christmas wreath hanging on the door and thinking how strange that this was no longer my home, as it had been the year before.

"Ready?" George said an instant before opening the door. As

Falling

soon as we walked into the warm and loud house, we were greeted with hugs and wishes of Merry Christmas. My favorite holiday, this year it felt extra special.

Mom, seemed to be warming up to George, enveloped him in a hug after hugging me. George looked stiff and uncomfortable. Pulling away, she looked up at him. "You're doing a good job; my girl looks happy." Mom grabbed his coat and mine and hung them on the coat tree.

"Margaret, dear, let me have that pie. It smells wonderful! Did you use those cherries I gave you?" Mom continued talking as she walked to the kitchen, expecting me to follow, of course, and not exactly waiting for a reply. Hosting family get-togethers gave mom a chance to shine, and she took pride in it.

I gave George an apologetic smile and followed her, leaving him to the rest of my family. I didn't think he minded, though, as my mother always seemed to annoy him. He enjoyed talking to Liam and Harry anyway.

In the kitchen, everything was ready to be placed on the table. The smells were all delicious and seemed to compete on what would be the strongest, the one that made your mouth water the most. At the moment, the turkey was overpowering. Usually, I would be excited to taste it, as my mom knew how to cook a bird. This year, however, I planned to stay clear of it as another wave of nausea passed through me.

"You look sort of peeked, Margaret, are you feeling okay?" Mom asked.

"I'm just tired. What would you like me to take to the table?"

"You can grab the beans; I'll grab the potatoes." She looked at me suspiciously.

"What can I help with?" Harry appeared in the doorway. Not waiting for an answer, she grabbed the yams and walked out to the table to set them on. Mom and I followed her with our hands full as well.

"I swear George and Liam could talk all night about what this

Ellie Lynn

person did, how that person was arrested, and so on. They gossip more than us women." Harry said with her fists on her hips right before walking back into the kitchen to grab more food. Full of energy and as eccentric as ever, she wore a bright red dress that sported a white furry collar. She looked like a female, red-headed version of Santa Claus.

"Well, I'm glad George gets along with Uncle Liam so well, and you know, has something in common with him." I said, as I shrugged my shoulders before changing the subject. "Aunt Evie looks well, how has she been, Mom?"

"You know, Aunt Evie, she's as strong as an ox. I imagine she will outlive even me." Mom said mischievously but also with a serious edge.

"Mom! I'm so happy to see her. I haven't seen her since before George and I married. I wish she could have come to the wedding." Aunt Evie's son Alroy was a selfish man who rarely took Aunt Evie anywhere, which was unfortunate, since Aunt Evie never learned how to drive. Seeing her for Christmas made me feel thankful that Harry and Liam picked her up this year.

As the last dish was placed on the table and the sweet tea glasses were filled, Mom yelled out to the family room for everyone to come to the table to eat. The one time when no one seemed to mind her loud and obnoxious yell. The call for supper on Christmas brought excitement given the room was filled with delicious smelling aromas. All the aromas this year seemed to make my stomach turn.

I nibbled on what I could. The freshly baked rolls were heavenly with their melted butter. I also took the time to look around and fully appreciate the gift of my family there with me. I don't know why I never sat and noticed this before. Probably because I usually kept busy stuffing my face with my favorite dishes as well, but at this moment I felt a true and deep appreciation for my family.

Harry looked at Uncle Liam and smiled at him as he tried her apricot glazed carrots. He took a bite, his eyebrows lifted, and he nodded in approval. This made her happy. Mom chatted with Aunt

Falling

Evie in between passing the salt, passing the mashed potatoes for seconds, and of course playing her part as hostess. I don't think it was in her to sit and eat her meal without helping everyone else. She played the part of taking care of everyone so well that no one usually noticed. Then I turned to my side and looked at George. He sat quietly, eating his meal. He turned to me and smiled. I smiled back. This was my family.

"George, this must be nice for you to have a warm meal at home with family this year. I imagine your last few Christmases weren't as nice, you know, with the war." said Aunt Evie with a stern stare. The room went quiet for a second, all eyes focused on George. My heart literally sank. I couldn't believe she said that. Bringing up the war on this beautiful Christmas day seemed... well, wrong.

Finishing chewing, George replied slowly, "Well, last Christmas wasn't so bad, although I spent a quiet evening alone. Which wasn't such a bad thing." George chewed another bite of his turkey before speaking again. Everyone seemed to be holding their breaths. "The Christmas before that was a little rough. I was a prisoner, and we didn't exactly get a full Christmas spread if you know what I mean." This he said with a wink before continuing, "I ate a piece of milk chocolate though that the Red Cross sent us. At the time it was enough."

"I hadn't realized you were a POW George," Uncle Liam broke the following silence to say. "Maggie never mentioned it. I imagine that was rough." He glanced at me as he said my name.

George simply shrugged. "Yes, well, it was quite an experience."

George had been a Prisoner of War! How did I not know this? Why hadn't he told me? My mind seemed to spin with questions.

"Was it the Japs or the Nazis, George?" Aunt Evie asked matter-of-factly. I loved her dearly, but I couldn't decide if I wanted to sink under the table or seriously tell her to mind her own business.

"The Nazis captured me..." George started to say.

"Those Nazi bastards!" Aunt Evie exclaimed in her loud elderly voice while also pounding her fist on the table causing the glasses to

Ellie Lynn

rattle. "I never did like those Germans. I had a friend once who dated a German. He was a dirty swine back then, and that was before the war. Well, I guess it could have been worse. You could have been a prisoner of those Japs. What with their weird customs and all that fish. I hate fish." Then, when her tirade was over, she simply went back to eating. I was pretty sure this time that Aunt Evie was losing her mind. Her words were becoming more outrageous the older she got.

"Aunt Evie, I'm sure George doesn't want to think about that right now. We should all just enjoy the time we have with each other on this Christmas day." I said, knowing I sounded like I was chastising a child. Harry took the cue and asked Aunt Evie about her son, Alroy.

"Oh, he's fine. He's happy as a pea in a pod with that little young wife of his. I can't say I like her much, though. She talks to me like I'm deaf or about to keel over. I think she wants all the money he's supposedly bringing in from his shop. Little does the harlot know that financially he's not doing so well. He borrowed money from me last month to cover his mortgage. Ha!" Aunt Evie snickered. "The joke is going to be on her when my son dies, and she's left with nothing but debt. And I'll be telling you, if that son of mine doesn't lose some weight he's put on, he's going to have a heart attack or something. But what do I know? I'm just the person who gave birth to him." The last she said in a mumble. Her annoyance was quite apparent.

My Aunt Evie was outspoken and completely inappropriate, which in a way seemed to endear her to us even more. You almost expected it from her, even if she still made you feel caught off guard. My Grandma Faye would have been red in the face by now with embarrassment. I looked to my mother, who had inherited much of her mother's characteristics. Yep, red in the face.

After everyone ate their full, we all gathered out into the family room to relax by the tree. I had thankfully eaten some food without feeling too nauseous. It was good because I wasn't ready yet to explain what I suspected. George sat on the sofa next to me and

Falling

laughed as Uncle Liam told us of a case he recently tried. Uncle Liam was a prosecutor and, according to Harry, a damn good one. Apparently, the accused criminal literally lost his pants while running from the drugstore he just robbed. The man snagged his pants on the door in his haste while leaving. As he ran away, his pants fell around his ankles, tripping him.

It slowed him down long enough to be caught by the store clerk, who was an older, heavyset woman. She came running after him and beat him silly with her cane. The police, after putting the handcuffs on, dragged him bare assed to the squad car. Everyone chuckled at the absurdity of it. George hadn't been one of the arresting officers but already heard the story from his fellow policemen.

"I would like to have seen that." said Aunt Evie with a small grin on her face and a faraway look.

"Aunt Evie!" Mom scolded.

"Well, I would have." Aunt Evie shot back. "It's been a while since I've seen a young buck's backside."

You could hear Harry trying to hold back a laugh under her hand pressed against her mouth. Uncle Liam rolled his eyes.

"Maggie, how is married life treating you? You look happy." Said Aunt Evie, clearly changing the subject since mom looked to be slightly frowning now.

"Thanks Aunt Evie, I am happy." I said this as I turned to George and smiled. He grabbed my hand and kissed it before turning back to Aunt Evie. "George is a wonderful husband; he makes me very happy."

"Well, he better." Aunt Evie said sharply.

She then turned back to Uncle Liam and asked what other types of cases he's been working on. Mom and Harry began to talk as well, and the room became full of chatter. George leaned in closer to me and whispered, "I like Aunt Evie, she cracks me up."

"I knew you would." I replied, then on a second thought, "I'm sorry for her bringing up everything during supper. I know it probably made you feel uncomfortable."

Ellie Lynn

"It's fine." Came his simple reply. Then he squeezed my hand and kissed it again.

As I sat there listening to my family talking, bickering, and laughing, I felt a sense of being at home. It was amazing being able to share this with George, as I knew he hadn't experienced many of these types of family gatherings. I hoped he would grow to love them all as I did. I felt a small wave of nausea, reminding me that next Christmas would be different. There would be toys under the tinsel covered tree and a sweet baby to hold. I didn't mind the nausea; it meant something amazing was happening.

I felt another slight squeeze on my hand and when I turned to look at George; I realized he was probably having the same thoughts. His eyes were intense and longing as he looked into mine. I smiled in return. This was our little secret, even for a short time. I felt the little life inside already bringing George and me closer together. This was all I ever dreamed of. The excitement of telling my family of our news gave me butterflies, but for now I would enjoy this moment as being ours.

"Ahh, just look at you two. To be young and in love again, whispering secrets to one another. That kind of love doesn't come around very often you know."

Both George and I broke eye contact to look at Aunt Evie, who spoke so sweet and quietly that I couldn't believe it came from her. I smiled; George smiled as we looked at the family, who were awkwardly looking back at us now. I felt my cheeks burn.

"Thank y...." I started to say while George said, "We're having a baby!"

I turned swiftly to look at him, feeling surprised at his revelation. He looked back at me apologetically and then shrugged with an enormous smile. It was hard to be angry with his excitement. The room instantly erupted in cheers.

Chapter Seven

Maggie

February 3, 1947

For the first time since plunging backwards into the open space of nothingness, I feel a sensation of peace run through me. My family seems to surround me even as I fall a long way from their personal beings. I smell the food from that night, hear the laughter, and feel their presence. I can feel the gentle love of my husband and remember our hopes and dreams that we shared. It's hard to understand why I'm falling as I look up into those deep brown eyes. Preparing myself to be strong, I know the end is close but there is more still to remember. The rocks below me won't pierce my skin yet. The pain is in the memory that I know is surely ahead.

Growing up, there were many times that Anna Beth and I enjoyed sleepovers. We did this so often that mom used to say that we might as well be sisters. We would stay up at night talking about school, boys, girls we didn't like, and of course our futures. They were always intertwined, and we knew we would always be close. It's a comforting feeling knowing that you have a friend like that.

Our fifteen-year-old selves imagined getting married to the cutest boys and having the cutest babies. Our babies would be close in age, of course, and they would play together and become best friends. Just like us.

We got married months apart. Apparently, we were going to have babies' months apart as well. Anna Beth told me of her condition after Thanksgiving. She was due at the beginning of April and expected twins. Twins... I couldn't imagine, but I was so thrilled for her and Hank. We exchanged letters weekly, but I hadn't seen them since early that fall. I was eager to see Anna Beth's rounded belly and her glowing smile. I couldn't wait to talk and plan and share in each other's excitement. I hoped and prayed that George and Hank would like each other and become friends as well. They met only a few times before but spent little time talking with each other. This is why Anna Beth and I planned this small visit. They would stay with us for the night before going to visit Anna Beth's family.

Ellie Lynn

I sat at my kitchen table drinking a cup of Earl Grey tea while waiting patiently to hear their car pull up our driveway. George wouldn't be off work for another couple of hours, so I waited quietly by myself. I spent the day before thoroughly cleaning the house and made up a bed in the room that would be the nursery. A pot of hot water sat on the stove for hot tea, and I had made some shortbread cookies to snack on. Everything was perfect and ready.

Another ten minutes of waiting before finally hearing tires on the gravel in front of our house. With a light, childlike squeal, I jumped up and half ran to the front door. Opening it, I saw Hank climbing out of the driver's seat. He gave me a quick wave as he made his way around the car to open up Anna Beth's door. Hank, a handsome man in his late twenties recently finished medical school and worked as a resident at Wesley Hospital in Oklahoma City. Opening Anna Beth's door, he held out his hand and assisted her out of the car. My eyes instantly went to her large, rounded belly. She looked adorable in the only way that Anna Beth could while being six months pregnant with twins. Her blonde hair was up in a perfect chignon, her blue eyes sparkled, her maternity dress was fashionable, and even her waddle had a charming sophistication to it.

If she hadn't been my best friend and the kindest person I knew, I would have been instantly green with envy. Even being so, I couldn't help but feel inadequate compared to her. The beautiful pregnancy glow everyone talked about had yet to hit me. My hair seemed more frizzy than usual, and my belly didn't have that perfect pregnancy shape. I looked like I simply put on some unflattering weight.

"Maggie Magpie!" Anna Beth cried out as she walked up the couple of steps to the front door. We embraced in the doorway as Hank held the door open. It felt so good to hug her. As soon as I stepped back, I placed my hands on her belly and giggled.

"You look amazing, I can't believe how big you are...uh, now I don't mean that in a bad way." I hurried up to assure her.

"I know you don't. It happened recently. I barely showed one day and the next it looked like I swallowed a watermelon." Anna Beth

Falling

smiled as she laid her hands on each side of her belly. As we moved further into the front room, Hank closed the door and Anna Beth continued. "You look wonderful, too! I can't believe we are going to both be having babies!"

"Well baby for me, babies for you." I corrected her with a laugh. Then I turned to Hank and gave him a quick hello and a hug. We all chatted for a few minutes before I showed them upstairs to the spare bedroom. After depositing their bags, Hank excused himself to use the restroom. It thankfully gave Anna Beth and me a few moments to talk.

"I hope you and Hank will be comfortable in here for the night. It's not much to look at, well, at least not yet. This is where the nursery will be when this little one comes." I told her as I patted my only slightly rounded belly.

"It's perfect. I imagine it gets the best morning light," said Anna Beth. Then she grabbed both of my hands and pulled me to sit next to her on the bed. It was as if we were teenagers again in her bedroom. "It's so good to see you. I know we write all the time, but it's not the same. I miss you."

"I miss you too." I couldn't help but tear up a bit at this because I deeply missed her. I missed our long talks and simply being around her. For some reason, in her presence, I felt prettier, smarter, more confident, and just a better version of myself. I loved being married to George and he was a friend as much as my husband, but he didn't know me quite like Anna Beth did. I guess I hadn't allowed him to yet.

About fifteen minutes later, we were all down at the kitchen table, enjoying a cup of hot tea and cookies, while we continued to catch up. Hank spoke about his work and the long, tiring hours of being a resident. While he talked, Anna Beth beamed at him. She looked truly smitten by him, and obviously about everything he said and did was perfect in her eyes. When he would pause in conversation, his eyes would meet Anna Beth's and you could read the adoration in them. I couldn't help but hope I didn't look so completely

Ellie Lynn

besotted with George. Good for them; I mean... Anna Beth seemed made for a fairy tale type of life. As for me and George, I enjoyed the realness of marriage. At least I did so far.

We talked for a few more minutes until we heard the front door open, and George called out for me. I got up and hurried through the kitchen doorway out into the small front room to see George standing inside. Anna Beth and Hank followed behind me, albeit slower. George wore a large grin to welcome me as I rushed to give him a hug and a quick peck on the cheek. I couldn't help but feel immensely proud of him as he stood there dressed in his police uniform.

"Hmmm, smells good, whatever you are making. Oh hey, Anna Beth, Hank! It's good to see you. Welcome to our home. Maggie here has been running around like a chicken with its head cut off getting things ready." George said as he walked over to shake Hank's hand and give Anna Beth a small hug.

"Oh George, that's a terrible vision, but yes he's right, I've been excited." Then as an added thought, "And I made a beef roast with carrots and potatoes which should be ready in about a half an hour."

"Sounds amazing and smells even better. I'm going to go get changed out of my uniform and I'll be back down in a few." George said before he headed up the stairs, turning back around at the top to give me a wink. An hour later, we all sat full and content at the dinner table. We listened to some music as we talked. Our chuckles were all dying down from the latest story George treated us to.

Just then *Till the End of Time* came on the radio by Perry Como. George jumped up from his seat to turn the volume up before walking back to me.

"May I have a dance with my beautiful wife?" He asked as he held out his hand to me. My breath seemed to catch, and my stomach fluttered which didn't have anything to do with the baby resting inside me.

"Of course, darling." I replied, admittedly a little embarrassed by the attention. I could hear Anna Beth sigh behind me as I clumsily stood up to follow my husband to the floor in the front room, which

Falling

was open to the table in which we sat. George's arm encircled around my slightly enlarged frame as his free hand grasped mine and tucked it in close. We swayed, we half circled, we parted and came back to one another all with never leaving eye contact.

I felt like the world melted away. I didn't care that Hank and Anna Beth never joined us or that they watched on. I cared that George and I were close and completely focused on one another. It seemed like since marrying we had less of these wonderful moments and would probably have even less after our baby came. I guess I did like a little of the fairy tale stuff as well. The song ended with Anna Beth clapping her hands and laughing.

"Beautiful. You two are the sweetest, don't you think Hank?"

"Uh, yes of course. We would have danced but with Anna Beth's condition and all..." Hank trailed off at the end. The rest of the evening we spent talking and laughing. Hank and George drank a little, which helped to animate Hank a little more, and George smoked a few cigarettes. They seemed to get along fine. I didn't think they would ever become best buddies or anything, but it was enough.

Later the next day, George and I stood on our front porch in the cold, waving as Anna Beth and Hank's car drove away.

"Hank's a little odd, don't you think?" George asked as the car was getting further and further away.

"Well, he is a little different, I guess, but he's nice. And Anna Beth seems so happy with him. He's the type of person I always imagined for her. Can you imagine her marrying someone as bright and bubbly as she is?" I asked as I turned to follow him into the warm house.

"Yes, it would be nauseating." He replied.

I laughed at that. Boys always fawned over Anna Beth in school, so it still surprised me that George didn't fawn over her as well. He liked me. No, he loved me, and I couldn't be happier.

Chapter Eight

Maggie
February 18, 1947

It was a cool February afternoon and I spent the day with mom and Harry picking out fabric for the nursery. Mom decided to sew some pretty yellow curtains to hang in the room that George and I picked for the baby. Not only did we manage to find the perfect fabric in a pale yellow, but some other cute baby items as well. Harry insisted on purchasing the cutest pair of baby booties with a matching hat. They were cream colored with bright green ivy vine stitching. I could almost hear my grandma say, "What a fine Irish baby you will have, Maggie."

After coming home from shopping, I laid down for a nap as I felt tired and had been having small cramps in my belly all day. It felt similar to starting my menstrual cycle. I asked mom about it while shopping, but she reassured me that everything was probably fine. Some cramping could be normal. Plus, I was due for my next doctor's appointment the next day to check on the baby's progress, so I tried not to worry. George was busy working outside, chopping wood from an old tree that lost a large branch because of some heavy, wet snow the week before.

The bedroom was cool and dark, and in the warmth of the blankets, I fell asleep quickly. Sometime later I woke up to sharp pains in my stomach. I felt a little groggy as I tried to reason with what started happening. As I sat up and hugged my stomach, I felt a warm stickiness between my thighs. On an anguished moan, I climbed out of bed and walked to the bathroom. Shaken and scared, the spasms of pain continued, one on top of another. I lifted my dress skirt up to see thick blood running down my legs and soaking into my stockings. I quickly sat on the toilet and pulled off my stockings to hold a wad of toilet paper against me to stem the bleeding.

I knew at this point what all this meant, but I didn't know what to do. The pains continued, and I knew I needed some help, so I walked back into the bedroom while holding the toilet paper with one hand and cradling my stomach with my other. Opening the window, I yelled for George. I wasn't sure if he could hear me with the sound of

Ellie Lynn

the ax splitting the wood. My yelling sounded more like an anguished wail than anything with substance. Soon panic kicked in and I managed a loud scream that thankfully got to George. I heard him call out my name. I slid down to the floor beneath the window. A chilly breeze drifted in from the window, billowing the curtains above me. I looked up and watched them through my haze of tears wishing they would take away this nightmare. Moments later, I heard George coming through the front door and racing up the steps.

The tears were coming down in streams on my face. I hurt physically, yes, but the anguish that I felt deep within my soul tore me to pieces. I was losing my baby. I looked up from staring at my blood-stained dress to see George rush into the room. He looked worried.

"Maggie, what's wrong?" He said as he crossed the room quickly to reach me, sitting on the floor under the window and on the other side of the bed.

"Maggie..." he said more urgently until he saw me in full view. "Oh my God, Maggie!" He shouted. I could only imagine what he thought as he saw me sitting there, pale, bleeding, and crying in between gasps. His face went white and still as he walked towards me to pick me up as if I were a baby. He laid me down on the bed and then walked off to get a couple of towels.

The pain in my abdomen continued as the cramps became more intense. I felt my body trying to expel the tiny baby from me. Everything began happening so fast, and I felt that if I could just close my legs and keep it from happening, everything would be okay. Tightening my muscles only seemed to increase the pain. The inevitability of loss slowly dawned on me as I felt the pressure between my legs increase. George reappeared and stood next to the bed. He placed the towel under my hips. He then grabbed both of my hands, one in each of his, and placed his forehead against mine.

"What can I do, sweetheart?" he asked, before lifting his head up to look at me. He seemed so calm, but I could also tell that he was hurting, too.

I couldn't stand looking at him at that moment. So I turned away,

Falling

"no, no, no, no..." I repeated over and over as I felt something move between my thighs, slick and warm. I knew with every part of my being that I no longer carried that little life in me. I felt like a part of me died and left as well and I never felt so empty in my life. I began to cry heavily with deep sobs. The fat tears rolled down my cheeks unnoticed as I sobbed into my pillow. I vaguely heard George try to sooth me as he wiped a cool cloth over my forehead. I swiped his arm away, as I couldn't stand to be touched in that moment. I wanted to sink into a void of nothingness where I couldn't feel any longer.

George began quietly touching my legs, and I could hear the faint sound of the rustle of blankets. George worked silently. He cleaned me up, he wrapped the baby, and then he kissed my forehead and told me he would be right back. He needed to call for Dr. Williams. I said nothing. I couldn't. I laid there for what seemed like hours trying to gain enough strength and courage to open my eyes. I felt like if I did, I would be right back in the reality of my nightmare. Taking deep breaths in, I slowly opened my watery eyes to look at the small bundle lying next to me.

I lightly shook with fear and sadness, but the small bundle wrapped in a blanket sitting so still called to me as if it had a voice. I leaned up on my elbow as my hand reached for the blanket to uncover the front. The blanket silently sat lightly stained with blood. My hand shook but I needed to see my baby. I grabbed the edge of the yellow cotton blanket and pulled it away to reveal a tiny, perfect little face. I continued pulling the blanket as I looked at little hands so tiny. I imagined the past few months those hands gripping my finger. I realized a second later that I was looking at my daughter. We would have called her Annabel.

"I'm so sorry," I said in a whisper. "I love you and I am so sorry." I couldn't help but feel guilty. At that point I failed my one job as her mother which was to simply carry her in my womb until she could survive outside of it. Somehow my womb failed her. I failed her. I began to cry in earnest once more as the pain from such a loss overwhelmed me.

Ellie Lynn

"I called the doctor Maggie. Dr. Williams should be here within a half hour. Are you in pain? Are you still bleeding? I could take you to the hospital..." George said as he walked back into the room. I slowly looked up at him. He looked beautiful bathed in the sunlight streaming in from the window. It started out as an overcast day, but the clouds seemed to have broken for that moment. He looked so calm.

"We had a daughter, George. Our little Annabel. I don't know what to say, I don't know what happened. I am so sorry." I said between gasps.

"Shhh, Maggie. It's not your fault. You have nothing to be sorry for. Things like this just happen." George said, trying to comfort me.

"It happened so fast. I don't know what happened." My voice broke as I began to deeply cry again. My heart felt split in two as George gently held me in his arms.

"My uncle once told me that people are like leaves on a tree. At some point they all blossom, fade, and then fall to the ground. Some are plucked sooner than others. Some never get to blossom at all." George's voice cracked with emotion.

His hand reached up, and his thumb wiped at my tears. He bent his head and our foreheads touched. I could feel his shoulders slightly shake as he silently cried with me. Our tears mingled with our mutual pain. A pain I didn't think would ever go away. We didn't just lose our daughter; we lost our dreams of her and hopes for our lives together. It was all gone now. The little girl fishing and smiling with her daddy would now turn into an unfulfilled dream. Feeling much more than I could bear, my body seethed with anger and raw grief.

The doctor came and after being cared for medically he gave me a medication to relax me... to make me try to forget. Like I could ever forget about what happened and especially forget about her. I cried and then I slept with my silent baby next to me. When I awoke, she was gone. George said the doctor took care of everything and that I would be okay. I felt oddly betrayed by this. I never would be.

Falling

The days seemed to pass afterwards as if they were all a seamless passing of time. I didn't care whether it was day or night, Friday or Monday. I simply and not so simply grieved. Physically I healed, but as for life, I wanted to shut it all out. Before I knew it a month passed. My mom and Harry came to visit me daily, trying to get me out of bed, to wash up, to eat, but I couldn't always do it. I didn't want them to dote on me, and I certainly didn't want them to tell me what to do. They couldn't possibly understand how deeply my feeling of failure ran.

As for George, he became distant as well. I didn't know if it was from the pain he felt or if he couldn't stand to look at me anymore. It seemed as if I rarely saw him as he kept busy with his work. He continued on, whereas the grief consumed me. I felt like we were slowly drifting apart. We exchanged words at supper and at bedtime, but everything seemed different. I was different, and I no longer felt happy as the anger consumed me. I felt anger towards everyone and everything including George. He never woke me to say goodbye to her. Besides the few months of memories, it was as if she never existed.

I woke up feeling groggy and could tell it would be a rough day for me. All I could think of was my baby girl. I pulled my blankets to my ears, I hadn't bathed in days, and the house looked a mess. I didn't care at that moment on what a terrible wife and homemaker I had become. All these things seemed inconsequential to me. My pain overwhelmed me too much.

Earlier that morning, I received a card from Anna Beth. A beautiful white card with little pink flowers printed on it. On the front it said With Sympathy in a gold script. Inside the card, she expressed her sorrow for my loss in a couple of brief sentences. It made me angry. I knew I shouldn't be, but I was so angry that all I got were a few words as she prepared to welcome her two babies into the world.

Ellie Lynn

It seemed so unfair. I loved her, but for the first time in my life I also envied her. Why me? Why my baby?

A little later, I heard a vehicle pull up to the front of the house. The sound of the wheels against the gravel woke me. I could then hear voices downstairs and I heard George say, "I hope you can do something because she won't talk to me." Inwardly, I groaned. I couldn't stand another "I'm sorry" or "it wasn't meant to be". I didn't want to hear how I needed to grieve, how to cry, how to pretend that everything was okay. The sound of footsteps echoed up the stairs before the door opened and Harry walked in. Her poignant perfume followed her in giving no question to the identity of my visitor.

"Maggie, we need to talk." She said in her matter-of-fact way.

"Harry... I... just can't today. It's not a good day. I'm sorry." I tried to say as I waved my hand, as if to tell her to leave.

"Maggie, I'm not here for a social call. You need to get your butt out of bed and quit feeling sorry for yourself!" Harry said sternly.

I sat up, brushing the greasy hair out of my eyes. "How dare you! Maybe I am feeling sorry for myself, but I think I have a right to. I lost my daughter and no, I will not forget about her!" I shouted. Oh, I loved Harry dearly, but I couldn't believe the nerve of her to walk in my room and say something like that to me.

"Yes, you lost your daughter, but so did George. Do you think you are doing anyone any good, especially yourself, wallowing in here in self-pity? You have a husband who loves you and who is grieving as well. You have your mom, and... well... you have me. Maggie, you need to find a way to get out of bed, wash your hair for goodness' sake, and start living again." Harry paused with a deep sigh and finally taking her hands off of her hips, she walked to the bed and sat next to me.

"You don't understand Harry. You do not know what I'm feeling and what I'm going through. I love you but you have no right to tell me how I should be feeling." I said, truly hurt.

Harry reached out her hand to wipe the tears from my cheeks. "Yes, Margaret, I actually do. Your uncle and I tried to have a baby

Falling

for a few years. The problem wasn't getting pregnant. That was always the easy part. The hard part seemed to be staying pregnant. The first baby we lost devastated me. I wanted to crawl into my bed and never get out. Finally, I did. I had to. I didn't have a choice because I couldn't give up on my dream of being a mother. I couldn't give up on Liam. A few months later, I became pregnant again. This time I almost made it past the first trimester. I honestly thought I was in the clear, that I would hold my baby at some point. I truly wanted to die after that because deep down in my soul, I knew it was never to be. My dream would never come true. I had a couple earlier on miscarriages after that, but I'd gotten to the point where I wasn't shocked when the bleeding started. We finally gave up. It was the hardest thing I have ever done, but also the best. I no longer felt the pressure and guilt of not being able to carry a child."

Harry sat and quietly wept. In the shadows of the room, I saw the tears streaming down her face. I felt shaken to the core because I never once saw Harry cry before. I didn't know of her losses and assumed she just couldn't get pregnant.

"I'm so very sorry Harry. I didn't know." I said in between my own tears. Harry leaned towards me and pulled me into a hug, and we cried together.

I pulled away slowly when our tears ceased. "How did you get through it? I never got to know her, but I miss her so much." I said, feeling the tears come to my eyes once again.

"My faith and my husband got me through. Once I realized I was not alone in my grief, that I needed to be there for Liam as much as he for me, that we needed to grieve together. Praying together helped and I realized I didn't have to take the weight of pain entirely on my own. So I gave some of it over to God to help me through. Once I did that, the most important thing happened. I realized and accepted that it wasn't my fault. I was a wonderful mother who carried my babies as long as I could. It wasn't my fault, Maggie. It's... it's not your fault either." Harry whispered.

She knew the raw guilt I carried inside. "I'm not telling you not to

Ellie Lynn

grieve or to forget, as I know that is so much more impossible than people would understand. I'm not telling you that you will not have days where you don't want to get out of bed. But my dear, you cannot completely give up on life. There are too many people who care so much about you. Take your sweet baby into your heart, never forget her as she will always be a part of you and take those steps to start your life again. If you don't, all this pain and guilt that you are feeling will eat everything that is good and wonderful about you away."

I closed my eyes. I knew she was right, I needed to work through the pain and not suffocate in it. Harry then patted my hand and kissed my cheek. "Now, I'm going to leave you. It doesn't have to be today if you can't do it but think about what I've said. Get out of bed, spend time with your husband, and for goodness' sake take a bath."

We both chuckled. "I love you, Maggie. I love you as if you were my very own daughter and I always thought of you as my own even though I would never say so to Aileen." She said, choking back tears.

"I love you too Harry." I whispered. "Thank you." Then as an afterthought as she opened the door, "Oh and Harry, you would have made such a wonderful mother."

Harry turned to me with a sad smile and then left, quietly shutting the door. Afterwards, I thought for a long while. I thought of Harry and her losses; I thought of my own, and then I thought of George who carried on quietly yet attentive the last month. Almost as if he went with the motions, caring for me, going to work, living life as if nothing happened. I realized I hadn't asked about his feelings. My anger towards him blinded me to the fact he experienced a lot of death in his life. He probably learned to cope the only way he could. We hadn't deeply talked since the miscarriage. My grief took over, and I completely shut him out.

Suddenly it felt very important for me to see him, to hear his voice and feel his arms around me. I needed to know that he grieved as well and that we could grieve together. I needed to forgive him and, more importantly, to forgive myself. The tree metaphor took

Falling

root. There are some things that cannot be changed because it's part of life no matter how much we may hate it.

Chapter Nine

Maggie
March 29, 1947

My sweet baby girl. Oh, how I always longed to hold your warm body close to mine and take in the sweet baby scent of you. I'm getting closer and soon my sweet, mom will be with you. There will be good that will come of today.

I sat in a warm tub, cloudy with soap watching small bubbles swirl and dance with the slightest movement. A week since my last bath, it felt amazing to wash my tangled and grimy hair. The water eased my tense muscles and, in a way, helped to make me feel alive again. I felt more focused and clear than I had the past few weeks, which also made me aware of the deep ache in my chest. I imagined it would be there for a while and would probably fade over time.

Stepping out of the tub, I grabbed a yellow terry cloth towel to dry off. Yellow. The color of the nursery. I closed my eyes and took a deep breath. I would not go back to bed. I padded my way back to the bedroom, walking on my toes since the floor was cold. Slipping on a sweater, trousers, and wool socks, I headed to the door. I stopped as I reached for the knob to turn and with a small smile I walked back into the bathroom to comb my hair, pinch my cheeks, and put a light coat of lipstick on.

I headed downstairs to start on supper, knowing putting the lipstick on was silly but I knew George would appreciate the change. I was serious about the change for him. And for me as well. I walked down the wood floor stairs, careful not to slip in my socks. A fire already crackled in the fireplace, chasing the light chill away. The family room stood empty except for a loveseat, coffee table, and a few other mismatched pieces of furniture. I smelt some freshly made bread coming from the kitchen and figured Harry must have brought some when she came to visit.

An hour later, I stood stirring the chicken noodle soup that had been simmering for a while now. I put big chunks of chicken, carrots, and celery in the chicken broth, along with an array of seasonings. The meal sounded like the perfect warm match to the loaf of honey wheat bread. The entire house smelled wonderful. A few minutes later, George came through the back door into the kitchen. The old door creaked open before closing shut just as quickly and noisily. The pretty flower printed curtains hanging on the door window swooshed with the wind and settled peacefully back in place. I looked up from stirring and over to the door to see George. He looked tired. I smiled at the look of surprise on his face as he looked from me to the big pot of soup and back to me again.

"I figured you would be hungry, George." I said with a small smile. He said nothing. He simply walked over to me and gathered me in his arms to hold me tightly. I relaxed against him, enjoying every moment of the embrace as my wooden spoon held limp in my hand dripped sauce on the floor. At that moment, this was all I needed. I pulled away slightly to look up at his face. "I'm sorry George..."

"No more 'I'm sorry', Maggie. I need you back. I need my wife back." He said, lightly chiding me. He wore a small smile that didn't quite reach his eyes. I blushed a little as I tried to not feel hurt at his words and tone. I tried. I would try harder now. Not trusting my voice with the lump in my throat to say anything more, I simply nodded.

We sat in silence for a while at the table, enjoying our soup. George rubbed the inside of his bowl with a hunk of bread sopping up the last bits of broth. The bread was crusty, and I watched crumbs flaking off as he bit into it. He seemed to enjoy it by the sounds he made. I smiled at that. It seemed to be so long since we sat at the table together and simply enjoyed a meal. Mom and Harry helped by bringing over food and helping around the house. I suppose I dropped everything and I shouldn't have.

It was almost like we lived as strangers for the past month after the miscarriage. We spoke little, at least with very little substance. I realized I missed him. I missed our easy-going time together, where we could talk about almost anything. Or not talk at all and still be

Falling

comfortable in each other's company. Now things felt a little strained. I needed to fix this.

"George," I said in a hoarse voice before I lightly cleared it. "I thought that maybe after supper we could sit up in the barn together and look at the stars, like we used to." At his hesitant look I continued quickly, "I know it's getting chilly, but we could bundle. You could keep me warm." I smiled at him as my eyes pleaded with him.

"That sounds wonderful, but we wouldn't be able to see much. There is a lot of cloud cover right now. Maybe tomorrow night we could try?" He said as he gently smiled back at me.

"Yes, maybe tomorrow night then." I replied as I returned my attention back to finishing the last bites of the soup. After a few moments, George stood up with his bowl and walked over to pick up mine. I hesitated on giving it to him when he leaned down to kiss the top of my head.

"I'll take care of the dishes tonight, my love, while you rest." George said in his usual sweet way.

"George, I feel rested enough I can wash the dishes." I tried to protest.

"It's okay, I got them. I've realized over the past month that I don't help you out enough. It's a lot of work keeping this home together. Besides, Harry left you a new book along with the bread. Why don't you start it?" Then he walked away with the dishes in hand.

Next, I could hear him lightly whistling as he ran water. I simply sat there and closed my eyes, completely engrossed in the sounds of him washing the dishes. It was much more relaxing than sitting in silence. My thoughts were too loud when everything was silent around me. This I could focus on. The sounds of the water splashing, the scraping against dishes, the rinsing. The small sounds George made as he worked. A clearing of his throat, a hum, a whistle. I loved this man with every ounce of my being. It was then that I smiled, because I knew everything was going to be okay.

Chapter Ten

Maggie
May 10, 1947

How would everything be okay? I see him standing at the edge, looking down at me. His clear face and eyes looked devoid of emotion. As if he simply flicked off an annoying fly from the sleeve of his jacket. Falling while looking up, I did not know how close the ground was to my back. I knew that any moment I would reach it and the musings of my life would be over. Yet somehow, I knew it wasn't time yet. I hadn't gained understanding... and of what I did not know. The one thing I knew, time wasn't infinite on this earth and at some point it would end. I was, after all, falling to my death.

The days continued and life became routine once more. I would wake when George did to pack him a lunch as he readied himself for work. We both drank coffee in a usually comfortable silence. I scrambled some eggs and buttered toast as he read the paper, occasionally making a comment or two about an article he was reading. We'd kiss and he would leave for the day. He worked long hours at the police department, and I spent my time with chores around the house, baking with mom, or helping Harry with her charity work.

The routine became comfortable once again, although truth be told, I sometimes missed working like I did during the war. I brought up the subject a couple of times with George about joining the workforce again. He spoke up completely against it. According to George... and well... a good amount of other people, the woman's place was still in the home. I didn't know if I disagreed with this, but I still missed working and the sense of purpose it gave me. George said that my finding a position would take away a position for a returned soldier. I suppose he was right about that.

The nights, however, became anything but routine. George continued to suffer nightmares and would twist and moan in his sleep. They seemed to have increased a lot lately and were scary. I felt completely helpless, wanting to help him. I learned that the best thing to do was to roll onto my side away from him, hoping he would settle down and try to get as much sleep as I could. I learned one night that trying to wake him wasn't a good idea.

George came home late and seemed tired and quiet. Most nights during supper he would tell me bits and pieces of his day, and I would share some of my day with him as well. There were other nights that he didn't want to talk at all.

Looking across the table at him, he seemed distant and quiet. He sat trying to pretend interest in what I talked about, but it became obvious that his thoughts were elsewhere. I still continued telling him about how Harry had gotten into a nasty argument with Mrs. Westerly the last time she brought the family a bag of potatoes and rice from the church charity. She acted upset about the confrontation and I spent a few hours that day with Harry and mom while helping to sew. Despite her insistence to the contrary, Mom's hands hurt terribly and sewing started to become harder and harder.

Deep in his own thoughts George could barely manage a nod at my ramblings. I didn't take offense. I had become used to George's moods, and I knew his job could be difficult at times. After eating, George left the table to go upstairs to take a bath. I cleaned up the kitchen and walked up the stairs to go read in the bedroom for a while. Everything was so quiet I could hear every creak on every stair as I climbed them. Upstairs, I walked down the small hallway where pictures were hung. A couple from our wedding and a few others of family. I walked past the door that was to be the nursery and pushed aside the pain it caused. I ignored the door and continued to George's and my bedroom across from the bath.

Standing outside the bathroom door, I listened to hear any sound of George, but the room sounded completely quiet so I lightly rapped on the door.

"What is it, Maggie?" George asked quietly. "I will be out in a few, I'm just relaxing."

"It's fine, George. I wanted to check on you is all. I'm going to read for a little, anyway." I said, sorry that I disturbed him.

Walking into the bedroom, I grabbed my book from the night-

Falling

stand and climbed into the cool sheets. Feeling sleepy after a while, I creased the page I finished reading and set the book back down on the nightstand. It was then that George emerged from the bathroom. He stood bare chested, and I could see small drops of water still stubbornly clinging to the dark hairs splattered across his chest. His arms and face were tan. His dark hair still damp and combed back away from his face.

He strode towards the bed and placed a half empty bottle of whiskey on the nightstand before climbing into the bed and turning off his lamp. I turned off mine as well and leaned over to give him a kiss on the cheek. I could smell the faint odor of alcohol on his breath, and I swallowed away any alarm that the smell gave me. An alarm I seemed to be experiencing more often lately.

"Good night, I love you." I said next to his cheek.

"Good night, sweetheart. I'm sorry I'm so tired. It's been a rough day." He then rolled away from me to the edge.

I wanted to tell him it was okay, that I understood. But I didn't. I rolled over, feeling my tense body slowly relaxing. I pushed away any thoughts that I knew would keep me awake. Worry over George, concern over mom, Harry's problems with the Westerly's, and of course... *her*. Instead, I tried to think of nothing. I tried to feel my body relax as my head sunk further into the pillow. The pillow sheet smelled crisp and clean, and soon I fell asleep as well.

My mind felt cloudy with a dream as I struggled to wake up. It was like walking through a spider web whose fine threads continued to grab at you... to trap you. Still, I pushed through. With one deep moan coming from my side, I jolted awake. Looking over at George, I could see he was deep in another nightmare. George started lightly gripping the sheets in his fists as he turned his head from side to side. I could hear his mumbling, his moans, and anguish. Feeling sluggish and tired as well, I placed my hand on his upper arm and tried calling out to him.

"George, sweetie, you're having a nightmare. Wake up." When I got no response, I tried again. "George, wake up, you're having a nightmare." I said as I shook his arm a little more firmly in my attempt to wake him up. Before I had time to think or react, I found myself lying on my back with George above me. His hands were around my neck, pushing down into the bed. I couldn't breathe. After a moment of shock, I pushed at his hands with mine. I could feel my fingers clawing at him to release me. I kicked at him with my legs. He was steadfast in his assault. His face was angry, even in the darkness. I could feel the blood in my eyes as they felt as if they would explode. I thought maybe I would die.

Then, it ended as quickly as it started. He rolled off of me and I could breathe again. I laid there gasping in deep breaths, scared of what happened and scared of what could happen next. I heard him breathing fast as well. Then he groaned and was once again over me. I tried to push back as far as I could go into the bed. I had to get away from him, but then he grabbed my face gently between his hands and spread kisses over my cheeks. Over my forehead and lips. All the while saying, "I'm so sorry" over and over. My fear resided, and I cried. I no longer felt scared of him, but bruised and hurt inside. I wanted to reassure him I was alright, but I wasn't so sure I was.

"Maggie, sweetie, I'm so sorry. I don't know what happened. I was having a nightmare and when I awoke, I already had my hands on you..." George tried saying, before getting choked up. I could hear in his voice how sorry and anguished he was.

"It's alright George," I said in a raspy voice. "I shouldn't have woken you from your nightmare. It's not your fault." I gathered him into my arms. His body felt heavy and warm on mine, but also strangely comforting, given what happened. I could feel a deep shiver running through his body. I suddenly felt so sad for him. He was such a strong man and yet in my arms, racked with sobs, he felt so vulnerable. After a little while, he slowly moved off of me and gathered me into his arms. My back up against his chest, I could feel his deep, even breaths as he relaxed and then fell back asleep. Sleep didn't come as easily for me.

My entire body felt on edge, and I couldn't bring my muscles to

Falling

relax. My mind kept replaying what happened over and over and my breath caught at the intense fear I felt. I couldn't stop the tears from rolling down my cheeks as much as I kept telling myself that it was simply a mistake. This isn't how any of this was supposed to go. I could see my dream of what I imagined my life with George would be like, crumbling away.

I could feel George pressed up behind me, warm and relaxed in his sleep. His deep, even breathing betrayed his now quiet dreams and thoughts. I almost laughed at the irony of it, although all I could muster was a watery frown. I awoke him to save him from his terror, only to have it brought upon me.

I had to admit, I also felt guilty for having such selfish thoughts. What horrors must have George been through to cause such brokenness? Such terror when he let his guard down and slept? I tried to squash down stinging resentment at his unwillingness to talk with me about what he felt and been through. I needed to fix things. I would help George. Our love, our life, our marriage was too important to ignore the troubles. I knew instinctively that things would only get worse if the problem didn't get faced head on. Finally, determined to do something and despite my troubled thoughts and sore throat, I fell asleep.

The next morning, it was as if nothing out of the ordinary happened the night before. George woke before me and sat at our kitchen table drinking coffee and reading the newspaper when I walked in. He gave a slight wince as he noticed the bruising around my neck. I examined the bruises in the mirror before coming down and they didn't look as bad as I expected them to, as bad as they felt.

"George," I paused as I tried to clear my tired throat. "Would you like me to make you some eggs?" I continued before he answered, "Also, I have some fresh raspberry preserves I could spread on toast for you."

"Hmm, just coffee this morning. I'm not that hungry. God Maggie, about last night... I'm so sorry." He choked out in an anguished voice.

Ellie Lynn

    I stood there for a moment realizing I felt a little angry and not exactly knowing if I had a right to be. "It's alright George. It wasn't your fault. You didn't realize what was happening. I think though, maybe it's time we try talking about your nightmares. Maybe it would help." I said the last a bit defensively, as I knew he would disagree.

    "Maybe, I'll think about it. I need to be leaving for work. I have things I need to do. I'll see you later and we can talk about it more then." George replied in his dodging way before getting up and leaning down to kiss my cheek goodbye. Then he straightened back up and walked to the door. As he opened it, he turned around and looked at me. He seemed on the verge of saying something else before changing his mind and walking out.

    Annoyed and hurt, I sipped my coffee and pondered going to visit my mom. I really needed to talk with someone, and I hated to admit it, but I needed some sympathy. Some acknowledgement of my pain. Then I realized I sat there swimming in a pool of self-pity. If I stepped one foot in mom's house and she saw one single bruise, then I would never hear the end of it. She wouldn't understand that it was an accident. No, being a married woman now and no longer a child, I wouldn't run to mom when hurt. I needed to be a good wife to George, take the bad with the good and help him with his troubles. His troubles were now mine.

Chapter Eleven

George
March 5, 1943

After taking one last draw from the cigarette now dangling between my fingers, I held the smoke deep in my lungs before blowing it out. It made small rings that ended up swirling together as they drifted away. My friend Benny taught me the trick, and I seemed to pick it up quickly. Despite hating the smell of cigarettes most of my life, I learned that it was the thing to do in the army if I wanted any friends. I found it ironic that if I ever made it back home, pa and I would have something in common for once.

Leaning back against the thick wooden post of the mess hall, my eyes drifted up to look at the stars. Here the whole damn sky seemed to fill up with them. I never noticed the stars much or cared enough to stargaze before, as it always seemed like a waste of time. My Uncle used to teach me the constellations during my visits to the farm. Uncle Edmund always wished he could have gone to school to become an astronomer. He dropped out of school by the sixth grade and instead lived a simple farmer's life.

Now, however, I couldn't seem to peel my eyes away. Something seemed peaceful and "at home" about it. Despite being so far away and in the middle of a damn war, the night sky was the same here...as it was at the farm. I could hear distant chatter and muffled laughter, but I barely gave it much thought. My mind swirled with grief and disbelief, and I simply wanted some peace.

Last week my friend Benny and I stood in this very spot smoking our cigarettes together. Benny animatedly telling me a story of how the night before he went for a walk because he couldn't sleep. He came across a young dark-haired nurse who also seemed to be enjoying the night air. She propped herself up against a truck wheel and drew in deeply from her almost finished cigarette held lightly between her fingers. According to Benny, the moon shined on her hair hanging loosely down her back. Her eyes seemed to sparkle in the moonlight and she was beautiful. Her blouse partially unbuttoned showed she had a pair of the biggest breasts Benny had ever seen.

He walked up to her, and they talked for a little while. He offered

Ellie Lynn

her another precious smoke and cupped his hand over the cigarette to light it for her. They talked, they laughed, he stroked his finger along the outside of her arm as he stared at her. She gave him a shy smile that spoke volumes of her want of him and so he leaned in for a kiss. She wrapped her arms around his neck and pressed her chest into his. Sliding his hands down her arms and then up her waist, he cupped those beautiful breasts spilling over his hands. They kissed like that for at least twenty minutes before she said goodnight and went back to her bunk. She left him aching, but he swore that if he died the next day, he would die a happy man.

I wasn't sure that I believed him, but it made a nice story to talk about as we smoked our cigarettes. I could almost feel the girl's breasts under my own palms and dreamt of them that night. I insisted it didn't happen. He laughed and insisted it did. Benny, with the red hair, freckles, big ears, crooked teeth, and crystal blue eyes, always seemed to have some story to tell. You never knew for sure if his story was simply a work of his active imagination or if he truly was the ladies' man that his stories made you believe. Thinking of it now, it didn't matter. You listened, you imagined, and it became real.

I wish this is how I would remember him. Sitting here now, looking up at the stars, all I can see of Benny is his brains being blown out in front of me. The brain matter splattered onto my face and the bullet sliced through the edge of my left ear. Benny dropped where he stood and, for probably the first time in his life, fell silent. The craziest thing is that even in the middle of this war, Benny's tragic death had been an accident.

Private Jimmy Stonewall was a short and stocky man with a hair-trigger temper. One of those men who probably kicked the shit out of the weaker kids at the schoolyard, excelled at basic training, and thought he would die in a blaze of glory on the battlefield after killing a dozen Nazis.

Only being in North Africa for a couple of months, it didn't take long for reality to sink in. This was not the school yard and Stonewall was not as tough as he believed and he sort of faded away. His eyes

Falling

looked distant, and he became more withdrawn. I saw it in other men as well but most seemed to snap out of it. Not Stonewall.

The brutal fighting in North Africa was a mud filled hell with powerful German tanks and sprays of gunfire. It is the real-life training on how to kill or be killed. You quickly learned that dying had little to do with skill and much more to do with luck. Either the powerful German gun shot its rounds through your chest or the chest of the man sitting next to you. It really was that simple. The toll this takes on a human being is not.

Benny and I both worked in Mine and Demolition. It was pretty much every boy's dream to blow shit up. If it wasn't for the war, it would be a dream. Instead, everything is like a nightmare that continues on and on. Benny and I worked well together. Our work, precise and accurate, like the turning wheels of a clock. For a clock to tell the time and chime at the precise moment, everything needed to be in order and had to run smoothly. The same went for our job, except if things were off or didn't work right, *times up* held a much different meaning.

That fateful morning a storm brewed while Benny and I walked back to our bunks to catch some sleep after having been up for the past nineteen hours. We were both exhausted, mentally, and physically. The sky took on an eerie look, with dark clouds threatening to open up and spill. You could feel the electricity in the air and knew that along with the heavy downpour the storm would bring, it would also leave behind thick, swallowing mud for the next morning. The kind of mud that pulled at your feet as you walked like a monster in a graveyard with fingers gripping. It was unbearable and played a major problem in combat.

Benny, like usual, talked as we walked. The man never shut up and I'm sad to say about what I don't know. I felt tired and wasn't paying attention. We could hear a boom of thunder hit behind us so loud it seemed to shake the earth. Shortly after, another shot rang out, but this time it wasn't the thunder.

Benny dropped in front of me. I wiped the blood and brain

Ellie Lynn

matter from my eyes as I felt the first drops of the rain hit. Up ahead of us stood Stonewall with his gun leveled straight at my head and where Benny's head used to be. His hand shook, and his pupils looked huge in his sunken eyes. His face pale as rain poured down it. He lowered his weapon and stammered an apology. I stood there for a second until the loud ringing stopped in my head. Everything seemed fuzzy and in slow motion. I looked down at the body lying in front of me in the dirt. The bright blood stood out shockingly next to his flaming red hair. His blue eyes were open and sightless. He lie motionless. Benny was dead.

I heard shouts and movements from my side, and I looked over to see men running towards us. That's when I heard another gunshot ring out and I looked forward to see Stonewall fall to the ground. He turned the gun on himself. Probably a good thing too, as there was no place in the army and in this war for a fucked-up coward.

Lighting up another cigarette, the stench of the fumes envelope me. The smoke burns my lungs and eyes and I slowly release it in small little rings. I almost wish that I hadn't started smoking. It wasn't a good thing to make friends during a war.

Chapter Twelve

Maggie
August 2, 1947

Over the next few months, I tried so hard to be a good wife. One who's understanding, loving, and patient. The more I tried, though, the more George pulled away and turned to drink. It seemed as if distance grew between us as time passed. I tried to gently encourage him to talk with me about how he felt and asked ways I could help him. This only seemed to annoy him.

I laid awake sometimes during the night, listening to him groan and thrash as he fought off his invisible demons during sleep. Never once did I try to wake him again. Too scared for that I felt desperate. I also missed my flow for the second month in a row and now felt certain that I carried another child. My nerves seemed to be on edge and at times sick, but I also felt determined to keep it a secret for a little while longer.

Everything in me wanted to tell George, but it scared me to. I feared getting his hopes up again to end up losing the baby. To be honest, I feared getting my hopes up as well. I knew I couldn't keep it a secret for too much longer, but selfishly, I felt that a few more days, maybe a week or two, wouldn't hurt. Plus, I hadn't made much progress with George. We seemed to have fallen into a routine of sorts once again and disappointingly we were spending less time being together. George worked a lot and I kept busy with the housework, cooking, and helping mom and Harry. It seemed so early in our marriage to already be at this point.

I stepped outside to grab the glass pitcher of brewed sun tea. The sun warmed my skin, and the tea looked to be a dark amber color glowing in the sunlight. I was eager to surprise George with a glass of it while he worked in the barn. After chipping away at the ice block and sweetening the tea with sugar, I walked back outside into the warm sunlight and headed for the barn.

I knew today would be a good day. I woke up feeling refreshed instead of tired and nauseous, and I felt determined to spend some quality time with George. Opening the barn door, the smell of old hay and gasoline instantly greeted me. It's sweet scent invoked a feeling of familiarity that I secretly loved. George whistled while on

Ellie Lynn

his back, under the truck. I recognized the song and joined in as he scooted out from under the truck to stare up at me. I gave him a smile while holding up the glass of sweet tea. He smiled back and stood, wiping his dirty hands on his old overalls.

"Thanks, darling. I needed this." He grinned as he reached for the tea. "That and to see your beautiful face, of course."

I blushed and smiled back. Then I handed him the glass watching him take a big drink as I clasped my hands behind my back and swayed back and forth, the song still in my head. After drinking his fill, George sat the glass on the wooden stool sitting next to the truck. Turning to me, he wore a different smile on his face. A mischievous one with a twinkle in his eye. The sight of it made me giggle. George was in a great mood. As if we were still dating, our bodies hummed when we sat too close and were alone.

George snaked out a hand and pulled me closer to him. I still had my hands clasped behind my back, so the full front of me met his hard chest. My skin tingled, and my hands found their way to the front of his shirt. He smelled amazing, despite having been working in the old barn on the broken-down truck.

He pressed his mouth at the curve of my neck where my shoulder meets. The blouse that I wore allowed his lips to brush my bare skin. Shivers ran up my back. His lips pressed a wet trail up my neck to my ear. I could hear his breath, heavy and intoxicating, as he kissed me. This was the George that I fell in love with. The George I was trying so desperately to get back. If I could, I knew we would be happy forever.

My hands traveled up his chest to grasp his cheeks, pulling his head in front of mine. I wanted to see his brown eyes, and I wanted to see them happy and wanting me. We needed this. Appeased, I pulled his head towards mine and pressed my lips against his. Our kiss was soft at first, but soon grew hungry. His fists gripped the sides of my blouse, pulling the end out of my skirt. My hands tangled in his dark hair, keeping his lips on mine. We were both hungry and desperate for each other.

Falling

Before I realized it, I was sitting on the edge of the car hood and George was between my legs. Our lovemaking was frantic and wild. I didn't care that I sat on a car or that George was dirty from the barn and car grease. It only added to the excitement of it all. It was as if we both had our fill of polite distance from one another. That was all that the last few months seemed to be. Our lovemaking hadn't been like this since when we were secretly together before saying our vows. We somehow lost this wild abandonment. This fun and excitement at being with one another.

I didn't realize how much I craved it; how much I needed it until now. When our breathing slowed, George pulled me off the car and I slowly slid down the length of him. My skin still felt sensitive, and I felt the urge to let out a long sigh as my feet touched the ground. George's hands were still around my waist, and he wore a lazy grin on his face as he looked down into mine.

"Sorry sweetie, looks like I got dirt smudged on your face." George chuckled. Reaching his hand to my face, he tried to rub off a streak of dirt, only to give up, as he only made it worse. He sighed, kissed my forehead, and then pulled away. I could instantly feel the cooler air without his warm body up against mine.

"It's alright, I'll wash up in the house. Are you going to be out here for much longer?" I asked, hoping not to sound too needy. I wanted to spend time with him, but I didn't want him to think I was so desperate for it.

"Not too long. Just have a few things I need to work on. I'll be in before supper, I promise." He said with a wink.

Appeased, I walked out. My legs were a little weak and shaky, but it felt good. I giggled a little and thought I would never stop smiling. Things felt like they were right back on track. There seemed to be a new lightness in my step as I walked back to the house. I upturned my red lips with a smile that I couldn't repress. This was the first time in a while that George and I had shared a spontaneous and intimate moment. Things had become so routine and even worse, there seemed to be this distant strain between us I couldn't quite understand. I didn't know if the feelings were mine alone or if George also felt it.

Stepping into the house, I took a deep breath and sighed before walking into the kitchen to wash the dishes from lunch earlier. As I dried the last dish before placing it in the cupboard, I heard tires on the gravel as a vehicle pulled up to our property. I dried my hands and went out to see who it was. As I walked out onto the front porch, the sun was blindingly bright, so I shielded my eyes with my hand until they could adjust. George stood talking with a gentleman.

Hearing me on the porch, George looked over towards me, along with the man by his side. The visitor looked handsome, with dark blonde hair and chiseled features. He dressed smart as well in gray trousers and a white button-up shirt that seemed to perfectly display his athletic build. I felt a little breathless as I descended the three steps leading down to the driveway. The two men watched as I approached.

George introduced us in a clipped tone as he drew his arm around my shoulders, pulling me up to his side. "Maggie, meet Taylor Bird. We work together at the police department."

"Nice to meet you, Ma'am." Taylor said in a deep voice as he stretched his hand out to shake mine

"It's very nice to meet you as well, Mr. Bird." I shook his large and callused hand and it felt warm in mine. George's arm fell away from my shoulders as he turned away from me, motioning for Taylor to follow him.

"Please, call me Taylor." He gave me a flirtatious grin.

"Maggie, sweetheart, how about getting Taylor a glass of that sweet tea hmm?" George asked as Taylor, and he started walking towards the barn.

"Sure." I replied to their retreating backs.

Walking back into the house, I worked quickly at chipping ice and pouring the sweetened sun tea in a glass to take out to the barn. My heart beat excitedly and I felt a small drip of sweat roll down between my breasts. Taylor Bird certainly looked handsome, plus I

Falling

admittedly felt curious about the visit. George rarely invited anyone over.

When I walked up to the barn, I faintly heard them talking and debated about lingering outside to eavesdrop. Shaking my head and silently chiding myself for even thinking of it, I opened the barn door and quietly walked in. My cheeks probably looked pink.

George and Taylor stopped talking and looked towards me as I walked in, holding the glass of tea. Taylor walked a few steps towards me to take the glass as he thanked me. George grabbed his empty glass sitting on his workbench and handed it to me.

"Maggie, dear, would you mind pouring me some more as well?" He asked with a small smile he usually used when wanting something from me. He knew they made me powerless to refuse.

"Sure, I could also bring in some of those blueberry muffins I made earlier, if you would like. Or you gentlemen could come inside where it's a little cooler.?" The day was exceptionally warm. I knew George would probably refuse, given his look, but it still would have been nice to have a proper conversation with a new guest.

"That would be..." Taylor started to say.

"That's alright Maggie, we're good." George said instead with a wink.

I felt dismissed. With a forced smile, I exited the barn and walked back to the house. I had some cleaning that I needed to do in the house, anyway. In actuality there always seemed to be cleaning and chores that needed to be done. Obviously, George and Taylor had something they needed to discuss. Walking out of the barn, I quietly closed the door and walked away when, like a magnet, I quietly crept back to the barn door. It felt shameful, but my curiosity got the better of me and so I pressed my ear to the door to make out what they said. The voices were muffled, and I could only make out a few words here and there.

"... wife seems nice.... good tea... muffins..." I heard bits of Taylor speaking.

"Thank you... stay away from... hear anything about... trying to fix the... truck..." George's firm voice definitely stood out from Taylors.

I moved my ear away from the door and turned around to head back to the house, a little ashamed of my eavesdropping but also desperate for any insight into the mystery of my husband. I couldn't help but feel a little annoyed as they seemed to chat about nonconsequential things. Nothing important or mysterious or even about anything from their work as police officers. Muffins and the truck. Things they could have easily talked of in the kitchen and in my company.

Shaking my head at my childish thoughts and behavior, I walked into the kitchen through the back door to fill George's glass with some more tea. I then walked back outside towards the barn and was about to open the door when I heard the tail end of George's profanity filled rant. He talked much louder this time, so I could hear pretty much everything.

"That fucking Westerly bastard better watch his back because if I see his ass again, I will make sure to blacken his other eye." George said loudly. He sounded dead serious.

"Yeah, well unfortunately there isn't any avoiding him. Trouble seems to follow him around. One day he will do something that will put him away for a long time, mark my words. That or he'll end up dead. Best though to keep your cool until that day comes." Taylor sounded as if he tried to reason with George.

"Keep my cool? He was drunk, belligerent, and refusing my orders. If one of my soldiers had been that disrespectful to me, I would have saved the Germans a bullet. You have no right to question me based on morality." George retorted.

I couldn't hear Taylor's response clearly, as he spoke in a more muted tone than before. Pressing my ear closer to the door, I couldn't make out much more than a few words, so I figured it was as good a time as any to walk in. I didn't want anyone to suspect that I'd been eavesdropping, so I opened the door as loudly as I could manage. Both men turned towards me as I walked in. I probably looked red

Falling

with embarrassment, but I hoped that they assumed it was from the sun.

"I brought you some fresh tea George." I said as I handed him the refilled glass. He grabbed it from me and, with a smile, downed half the tea in one drink. I could see his throat muscles working as he gulped it down. When he finished, he wiped the back of his hand across his mouth and gave a loud sigh.

"That was good, thanks." He walked over to a small stand to set the half-filled glass down and as he turned away, I couldn't help but glance at Taylor, to see him watching me intensely.

"Very refreshing, ma'am, and I thank you for your hospitality. George, I need to get going. I have an entire list of honey-dos before my shift starts on Tuesday." Taylor walked past me with a small smile and a wink. Our eyes locked and I felt my cheeks go warm. Stopping at the opened doorway of the barn, Taylor looked back at George and said, "Remember what I said, George. I'll see you later." Then turning towards me, "Ma'am."

He walked out and I stared after him for a couple of seconds before turning back to George, only to see the anger on his face. My smile slowly faded.

"Taylor is a charming man with a smile that apparently melts girls' hearts... or so I'm told. You are not one of those girls. He is not as much of a gentleman as he may seem Maggie. You would do best to stay clear of him."

"George," I gave a small nervous laugh, trying to lighten up the situation, "I don't know what you're talking about. Taylor seems like a nice enough man, but I only have eyes for you. I thought you two were friends..." My words trailed off and I wasn't sure what to say next, I felt confused.

George's eyes squinted at me as he walked the couple of steps towards me to grab my hand. "I work with him and we mostly get along, but that is it. He is not my friend Maggie."

George dropped my hand and walked out of the barn. No explanation. I stood there for a moment, suddenly feeling like I wanted to

Ellie Lynn

cry. George's mood changed so quickly. He usually acted so calm, patient, and good humored. He could be distant but that was all. I never saw his temper roused so quickly as it seemed to be today. I closed my eyes and took a deep breath.

Something obviously upset George besides me looking at Taylor. Something maybe from his work. Guiltily, I also felt a little ashamed of myself. I did find Taylor attractive, and I must have unintentionally let it show. That, combined with my eavesdropping, made me feel like the worst sort of wife.

Turning around, I too walked out the barn door to see George walking down the dirt road leading to the small pond about a half a mile away. George called it his thinking place.

I walked into the house to begin the chores that needed to be done. As I put the clean sheets on the bed, I took a deep breath and smelled the crisp scent of soap and sunshine. I earlier pulled them off the clothesline, and it was probably my favorite smell in the entire world. As a child, I used to run along the flowing white sheets hanging on the clothesline. When the wind would blow them, they billowed out like giant sails, and I would pretend that I was aboard a beautiful ship sailing far away. Caught up in my imagination of distant lands, I could block out the yelling from my father and the crying of my mother.

Looking down on the sheet that I spread smoothly over the mattress, I noticed a couple of small wet drops standing out. Then another one joined them. That's when I realized I hadn't been doing a very good job at stifling the tears. Once I realized this, I sank to my knees and cried. I didn't know exactly what I was crying for, but the sobs came from deep in my chest. Today had almost went perfect.

I didn't know what to think, how things had turned so terribly wrong. Being silent about my feelings only made things worse. So, as I sat on the floor wiping tears away, I made up my mind to talk to George later. Feeling determined and not as weepy, I stood up and continued to make the bed. Then I moved on to dusting the chest of

Falling

drawers and headboard. Like the laundry and dishes, dusting seemed to be an endless job.

I acquired my mom's obsession with having a clean house and took pride in making it tidy and neat. Even though George never really said anything about it, I'm sure he appreciated it as well. After the miscarriage, the house fell in shambles when left to him. It was my job to be a good wife, to keep our home clean, to have meals prepared, and to eventually be a good mother. It's what George deserved.

Certain if I could give George a baby everything would change. It would bring us so much closer together and we could finally be like we were before the miscarriage. We would be a true family, and I knew George would make an amazing father. I placed my hand onto my still flat abdomen and silently prayed for everything to be okay. I prayed the child growing inside me lived and that my body was strong enough to carry it.

I stood in the kitchen chopping carrots for the chicken I planned to place in the oven, when George opened the kitchen door. He looked flushed and sweaty from his walk. I stopped chopping as he walked over to me and planted a kiss on my cheek.

"George, what were you yelling about in the barn? You sounded worked up which seemed to put you in a bad mood afterwards." I turned to face him with my hands on my hips. I tried to make sure my voice sounded steady and strong, although I'm sure he could probably still hear the hurt in my words.

"It's just work stuff. Nothing for you to worry about. I'm sorry it put me in a bad mood. You didn't deserve that." George replied before turning around to leave.

"George!" I cried out. I felt grateful for the apology, but it wasn't enough. "Is that it? No other explanation?"

George turned back around to face me and sighed with resignation. "Taylor wanted to talk about work matters involving Mr. Westerly. Mr. Westerly is and always will be a pain in my backside, as he

Ellie Lynn

is to most other people that live here, but my job makes it hard to avoid him. That's it."

Then, without another word, George turned around and walked out of the kitchen. I didn't realize I held my breath in until I exhaled as he left. The smell of his warm sweat lingered briefly in the kitchen like a cloud. I unconsciously breathed in deep and I longed to go to him, but knew he needed his space. Instinctively rubbing my stomach, I decided right there to tell George of the pregnancy that night.

Later that evening George and I sat side by side on the loveseat enjoying comfortable silence. George looked busy reading an article in the Reader's Digest magazine that he picked up that morning. I sat busy crocheting a new blanket. I only started it but was pleased to see the soft green shades in pretty little rows. Making a blanket for the baby, may be a little foolish I knew but I couldn't help myself from being excited anyway.

Closing my eyes, I took a deep breath and gripped the starting of the blanket against my chest. I didn't know why telling him felt so hard. I guess I feared his reaction. I worried it would be so different than the last time and I worried he wouldn't believe I could do this. That I would lose this one as well.

Feeling as courageous as I was going to feel, I decided now was the time. "George, I... I have something that I uh... that I want to tell you." I started out.

Looking up and at me from his magazine article, George lifted one eyebrow waiting for me to continue.

"I love you so much. You truly are my everything, and well, I guess I'm just going to come out and say it. I'm pregnant George." There, it was out, and I couldn't help but watch him waiting for any sign of judgement, fear, or anger. The first time he'd been so excited, but I couldn't help but feel that this time things would be a little different. We were a little different. Another pregnancy meant a possibility of another heartache like we experienced before. Holding my breath, I waited for George to react.

At first George looked shocked, but that quickly turned into a

Falling

huge grin, with his eyes sparkling. He sat his magazine down next to him and reached over to me, pulling me onto his lap.

Nuzzling my neck, he chuckled, "You should have told me earlier, otherwise I would have been gentler in the barn. You got me so excited." He said in a breathy whisper.

"How far along are you?"

"About ten weeks, I think. So still early." I pulled slightly away from him to look into his eyes. "George, I believe everything will work out fine this time. I don't want you to worry too much."

I'm sure he could read the worry in my eyes, but he didn't comment on it. Instead, he pulled my head down for a lingering kiss. I could feel my breaths getting faster as his hand inched up the skirt of my dress. I positioned myself so that I was straddling his lap and could better feel the friction between my legs. He unbuttoned the top of my dress to pull it down over my shoulders, spreading wet kisses over my neck and shoulder bones as he went. It always amazed me how I could suddenly and completely need this man so quickly. I felt on fire and the life growing between us seemed to help fuel the flame.

Later that night, while in a deep sleep, I dreamt of friction and heat once more. My body withered with pleasure as the man above me rhythmically ground his hips against mine. I heard him moan with pleasure in between my breathy gasps. I kept feeling myself climb higher and higher towards the convulsing pleasure but couldn't quite seem to reach it. It seemed just out of my grasp the closer I got. The need almost became painful as I scratched my nails down my lover's back and bucked harder against him. His head on my neck, I reached up to grab his hair, to bring his lips to mine, when I froze. The man above me had dark blonde hair and a chiseled, handsome face. It was the face of Taylor rather than George's, and he gave me a knowing smile as though we shared a secret. As though we were children who had just stolen candy.

I sat up quickly coming more awake out of my dream. My skin drenched with sweat, and I could still feel a swollen pulse in between my legs. Despite the shock of the dream, I still felt painfully close to a

Ellie Lynn

release, but I didn't dare move and instead hoped that it would fade unfulfilled. Hearing a moan, I turned to look at George fast asleep, but caught up in another nightmare. He lay there sweating as well, and his head turned from side to side as he moaned. I could feel the nausea build as saliva filled my mouth.

Climbing out of bed, I quickly padded my way to the toilet across the hall to empty the contents of my stomach. I was literally sick with shame. Hoping to not wake George, I quickly rinsed my mouth with cold water and walked back to the bed. Climbing in next to George, careful not to wake him. I couldn't help but think about my dream. I felt as though I truly betrayed George. His moans were of anguish and mine had been of pleasure from another man. It barely mattered that it was only a dream, it felt like a betrayal just the same.

Tears slipped down my cheeks as a feeling of helplessness overcame me. I truly felt helpless. As though my marriage was slowly failing, I couldn't seem to pass over this barrier that George built up between us. Or maybe it was I that built the barrier, or maybe both of us. Either way, it felt almost tangible, as strong and impenetrable as it stood. Things seemed so easy when we were dating; before the nightmares, the anger, the sadness... before Annabel.

The rays of the sun rising started to seep in through the curtains before I drifted back to sleep. When I awoke again, the bed felt cold I the only one still lying in bed. Grateful for the time, I sleepily walked to the bathroom to start a bath. My stomach rumbled, reminding me I woke late and hadn't eaten yet. Although the achiness in my body seemed to scream the loudest and my eyes burned from having cried so much the day and evening before. I decided a bath would ease my body and mind. Breakfast would need to come second.

Sinking in the tub, the steam rose to tangle in my curls as I let out a loud sigh. I could feel my muscles softening as the top of the water gently lapped against my breasts. My mind didn't relax as quickly as my body. I needed to fix things. I just wasn't sure how.

Chapter Thirteen

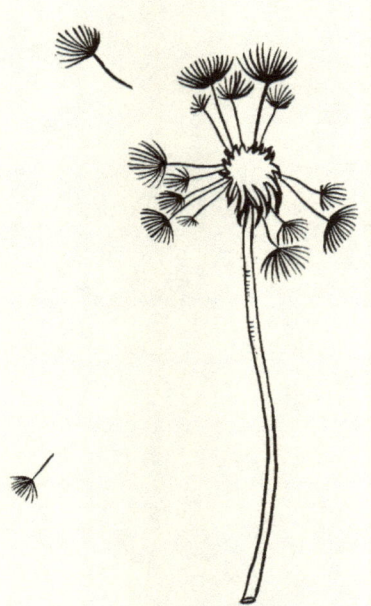

George
February 2, 1944

The acrid smell of gunfire filled the air, making it almost impossible to breathe. It made me feel suffocated, as if I was trapped in a cloud of it with no oxygen to fill my lungs. Instead of passing out from starving lungs though, my body somehow kept moving, straining, surviving.

The power of the German's defense in Cisterna was much more powerful than expected, although it shouldn't have been since we experienced a heavy loss in Anzio as well as our allies. We lost ships and equipment. The bigger loss though were many men, but that seemed to not matter as much to the men fighting the war from cozy offices.

It mattered... they mattered to me and to the other men choking on the thick, stinging air and sitting in dirt stained by other men's blood. We were not equipped to take Cisterna, and those in command highly underestimated their defense, proving to be a grave mistake.

While in Africa a call came out needing men to sign up with a new special force unit called the Rangers. I felt a duty to be one of the first to sign up. After Benny, I didn't care anymore as if my feelings were numb. At 2400 hours, our mission was to infiltrate Cisterna before the Germans knew what hit them. An incredibly important task, as taking Cisterna would stop the German lines of communication on Italy's western coast.

The operation did not work as planned, and we were no longer under the cover of darkness. The rising sun illuminated us as if the Germans turned a light switch on as we tried to secretly advance. Now we were exposed to those bastards as they rained bullets and artillery down upon us. We were basically sitting ducks. Crouched in a small embankment, I sat hunched with four other men. It took a good amount of time and cost the lives of three of our men to make it from our last semi cover to only about a hundred yards closer. We were close to Cisterna's southern outskirts. We were so damn close, but it didn't matter. The defense was impenetrable as if they knew we were coming and crouched waiting.

Ellie Lynn

Next to me on my right was Harvey Holsted. His hands were shaking, but his eyes seemed steady and focused, despite blood matting one eyelid from the gash above his brow.

"We should have been there before dawn, now we are fucked." He yelled matter-of-factly, as if this were any other fight. As if we all didn't feel the doom creeping in.

"We need to find a break..." I didn't even finish the sentence. It didn't matter, we both knew that there would be no real advancement to take Cisterna at this critical point. Our only chance, the cloak of darkness, disappeared with the rays of the sun. They did not outfit us to take on the likes of what we faced now. We fought with only so many men and ammunition. Without the support of other ground troops and heavier arms, we were, as Harvey said, fucked.

I turned to my left to see Jackson trying to shake Phillip Baisley off his arm. Jackson was a good guy, always wore a smile and a bawdy joke to tell. Baisley sat clinging to his arm frantically in a panic, preventing Jackson from being able to hold his weapon up. Baisley was one of the newer rangers, although it wasn't as if he hadn't experienced battle before. Heck, we all had.

"Get the hell off me, man!" Jackson yelled, pushing Baisley finally away in one hard shove. That's when I saw what was wrong; why Baisley was so panicked. One eye looked closed and caked in blood. The other eye grotesquely dangled out of its socket. It became obvious that he was in shock. Being blinded while in the middle of battle made him as good as dead already. The situation we were in was hellish enough. I couldn't imagine only being able to hear and smell the battle going on. The utter helplessness must be overwhelming. I looked forward again to gage our next move. It's funny how easily and quickly you learn to move past horrors.

Just then, the ground in front of us was sprayed in gunfire. You could see the disturbance of the ground as it became mutilated before hearing the whistling sounds of it. The only disruption in the sound of the gunfire is the occasional ping of a bullet hitting a helmet or the boom of heavier artillery.

Falling

The firing stopped in our direction briefly, becoming our only time to move.

"We gotta go!" Harvey yelled.

"Where the hell are we supposed to go? I don't see shit but dirt." Jackson said, looking at me.

"We gotta go." I said softly, mostly to myself and agreeing with Harvey. I scanned through the smoke and bodies trying to find some safety somewhere, except there was none. Literally in every direction, men fell around us.

"Oh my God, oh my God" Baisley yelled repeatedly.

"We die if we don't move!" Harvey ground out. Then he pulled himself up, ready to advance...to where I couldn't possibly discern. There were a few outbuildings within sight but being able to reach them seemed impossible.

Then it hit us. A mere second after Harvey lifted himself up, we were hit. I heard the massive boom from the tank right as the surrounding ground shook and ruptured. I felt myself being lifted and then slammed into the ground. It's all been for naught. This became my only thought before everything went dark.

My head buzzed in pain as I tried to open my eyes. The little slits of light pouring in through my lashes burned, exposing the dirt and debris filling my lids. My ears rang and I could feel a warm wetness dripping out of them. I didn't want to move. I wanted to fall through the earth and disappear. I heard screams and gunfire, but the noise seemed distant, almost as if I was underwater.

I felt small rocks digging into my back and the scratchiness of a weed laying against a partially bared leg. Somehow, I seemed to notice these details in my haze of fogginess and pain. Almost like my mind frantically tried to grasp out for anything but what was going on around me. Then, as quickly as the first blast hit us, a second blast close by seemed to "wake" me up like a violent shake to bring someone back from a nightmare. The only difference, I was being awoken to the nightmare.

I groaned as I forced my eyes to open fully. They burned and watered, and I tried to rub the dirt out of them. When I lifted my hands away and saw them, they were covered in blood and dirt. That's my blood. I slowly sat up, ignoring the pain racing through my body like a jolt. My head felt thick and dizzy, and my stomach churned. I closed my eyes once again and sat there for a moment to settle things. When I could open my eyes once again without too much nausea, I started desperately looking around to find someone else who could have possibly survived. I crawled the few feet to where I saw Harvey laying.

Grabbing his shirt front, I tried shaking him awake.

"Harvey, Harvey, wake up, man we gotta go. Now is our time," I cried to him. My voice sounded foreign, and I wondered what I was doing. Harvey was obviously dead, given the massive gaping wound in his chest, a missing limb, and a blank stare.

Feeling desperately alone in that instant, I closed his eyes and moved to Sam Gillard next to him. I only knew him because of the crucifix around his neck. Nothing else looked recognizable. Turning away, I crawled to where Jackson lay. His bloody hand lifted off the ground to his head as if to check to see if he still lived. I breathed a sigh of relief. He was alive and didn't seem to be gravely injured. Laying a few feet away from Jackson was Baisley's mangled body. Next to him was Leonard. Leonard just heard the news a few days ago that his young wife was expecting their first child, a child he would never get to meet.

I looked back at Jackson as he sat up, while holding his head and groaning. I felt his pain that moments ago I experienced myself. I noticed that the sounds of gunfire were dying down and I could hear the moans and screams of my fellow rangers now louder than an occasional shot. The beginning sounds of silence seemed eerie and ominous and produced a sinking feeling of dread. I crawled a little closer to Jackson so he could hear me.

"Jackson, we've gotta get the hell out of here. The Germans are coming. If we don't move, we will either be shot or taken." I said, spit-

Falling

ting out the words. My head felt dazed, but I was clear enough to know what was about to happen.

"For Christ's sake, George, where do you think we can go?" Jackson replied, sounding desperate. "Plus, I'm out of ammo. Ran out right before we were hit."

"Shit!" I replied as I checked my weapon. "I've got two rounds is all."

"One for each of us."

"Now is not the time to be funny…"

"I'm not. I don't want to die in a German prison."

It dawned obvious that Jackson was serious. Could he be right and would it be better to end it, than to be taken? All I could do was look into Jackson's pleading eyes. I felt like we were both stuck on a ledge waiting to fall or not. It was my weapon, my ammunition, it would be my decision.

"Du da drüben! Hände hoch!"

Too late, I looked forward and could see dust covered boots standing a few feet up the small slope in front of me.

"Hey, ihr da drüben! Hände hoch. Macht schon! Hände hoch!"

"Hands up." Jackson whispered to me. With little hesitation, I followed the foreign instructions. I laid my weapon down and put my hands up high in the air. Jackson did the same. The decision on whether we would die here in the ditch or be taken prisoner was suddenly seized from me.

"Jetzt steh auf und kommt zu mir. Zack, zack!" The German yelled to us, motioning his hands to direct us to him. I stammered to my feet, feeling the pain course through me. Pushing the pain aside, I climbed up the small slope to stand next to the German. I could see his cold blue eyes, his reddened, chapped cheeks, and a slight tilt to his lips in a perfect smirk. The few teeth I could see behind his lips were perfectly white, although crooked. Being the embodiment of evil and everything that was damn wrong in this war, he looked as if he enjoyed this.

Ellie Lynn

His eyes looked past me, down to where Jackson still struggled to get on his feet. He couldn't seem to manage it. It looked as if he couldn't put any pressure on his left foot.

"Steh jetzt gefälligst auf!" The German yelled down to Jackson. "Eins!... Zwei!..."

"Jackson, get on your feet now!" I yelled down to him, as if I could motivate him to hurry. Just then Jackson sunk down to both knees in defeat, unable to complete the task of standing up.

"Drei." The German said in a clipped and absolute tone. There would be no more counting, only a single gunshot.

I watched as a bullet pierced Jackson's forehead. His head snapped back, along with a spray of blood. His eyes were open as he fell backwards, awkwardly, and then to the side. I looked over at the German. He now wore a pleased grin. I wanted to hit him. I wanted to smash my fist into his crooked teeth to knock them out. I wanted to put a bullet in his forehead, as he had done to Jackson.

The German looked at me for a moment, daring me to say or do anything to give him a reason to dispatch me as well. Instead, I swallowed my anger like a dry lump of bread and buried it. Men who acted on their emotions did not survive.

"Er ist nicht aufgestanden." He said simply with a shrug of his shoulders, then motioned me in front of him. With my hands still raised and a gun pointed at my back, I finally stumbled fully out of the ditch and walked forward, leaving my men behind. Suddenly my father's words ran through my head. Not dying. Now I understood what he meant. I suddenly envied my dead comrades. I did not know what hell I was now walking into.

Chapter Fourteen

Maggie
October 12, 1947

There is something magical to me about the fall season. The changing colors, the light breeze rattling the leaves, and the crisp nights. Grandma Faye and I used to talk excitedly about the upcoming season, the stews, and chowders we would eat, the sweet potato pie, and the pure sense of revival the season seemed to bring to the both of us. This was something that we shared and felt special between us. Every season, I couldn't help thinking about my grandma and how very much I missed her. We were like kindred spirits, and I longed for the smell of her, the sound of her voice, and her soft hazel eyes.

Mom never understood our love of fall, as she only saw it as a time when her roses would soon wither. Spring was her favorite season since she saw it as the beginning of warmth, sunshine, and of course, the budding of her roses. Mom saw the colorful falling leaves as a time for work. Fall to her meant raking the leaves that always seemed to blow into her small yard from Mr. Thompson's enormous cottonwood tree looming next door. It also meant she would be very busy as a seamstress mending shirts and jackets with holes to be used for the winter. Being gifted at sewing and making long pants and wool sweaters fit again, mom's career took off after the war. Buying new clothes was simply not an option for most. Especially when clothes were scarcer than before the war.

On this unusually warm October afternoon, I sat on a chair pulling out threads from a pair of old uniform pants. The inseam and waist needed to be let out a bit to accommodate the weight that Mr. Scott gained since coming back from the war. The pants were in fairly good condition besides being on the tight side and it would be a waste to get rid of them.

Unlike Mom, though, I didn't have the skills to mend complicated items, but I tried. Quilting, on the other hand, I was good at and enjoyed. I guess I loved the creativity of it. I could remember a few times growing up when mom and I would sew a quilt together, usually as some sort of gift for someone. A wedding, a new baby, even

Ellie Lynn

a special birthday. Unfortunately, mom didn't need help sewing a quilt now, instead boring mending. Her hands seemed to tire and hurt more as she aged and it's mending that pays the bills. She agreed to my help, but only if I didn't dare mention her worsening arthritic fingers.

"So how is that baby coming along?" She asked casually.

I unconsciously placed my palm over my small, rounding belly. I recently felt the slight butterfly-like movements showing life. I couldn't help but feel thrilled at the slight movements, but terrified I'd lose the baby as before. I wanted to tell Mom this, that I didn't think I could handle another loss, and I was certain that my marriage wouldn't.

Instead, I simply told her everything was fine. Such a generic response I knew, but I could never speak my fears aloud. They were my worries and I kept them to myself like a closely held secret. Speaking of them aloud made them a possibility, and I was determined that everything would work out this time. George and I needed this baby so badly.

"Is George getting excited... about the baby?"

"I guess so." I replied quietly.

"What do you mean, you guess so? How can you not tell? Does he talk about it? Is he helping you out with things like chores around the house? You know with what happened last time, you really need to take it easy."

I felt the familiar lump rise in my throat. With what happened last time... I didn't quite know what to think about that. As if I had done something that caused the loss last time. Or did I? Plus, I didn't know how George felt. He talked about being excited, but I wasn't sure. Things were different from the first time around.

"Everything's fine mom!" I snapped impatiently while continuing to pull out little threads. Looking up after a moment of silence I found mom not working but staring at me with that "don't you dare talk to me like that" look.

Falling

"Margaret, you don't have to get all snappy with me. All I did was ask after my daughter and soon to be grandchild." Her stern look turned to hurt.

"Mom, I don't want to talk about all of that right now. The baby is fine, I'm fine." Then, not wanting to spoil this beautiful fall day with my mood, I added, "It's hard sometimes for me, you know? But I'm okay, I'm getting excited."

Mom's expression changed back to her normal cheerful self. She won. We sat in silence for a little while longer, listening to leaves rustle as a light breeze picked up. I absorbed the sound like it was the earth's magical song. Mom did not.

"That darn wind. I raked the yard yesterday and now it's going to be full of leaves again. If I didn't like the shade so much in the summertime, I'd chop that tree right down, you bet I would! I'd do it when Mr. Thompson wasn't home and couldn't say much about it."

I shook my head at mom's blustering. No one would ever chop the tree down. That tree was where Mr. Thompson's sons used to play any chance they could get. Charles and Phillip would climb high up in it and throw twigs and sticks down upon me and Anna Beth, while we would play with our dolls. They did this while cupping their hand over their mouths and moving it back and forth, making the sound of an Indian call. They were three and four years older than Anna Beth and me, but at a whopping seven years old, we would turn our noses up at them and explain in our most mature voices how immature they were acting. If Charles or Phillip had ever invited us up to play in that tree with them, we wouldn't have hesitated a second. They never did.

I guess we were just some pesky girls to throw their pretend arrows at. Phillip's interest in me seemed to change a little, though, as a few years passed and I matured a bit. One evening after supper I ran to my room to get ready for bed. I pulled my shirt off and stood in my bedroom with just a bra on. I looked out my window to see Phillip standing in his window, watching me. As soon as I caught him, he dropped out of sight, probably hoping I hadn't seen him. After that, he always blushed whenever I saw him.

Both Charles and Phillip died in the war within three months of each other, a complete devastation to Mr. Thompson. He lived there alone now, since the boys' mother passed from pneumonia when the boys were young. Sometimes Mr. Thompson would sit out on his porch swing watching that enormous tree. I guess he still imagined them playing in it. I know I did.

Thinking of the loss of my precious daughter, I felt a newfound respect and sympathy for Mr. Thompson. Knowing that both his sons fought and died in a war valiantly probably provided little comfort when he sat all alone, looking at that tree and hearing their laughter echo in the past.

I quickly swallowed the lump that suddenly formed in my throat to answer Mom... "Uh huh."

"Margaret, you're not paying a whit of attention to what I'm talking about, are you?" Mom scolded. "I told you I was planning on moving out east to join the circus. I'm wondering if you want to join me. I've heard that clowns are quite the thing. I have my red nose and big shoes already picked out."

My eyes got big as I seriously looked at Mom. Not because I believed what she told me, but because she said something completely silly and ridiculous. Mom never acted silly. The only hint that she wasn't serious was the small twitch at the side of her mouth. Seeing that, I couldn't help myself. My eyes watered and my hand covered my mouth as I laughed. By the time I finished, my side hurt, and tears ran down my face. I guess sometimes you need a good cry and sometimes you need a good laugh. Apparently, I needed both.

"Well, I didn't think it was that funny. Maybe I should tell jokes more often, I haven't seen you laugh like that in ages." Mom said with a smile. Her voice held a serious note.

"Sometimes it's hard to find something to truly laugh about Mom. I'm sorry I was wool gathering before. What were talking about?" I asked

Falling

"Well, what I said is that you should have seen Mrs. Mullkins hat at church service on Sunday. That thing is hideous. It honestly looked like she poured some glue on the thing, stuck some flowers on it, and then ever so gently put a nice little replica of a butterfly perched on the top. Twice I shushed Harry from laughing out loud." Then with an eye roll she continued, "Pastor Willis, though, gave the most beautiful service. You really shouldn't have missed it, Margaret... duty to the Lord... helping our neighbors..."

I could feel myself drifting away again in thought. I could hear her speaking, but what she talked about couldn't seem to penetrate my thoughts. My eyes drifted away from her face once again to see the leaves blowing off the tree and silently dancing to the ground. I felt the quiet dancing in my womb as well.

Looking back towards Mom's face, I tried to pay attention and nodded in agreement with the wise speaking of our pastor and the unfriendliness of Mr. Larson's new wife. Yes, yes, although I really didn't care now. All the small talk seemed... well, small.

Pulling out the last few stitches on the trousers, I now had two separate pieces in my hands. "Oh, I'm so sorry Mom. I guess I got a little too enthusiastic with the seam ripper." I said to Mom's open mouth agape. "As you can tell, I've been a little scatterbrained lately. I don't know what's going on with me." I trailed off in a mumble. I hadn't been feeling much of myself lately.

"It's called pregnancy Margaret. Women are usually more scatterbrained while carrying that precious life and I tell you it doesn't get much better after you have it. Then you get little sleep. Hopefully, your George will help some with that, although I wouldn't count on it. Now that has nothing to do with George but men in general. It will all be worth it though when you finally get to hold that child." Mom smiled with a knowing look. "I can finish this work; you go home and get some rest."

"Mom, but your hands..."

"They are fine, Margaret. I've been sewing my entire life. My hands will not fail me now."

Ellie Lynn

"Okay, I'll come and help tomorrow if I can." I said hesitantly. Then I got up and kissed mom on the cheek. I started to walk away but on a second thought I turned back to her and I grabbed her hands with both of mine. "Mom, did you know about Harry's babies?" I didn't know why it suddenly felt important for me to know. Plus, I realized the odd timing for me to ask such a question. There was no prequel. I hadn't even realized that it sat heavily on my mind.

"Yes, and I've never witnessed such suffering as that poor woman. Then, she accepted it, and dedicated herself to helping others. It also helped that she had you to love on. I think she's always seen you as the daughter she could never have." she said, her eyes looking a little glassy. "Margaret... everything is going to be okay." Then she squeezed my hands with her own and I believed her. Those simple words *everything is going to be okay* meant more to me than she could have possibly known. As if I were a child again, those simple words made everything better.

On the ride home, I thought of Mr. Thompson again. I knew mom took him over extra loaves of bread and plates of supper occasionally. Before meeting George, I occasionally took them over myself, but I thought little of it since moving in with George. Suddenly feeling selfish I realized I hadn't done anything to help anyone else for a long time. Harry took care of everyone around her and had the biggest heart imaginable. I guess part of the wisdom we get when we grow up is gained through some sorrow and hard times, and I suddenly needed to do something for him. I sat wallowing in self-pity long enough. The thought of doing something for Mr. Thompson made me feel almost giddy, and my soul felt lighter.

Winter would be here soon, and I knew what to do. Mom stored many scraps of old fabric in different colors, textures, and print. Some vibrant and beautiful, some dull and sturdy. Like leaves. Tomorrow, along with helping mom with the mending, I would gather the fabric needed to make a warm quilt to give to Mr. Thompson. On the front I would stitch together a big tree with all the colorful leaves. Hope-

Falling

fully, it would remind him of his sons. It would be something he could hold on to at night when memories flood his thoughts.

I instinctively knew this to be true. When I lay my head down at night, just before sleep overtakes me, my mind is usually flooded with thoughts of what could have been and memories I never got the chance to have.

A week later I was back at mom's house, but this time we were baking bread. Harry walked through the door as mom and I were measuring out flour. She put on an apron before placing a kiss on my cheek.

"Sorry I'm late this morning. I got called into the hospital for a couple of hours, so never mind me if I'm a little crazy. I've had five cups of coffee." Harry said matter-of-factly.

You would never know by looking at her. Like usual, she pulled her hair back in a long braid and her lips were red from lipstick. Even her eyes looked alert and awake, although that was probably from the large intake of caffeine.

"You are perfect Aunt Harry, we started anyway." I said cheerily.

"Maggie, your mom told me about the little project you started. I'm so proud of you, although frankly I don't know when you have the time. What with the pregnancy, keeping up with your home and husband, baking, and helping your mom?" Harry said with a hint of concern.

"I can do it and I'm enjoying it. I've always liked to quilt, and it's been helping me to deal with my anxiety I have from this pregnancy. I'm sewing a little at night before bed and after George is off to work. Did I tell you he has started working the night shift?" I asked.

"Well, you hadn't, but I saw him early this morning at the hospital at the end of his shift. We didn't get to chat much, but he did mention that he was ready to head home for some sleep. The poor man looked exhausted." Harry said while vigorously washing her hands.

Ellie Lynn

"Yes, he seemed exhausted this morning. He barely spoke to me when he got home but went straight to bed. What was he at the hospital for?" I asked curiously. Harry didn't answer for a little while. She completely dried her hands on the dish towel before walking back to the table where we started to knead bread.

"Well, he brought in young Harmony Westerly around four this morning. She was bruised and battered up pretty good and... well..." Harry swallowed a couple of times as if she couldn't stand to even speak the words. "... someone had raped her."

Both mom and I gasped with our flowered hands over our mouths. Harmony couldn't have been over fourteen years old and looked to be but a wisp of a girl. Her blonde hair looked thin and under her bangs were bright blue eyes. She was thin, tall, and sort of lanky. I always felt sorry for her whenever I saw her in town with her mother. That woman always seemed to holler at her for something as Harmony would dutifully follow from behind. Her head always bent downwards, with her hair tucked behind her ears.

"I feel sick. That poor child." Mom said with her hand still over her mouth. I shook my head, it was too horrible to even think of.

"Did they catch the bastard that did it?" Mom asked with almost a shrill to her voice. Mom never swore, but when she did, it was for good reason.

"I don't think so." Harry pursed her lips and poured her ingredients into a big glass bowl. Mom and I started kneading our dough again in silence for a little while, all deep in our own thoughts.

Mom finally broke the silence. "What is this world coming to when a young girl like that isn't safe? It probably had something to do with that whoring mother of hers. I mean, someone probably thought..." her words trailed off. Probably given the look that Harry directed at her.

"It doesn't matter what her mother is like, something like this should never happen. It should never happen, period!" Harry said in an icy and direct tone. If there was one thing about Harry, is she's

Falling

always direct and to the point, especially with injustices to those that are more unfortunate.

"I meant nothing bad by that Harry and I certainly wouldn't put any blame on poor Harmony. That poor girl." Mom stopped kneading the dough for a moment.

Harry exhaled with exhaustion before answering. "I know you didn't Ailene, it's just been a very long night."

Mom smiled knowingly at Harry. "I know. Did I tell you two that Aunt Evie is going to be coming to stay with me for a while?" An obvious change to the subject.

"No, you hadn't." I answered, secretly glad for the subject change.

"Yes, well, I got Aunt Evie's letter yesterday. Apparently, that worthless son of hers is having business troubles and has moved his wife and himself into her house. He declared that it would be overcrowded for them all to stay there so she is coming to stay with me."

"Why that little weasel. It's her house!" Harry said.

"Yes, I know, but I think she's going along with it to get away from them for a while. I suspect that she secretly detests her son. She may love him, but I don't think she likes him very much, can't say I blame her for that. Plus, it will be nice having her around. I think I will enjoy the company."

"What's he doing with his house, is he going to sell it then?" I shook my head at mom's comment on looking forward to Aunt Evie's visit. Those two mixed as well as oil and vinegar.

"Apparently, they must sell it." Mom shrugged before wiping her white hands on her apron to dust off some of the flour.

Harry clicked her tongue in disapproval. We all finished kneading our dough at this point and placed and covered them to rise.

"I'll make some hot tea if anyone would like some." I said as I filled a kettle with water and placed it on the stove. We would have time to sit and talk and Harry would have time to snooze if she wanted, although I doubted she would.

Ellie Lynn

We sat in heavy silence for a time while we sipped our tea. Mom also put out buttered saltines sitting on a pretty plate with scrolling roses around the edges. The saltines looked good, but I always hated when mom coated them with butter. Mom already devoured three of them and with crumbs speckling down the front of her blouse.

I looked over at Harry and she looked deep in thought. Thoughts that were obviously weighing heavily on her as her forehead creased in such a way showing her distress. Mom surprisingly sat quiet as well. Ignoring the heaviness for a moment I focused on Aunt Evie's upcoming stay. It would be nice to spend some more time with her. She always made me laugh and even though they were practically opposites from one another, she reminded me of my grandma.

My slight smile faded as I thought once again of Harmony Westerly. Rape was not something that polite society generally talked about. It sounded like a dirty word, although most times that had little to do with the pure evil nature of the crime. In society's eyes, a rape occurred usually because of something the victim must have done wrong. I hoped that Harmony's young age would spare her from this.

"Is she going to be okay Harry?" I asked. No need to mention who I asked about. I suspected she fell on all our minds.

"I don't know. She will heal physically but mentally... I don't know." Harry replied.

I didn't ask anything else. Neither did mom. After a few minutes of sitting there, the conversation turned to Aunt Evie once more. She would arrive next week for an indefinite stay. Despite them not seeing eye to eye on many things, I knew it would be good for mom to have Aunt Evie stay with her. Giving mom someone to fuss over besides me.

Later that day I kissed mom and Harry's cheeks goodbye and headed home. I wanted to be there for when George woke up, as I worried about how much the situation with Harmony affected him. Would it be yet another reminder of other horrors he'd seen? I heard

Falling

rape was sometimes another atrocity placed upon those already affected by war.

Although the truth be known, George talked little about his job to me. I suddenly wondered if he came across a lot of situations that brought memories flooding back. That his job could possibly help to create his continuing nightmares.

Chapter Fifteen

Maggie
October 19, 1947

There are moments in life where your entire world and existence simply change. What you once thought about the world, about others, about yourself all become clear. Life becomes clear. Tragedy and pain often remind you about the good in life. The love, the comforts, the joy. Without sadness, how could you feel bliss? Without anxiety, how could you feel tranquil? There is no moment quite like your impending death to bring about this clarity. The knowledge, the truth, is so very close I can almost reach it. It's not quite clear yet but I can feel it getting closer.

I put the meatloaf topped with ketchup in the oven to bake when George walked into the kitchen. He looked tired still and wore a shadow of whiskers on his cheeks.

"Did you not sleep well George?" I asked in my concerned voice. I did not know how he slept during the day and stayed up all night. Especially since he struggled with getting a full night's sleep, anyway.

"I slept long enough." he replied shortly while walking over to me, kissing my cheek while caressing my backside with his hand. A shiver went through me as usual when George touched me.

"I was thinking that maybe after supper we could take a small walk." At the look of his hesitation I continued, "It's nice outside this evening and I think the fresh air and exercise would be good for me and the baby." I smiled playfully as I turned more fully into his arms.

"I suppose we could take a small stroll, but I need to head into work a little early this evening so it will have to be right after we eat, okay?"

"Yeah, of course." I conceded. Just then I felt a small little kick inside my womb. I'd felt a fluttering feeling for a while now, but this was the first real kick I felt, and the exhilaration of it ran through me. I couldn't help but laugh a little as my hand went straight to my belly.

"George, I just felt our child kick. I mean I've felt movements for a little while now, but this felt like a small kick." I couldn't help but

Ellie Lynn

give a choked laugh as I felt a lump in my throat. I couldn't decide whether to laugh or weep.

George placed his hands on my small protruding belly to feel any movements. He smiled and seemed happy. After a few moments, his hands fell away, and he looked a little disappointed.

"It's probably too early still to feel movements from the outside. Soon though, my love." I said, as I placed a kiss on his cheek.

"Of course. I'm going to go get ready for work. When should I expect supper to be ready?"

"About a half hour... maybe a little longer." I replied.

About an hour later we sat at the table, almost finished eating. I drizzled some honey on my cornbread while George took a bite from his second one. Our conversation so far felt like mundane everyday things. The "look at this weather we are having" type of talk. George asked me about the quilt I started making. I told him about Aunt Evie's upcoming visit, and then of course he asked about my day baking with Mom.

"Aunt Harry mentioned she talked with you early this morning at the hospital. She told me about Harmony." I said matter-of-factly. The moment the words were out of my mouth, I felt the tension rise in the air. I saw the emotions changing in him as he looked up from his plate to me. I had a moment of doubt. I wondered if I did the right thing by bringing it up. Maybe it really wasn't any of my business.

Then, just as quickly, my resolve returned. George and I needed to talk about the hard things, despite what society said. I didn't agree with pretending. We needed to get emotional, work through problems, get angry, get sad, get support, and offer it. We needed to do all this together. Marriage was so much more than the niceties and safe conversations. I didn't always need to be protected, and I was tired of living in the bubble George created for me.

George finished chewing in no hurry to say anything. When he

Falling

finished, he wiped the sticky residue of honey off his lips and then laid his napkin down. I saw his tongue rolling around his teeth inside his closed mouth, dislodging any remaining food.

"What happened to Harmony is a terrible thing." George said, as he shook his head sadly. Then he placed his napkin on his plate and rose to place it in the sink. Walking back to me he said, "are you finished?" before grabbing my plate as well.

"Thank you, George I'll wash those dishes when we get back from our walk." I said, trying to make sure he didn't have an out to wiggle out of our walk and our chance to have an actual conversation. George protested, but I raised my finger to his lips and with a smile said, "you promised." Before turning around and grabbing a light sweater that I hung up next to the kitchen back door.

It was a beautiful evening for a walk as the air felt cool outside but not yet cold. Just before dusk, the sky already began darkening and I knew there would be a beautiful sunset soon. I looked over at George next to me, so handsome in his uniform. He looked a little intimidating if you didn't know how quick he was to smile and laugh. God, how I loved this man.

"George, tell me about what happened. With Harmony." I unnecessarily added the last, as if he didn't know what I was talking about.

"Maggie, why do you want to know? This isn't just some juicy gossip to share with Harry and your mother." George replied sounding a little annoyed.

"I know, George, and I wouldn't dream of telling them anything that you tell me. I promise. You can trust me. I just thought it would be good for you to share it with me...you know, for you." I said, as I squeezed his hand.

"Well, it's unnecessary, but... fine. About two this morning Mr. Collins spotted Harmony sitting on the side of the road, near to where she lives. He brought her to the hospital, where we were called. Someone beat her around the face, and it became obvious she had been the victim of an assault... sexually."

Ellie Lynn

I waited a minute for George to say more, but he didn't. His body was rigid, and he looked angry. I could almost feel it coming off him in waves. I couldn't say that I blamed him.

"Do you know who could have done this to her?" I asked.

"No." Then on second thought and much quieter, as if it came from a dark place in him, "yes, but not officially. Maggie, it's a fucking mess!" Then he looked at me apologetically for the language. I in return gave him a small smile. It's not like I hadn't heard that word before and even quietly muttered it under my breath a few times. "She's not talking. Which speaks volumes but also keeps our hands tied." George said quietly before pulling a pack of cigarettes from his pocket along with a match. We paused briefly in our walk for him to light it.

"Maggie, the gossip mills around town will have a heyday with this. Just don't... don't take part in it. The poor girl has been through enough and to top it, she will probably be whispered about for who knows how long." George then took a long inhale of his cigarette and blew out a long billowy cloud of gray smoke. Coughing a little, I reached out a hand to touch his sleeve.

"I won't talk to anyone about her, George, I promise. I'll say a prayer for her tonight, and I'll say one for you as well." I looked up at him with a small smile. He took another drag of his cigarette and then blew it out.

"I wouldn't waste your breath, Maggie, we both know I'm probably going to hell anyway." He looked at me and winked with a smile that was more of a smirk.

I smacked his arm and laughed a little. I didn't really like what he said, but I also understood that he said it in jest. Then, we both stopped walking and looked up at the brilliant sky; streaked with reds, pinks, and purples. The clouds made puffy little hills, making the entire sky look like some kind of fantastical world. It was beautiful.

"George, do you know what this reminds me of? You know that time at the barn when we first started dating? We sat on the edge

Falling

with our feet dangling and watched a sunset. Everything felt so simple then. I didn't think I could love you more than at that moment... but I do." Then I turned to look up at him. My chest tightened with my feelings for him. I loved him more than anything.

George looked down at me and smiled. A genuine smile that softened his eyes. I could see his thoughts before hearing the words. "I love you too, sweetheart."

At that moment, everything was perfect in our little world. The world around us may have been a completely different story. Heck, our own lives had many times been fraught with pain and sadness. But right then, right at that moment, everything was perfect. If only I could capture it to stay forever. As soon as George kissed my cheek and headed back to the house to grab his belongings to head into work, the spell broke. The real world began to spin again.

Chapter Sixteen

George
March 23, 1944

Sleep didn't come easy as I laid on my side looking towards the small charcoal stove sitting in the middle of the room. It was our only source of heat, and despite seeing the faint glow of it; it did little to ward off the chill in the room. I could feel it snaking its way up my back, bringing with it a small shiver, only to repeat once again.

Two men were snoring rhythmically. One wave of irritating noise quickly proceeded after another, like two clocks ticking out of sync, but much louder. One man wept. He tried to be quiet about it all, but you could still hear his shudders, his running nose, his deep breaths.

My bunkmate made the situation worse above me. He'd been plagued with dysentery this past week, and the smell of him kept creeping down to my bunk, making me want to gag. I struggled to keep pitying him, as all I could imagine was putting the poor man out of his misery... and mine. I wouldn't, of course.

All I could do lying there in my bunk was imagine walking out the door of our small barracks into the chilly night air, fresh air. Fresh air so cold and clean that it would make my lungs and throat ache. I would keep walking past the guards, past the barbed wire fence, away from the smell of unwashed bodies, shit, and blood. In my imagining I could walk forever if I had the freedom to do so. I would walk straight to Oklahoma, and rest my aching body in Aunt's rocking chair sitting on the porch. There I would gaze up at the stars on a warm winter night and everything would be right.

I think in all honesty the hardest part of being a prisoner of war was the inability to simply leave. The hunger, the cold, the sickness, and the fear all didn't compare with the realization that I couldn't walk out of here. I no longer had the freedom to do so, to do any of the things my mind and soul begged for me to do and there seemed plenty of time for begging, as there wasn't much else to do but dream of freedom.

Roll calls filled a good portion of our day where we would all parade out in front of the Germans in rows. We waited in the blistering cold just to confirm we still existed there in hell. It was a long process, and the Germans seemed to enjoy parading in front of us as

Ellie Lynn

powerful and strong in opposition to our weak and sick beings. Men puked, some shit themselves, others had to be held up because they were too weak to stand. Roll calls didn't make exceptions for anyone and for any reason. You simply didn't have the power to just walk away or not go as we all wished we could.

Yesterday I stood in the courtyard, feet feeling numb with cold, trying to ignore the surrounding misery. I heard a bird chirping above me. I looked up to see the little black bird dancing around in the sky. I felt amazed at how it flew around so oblivious to what was happening around it. It showed off its freedom to roam, dive, and flitter about, like a child does with a lollipop. I hated and envied that bird with every part of my being at that moment.

Then something amazing happened. Out of the cold gray sky came a black flash so quick I almost missed it. I would have if I hadn't been staring. The flash hit the little bird so hard that it quickly started to drop out of the sky. This didn't last long though, as just as the bird started to fall, it was scooped up in a tight talon grip. A Peregrine got its meal. I heard what amazing hunters they were flying at incredible speeds. I never actually saw one hunt before, and I stood awestruck.

Turning over and wrapping the itchy wool blanket more firmly around me. A profound thought raced through my head while thinking of the Peregrine and its amazing feat. I watched the bird being scooped up and taken away. I watched the Peregrine simply take what he wanted, what he needed. At that moment, I believed I saw this for a reason. My freedom had been taken from me, but I could still think, feel, imagine, plan...

The Germans thought they owned us, but they didn't. They illusioned themselves into believing that they could control us. As for me, I would no longer wallow in my self-pity, allowing them that control over me. Like the Peregrine I would take what I wanted no matter how hard of a feat or if it ended up costing my life. I wanted my freedom back.

Rolling over again, I tried to hug my body to trap in my body heat. I tucked my chin in closer to my chest and let out a long breath

Falling

of warm air, feeling its brief warmth circle around me. Directly following it my body shivered. Nothing really took the chill away. Instead, I tried concentrating on routines. Not mine, as there wasn't much to concentrate on. The Germans, however, had lots of routines. They worked like clockwork. I'm sure if I thought hard about it, concentrated on it, I'm sure I could possibly find a glitch. A small kink in the well-oiled machine.

Lots of time sat in my hands. As I tried to keep from gagging after another bout of wretched flatulence from above me, I remembered that the German with the glasses and blonde hair smoked a cigarette at 1100 hours every morning. The big German with the cleft in his chin looked at the POWs with a hint of sympathy, as he always turned away when one got beat. And I remembered the German who looked as if he worked as a schoolteacher and who was the cruelest of all, never patrolled the barracks after midnight. I had indeed a lot to think about.

As I categorized and made lists in my head, I felt drowsy like being read a bedtime story. There seemed to be a tightness in my chest and a lump in my throat so strong that it was almost painful. It was then I felt a strange wetness running fiery streaks down my cheeks, and I belatedly realized that I was crying. I hadn't cried since the day Benny died despite all the death, fear, and pain I experienced since. It was almost funny; I thought before succumbing to much needed sleep, that the one thing that could bring me to tears after everything I had been through, was hope.

Chapter Seventeen

Maggie
January 4, 1948

Guessing by the faint light illuminating the bedroom, dawn neared, and I once again sleepily strode to the bathroom since first going to bed hours ago. After once again relieving my bladder, I stretched my aching lower back, making my protruding belly stretch forward even further. To say I felt ready to deliver this baby was an understatement. Even though I knew I would greatly miss the specific closeness that was pregnancy.

Now at that uncomfortable point where my feet swelled, my lower back ached, and with each step I took, it felt like my baby would fall out of me. With each sigh and ache, bathroom trip and restlessness, I also felt incredibly thankful that I was feeling each discomfort that so many took for granted.

When I last spoke to Anna Beth, she told me she experienced the same symptoms before delivering her beautiful twin girls. Crawling back into bed, I couldn't help but feel a small tightening in my chest when thinking about them. Alice and Freya were perfect. And it was painful for me to see them for the first time a couple of months after they were born. George practically forced me to go visit, but once I saw them, cried, and held them, and cried some more... I was okay.

Anna Beth cried just as much as I did, and I never felt closer to her than I did at that moment. I imagined during my grief she stayed away to focus on the rest of her pregnancy. She stayed away to protect my feelings, knowing that it would be painful to see her then.

Feeling uncomfortable, I turned over to my right side and put George's empty pillow at the small of my back, trying to take the pressure off it. After finally getting comfortable again, or as comfortable as I could get, I felt the gentle pull of sleep.

A couple of hours later, I awoke to George climbing into bed. I started to pull his pillow away from where it sat wedged against me when he stopped my hand with his.

"It's okay, sweetie, I'll just share yours. It will give me an excuse to do this." George said as he snuggled in close, sharing my pillow. My head rested against his chest, and his hand curved gently around

Ellie Lynn

my belly. I felt him lightly nuzzling the top of my head with his chin and lips.

A few minutes later I heard his rhythmic breathing with an intermittent whistle like snore. I also felt a bit trapped, claustrophobic, and hot, despite the coolness in the air. To be honest, I didn't love to snuggle, so after about twenty minutes of trying to relax enough to fall back asleep; I decided to get up. A little while later I sat at our kitchen table in my dressing gown and slippers, sipping a cup of hot tea. I also devoured two pieces of banana bread smeared with rich creamy butter that mom made and brought over yesterday. Mine never came out as good as hers.

With my ravenous appetite, my belly wasn't the only part of me that had grown during this pregnancy. It didn't bother me though. The most important thing to me was to have a healthy baby. So, I gave into my cravings and figured I'd worry about any extra weight later.

Standing up, I grabbed my empty plate and walked to the kitchen sink to place it there. As I heard the plate clink, I turned away when on second thought I instinctively turned back around. Something out of place caught the corner of my eye. Right on the edge of the sink was a dark red smear. As I inspected, I recognized it as blood. I turned the faucet on and with a cloth wiped the small amount of blood away. I then rinsed the cloth and hung it on the middle divider in the double sink.

George must have gotten a cut on his finger or something, I thought to myself. Having a few chores to do in the house that day, I gave the blood no other thought. After dressing in our dark bedroom, I quietly crept out, pulling the door softly shut behind me. I then made my way to the nursery, where I left a box full of clothes to go through.

Yesterday I received the box of outgrown baby clothes from Anna Beth. She promised me she would months ago, and I was so grateful that she finally gotten around to sending them. I knew Alice and Freya kept her busy, but I worried that she forgot. We didn't have a

Falling

lot of money, but with family help we managed to get everything that we needed.

Looking around the nursery, I couldn't help but feel anxious about everything. We set the crib up against the wall. The pale-yellow curtains hung against the sun-filled window, casting the room in a soft glow. A wooden rocking chair sat to the side of the window, where I already imagined rocking my sweet baby as the room filled up with warm morning sunlight.

Turning to the mostly empty dresser, I walked over to the large box sitting there, still taped up. I quickly tore the tape off and opened the top, exposing the miniature clothes inside. Picking the top piece up, a small cream-colored gown, I couldn't help but bring it up to my face to breathe in the lingering baby smell clinging to it. This caused a small tingle to run down through my body. Normally this would have brought about a deep wave of grief. Today, I felt anticipation and excitement and of course a little nervousness.

Dragging the box over to the rocking chair, I sorted through the clothes. Before I knew it, I felt the rumbles of hunger telling me it was close to noon. I placed the last of the clothes in the bottom drawer of the dresser. I separated all the clothes by size and type, and also arranged the powders and creams. Folding the cloth diapers, I tried to imagine how to put the diapers on, pin them, and clean them. Laughing to myself lightly I told myself there would be a learning period for all of it.

Mom told me once I would be a natural mother. That I would know what I needed to do instinctively. What if she was wrong? I worried that once I brought the baby home, I'd discover that contrary to what my mom says, I'm not a natural. These types of worries filled my head but were concerns I never spoke out loud. They were too personal, too private, and they led me to that dark voice hidden deep within me that whispered I wasn't worthy. That there was a reason God took my baby from me.

Shaking off my bad thoughts, I walked out of the bedroom and headed down the stairs to the kitchen to make a sandwich. I just took

Ellie Lynn

a bite when our telephone rang. It caused me to jump a little as the shrill ringing sound pierced the silence.

"Hello, Harkin's residence." I answered.

"Yes, hello Mrs. Harkins. This is Taylor from the police department. I don't know if you remember me, but I work with your husband." The male voice on the other end said.

"Of course, what can I help you with?" I asked as my cheeks reddened a bit with long ago guilt.

"I need to speak to George please."

"He's actually sleeping..." I tried telling him.

"I need to speak with him, it's urgent. Can you please wake him?" Taylor said in a no-nonsense type of way. His voice carried a certain authoritative tone, one I'm sure he used in his profession often.

"I'll see what I can do." I said a bit curtly, not understanding what could be so urgent that Taylor couldn't wait until George was at least awake. I laid the receiver on the table and hurried as quickly as my enlarged body would allow me up to our bedroom. Walking in, I heard George still snoring lightly. He kicked off most of his blankets and slept there in his underwear and white undershirt.

Walking over to him, I gently shook his shoulder. I didn't want to startle him awake but Taylor seemed insistent to talk with him, so I hesitantly shook him again. The third time, I shook him a little harder, then stepped back cautiously. Sitting up, he rubbed his eyes before running a hand through his messy hair.

"Is it already time to get up? I feel as if I barely slept." He said with a loud yawn.

"George, it's not time to wake yet but Taylor is on the phone for you. He says it's urgent." I said, knowing how annoyed it may make him. But he wasn't. He looked at me for a moment in a still and pale sort of way, nodded while covering a yawn, and then got up and walked out the door. I brushed off a feeling of unease.

Following him down the stairs and into the kitchen, I walked back over to the small table to finish eating my egg salad sandwich.

"I hope you have a good reason for waking me." George said the

Falling

moment he put the receiver to his ear and sat in the chair sitting by the small telephone table.

As he listened, he rubbed the growth of stubble on his chin. His eyes were at first downcast, looking at the floor. He seemed casual, yet annoyed. That instantly changed as he looked directly at me. He suddenly seemed serious, and there was a slight tension in the air, something I felt. Whatever Taylor told him on the other line was indeed serious.

"Can't say that I feel bad for the son of a bitch... Yeah, well he had a lot of enemies... I'd be careful what you say to me as that sounds close to an accusation. I guess I'll be coming in early to talk to Captain. Okay, well thanks for the heads up. Okay, bye." After hanging up the phone with a loud clunk, George sat there a moment again, staring at the floor.

"Goodness, George, what was that all about?" I asked, bewildered.

George took a big breath and let it out slowly as his hand rubbed through his hair once again. Then he paused. I could see his indecision in telling me about his conversation. I heard his end of the conversation and he couldn't get out of telling me something. My insistent and unflinching stare at him told him as much.

"Westerly is dead. They found him this morning with a gunshot to his head behind his house." George said in a grave tone.

"Oh my, that is terrible... I mean, I didn't care for the man, but he certainly didn't deserve that. Why does the captain want to talk to you about it?" I wondered out loud.

"Because, like a few of the other officers, I had run-ins with and some choice words about him after Harmony was raped." Then, after running his hands through his hair again, he continued, "It's all protocol hun, just part of the investigation. They will talk to anyone who had much contact with him. More than likely Westerly ran his mouth to the wrong person last night. Who knows, there's probably a long list of potential suspects given Westerly's winning personality." George said dryly.

Ellie Lynn

Then, after a moment of silence, George stood up to lean over and plant a kiss on the top of my head. "Don't you worry your pretty little head about it, okay. All you have to worry about is cooking that little sweet roll."

I chuckled at this. Sweet roll. A cute little nickname George gave the baby. "Alright George, do you want something to eat, or do you plan on trying to get a couple more hours of sleep?" I asked, standing up to put my arms around his waist in a loose hug.

"Ooh, what do you have in mind?" George said deeply that was a mixture of sensual suggestion and joking.

"George!" I scolded as I laughed. "I'm as big as a house right now and besides, I feel as though this baby is going to fall right out of me any moment."

"Well, you look beautiful to me Maggie." He said seriously. Then, with another quick kiss on the lips, he continued, "I think I'll try to get some more sleep. I'm still tired and I can already tell it's going to be a long night."

"Okay. I love you." I replied as I watched him turn away and leave the kitchen. My insides still felt warm and tingly after his compliment. What was it about being called beautiful that made a woman melt? It held so much more to it than pretty, looking good, sexy, or attractive. It felt special and I lately felt anything but beautiful lately, and today was no exception.

After cleaning up lunch dishes and packing away food for George to eat later, I gathered up the quilt I had been making for Mr. Thompson and spread it out over the table. I finally finished it and needed to snip away loose threads, double check for pins, and make sure every detail looked perfect. I used a light cream and blue for the background. The tree trunk and branches were different shades of brown, from light to dark, intertwining around each other. Then there were the leaves. All were vibrant and colorful. Some stood out in a loud pattern, while others were soft and peaceful. There was no patterned order, no crisp lines and straight edges. The tree looked wild and free and so beautiful it made my chest tighten.

Falling

I pulled out many stitches and replaced many pieces of fabric to create what was in front of me and it looked perfect in its not so perfect way. It was the tree. It made me feel a sense of loss and hope all at the same time and a gift that I truly hoped Mr. Thompson would love. I felt a wave of anticipation at the thought of giving it to him.

I planned on this being tomorrow afternoon. Mom wanted to make a big fuss about it and plan an entire meal with everyone invited. I strongly disagreed with her as I thought putting him on the spot would be cruel. As a parent who lost a child as well, I knew this to be true. Instead, I planned to make a small stop at his home before going to Mom's to check on her and Aunt Evie.

Mom cleared out the small reading room on her main floor to accommodate Aunt Evie who didn't do stairs too well. Mom told me the other day that the longer Aunt Evie stayed with her, the more mom realized Aunt Evie's failing health. When around her, it was easy to forget her advancing age, given her spunk in spirit and sharpness of tongue. The reality of it, though, was that Aunt Evie was in her late eighties and every moment left with her felt like a blessing.

Giving the quilt a last inspection, I folded it up and wrapped it in brown paper tied with twine. As much as I enjoyed sewing the quilt, having it finished felt like a weight lifted. I didn't know how much free time I would have once the baby came. Giving the package a last pat, I took a deep breath. It felt good. I think I made the quilt as much for myself as Mr. Thompson. Like I not only closed the chapter of memories of the boys who played in that tree, but also in a way a goodbye to my baby girl as well. I would never forget her or stop loving her, but concentrating my grief into something good felt cathartic.

The next morning, I stood in front of Mr. Thompson's front door. Knocking two times, I faintly heard the shuffling of footsteps as he approached it. I was a little anxious as I stood there, waiting. I couldn't help but run my hand down my clothes to smooth out any wrinkles and pat my hair. Taking a little extra time getting ready this

Ellie Lynn

morning, I thought the gray smock-like dress I wore contrasted smartly with my light pink blouse. Unfortunately, you couldn't see the pink much as I had also put on a large gray wool sweater to keep warm on this chilly morning. I thought I looked like a dressed-up hippo.

"Margaret! Hello, what a pleasant surprise. Does your mom need anything? I promised her I'd come over to fix her squeaky door but haven't gotten to it yet." Mr. Thompson said as he opened the door.

His bushy gray eyebrows were long and slightly fanned out behind his round glasses balanced on the bridge of his nose. He had always been soft spoken, with keen intelligence. Mr. Thompson was one to observe, listen, and contemplate. He wasn't loud, outspoken, or demanding in his attention, but when he spoke, everyone usually listened. He had that presence about him. As rambunctious as his boys always were, I never heard Mr. Thompson yell at them. I always thought how strange that was growing, given the constant yelling in my home.

"No, no, Mr. Thompson, I haven't come on behalf of mom. I came by to see you." I said, feeling awkward. "Uh, I brought you something. A gift." I stammered on.

"A gift. Hmm, well you don't say. Why don't you come in if you'd like? I made some coffee if you want some." Mr. Thompson replied as he cleared a pathway for me to come inside while he held the door open.

"A cup of coffee sounds wonderful." I answered with a small smile.

"And now how is your mom doing? She asked me to fix a squeaky door of hers, but I guess I got caught up doing other stuff and forgot. I'll have to head on over there later today to fix it. Probably just needs to be oiled." Mr. Thompson asked with narrowed and concentrating eyes.

"Yes, well, I'm sure it's nothing to rush about." I replied, not wanting to point out that he already mentioned as much. Mom told

Falling

me a few months back that Mr. Thompson started having troubles with his memory, forgetting things and repeating conversations.

Mr. Thompson waved his hand towards a dark blue couch with a pattern of little white dots on it. "You're welcome to have a seat if you would like, and I'll fetch the coffee. Do you like cream or sugar?"

"Both please." I answered, before lowering myself to the couch, glad that the cushions were firm and didn't sink too much. A few minutes later, Mr. Thompson came back with two coffee mugs in hand. I smelt the faint aroma of coffee in the air mixed with the smell of the house. Not an unpleasant smell, but the unique smell that every house seems to have. All different but the same in having one.

Mr. Thompson sat down in a chair across from me and took a sip of his coffee, blowing in it before doing so. I did the same. Behind him stood a small table with pictures on it as well as two triangular wooden boxes holding the flags honoring his sons' service. The stars stood out proudly against the deep blue and the glass in which they were behind gleamed without a speck of dust. My chest suddenly felt heavy. I didn't understand why I hadn't come over before. I gave him a small hug and told him of my condolences after it happened, but besides dropping off food when mom couldn't I never came over and simply visited with him. I never tried to understand his total loss and sacrifice quite like I did at this moment. Those two flags were two out of so many that lost their lives. To really think about it was overwhelming. These two flags, though, they were from men that I had known. That I watched grow up and who I had basically grown up with.

Mr. Thompson sat patiently across from me, waiting for me to speak. The silence wasn't uncomfortable, more like we both waited until we felt ready. Trying to find the correct words I cleared my throat and took another quick sip of the coffee, so sweet and creamy that I was sure there were more than a couple of teaspoons of sugar in it. I quickly sat it down on the coaster sitting on the small coffee table in front of me and grabbed the brown package I placed to the side of me on the floor.

Ellie Lynn

"Mr. Thompson, as I was saying, I brought you a gift, something I wanted to make you. Here, I hope you like it." I said clumsily, all while inwardly yelling at myself for not saying what I really wanted to say and instead sounding like such a ninny.

"That's so nice of you. I'm not sure what could have prompted this but, thank you." Mr. Thompson stood and reached forward to grasp the package. After sitting again, he untied the twine holding the wrapping in place. He paused for a moment, grazing his hand over the top part of the fabric. He then unfolded the large quilt, stood up and draped it over the chair he just vacated. You could see more of the design this way; you could make out the tree and its leaves in all its colors.

"Did you make this?" He asked.

"Yes, I did." I replied quietly.

"I've never seen a quilt quite like this before. It's beautiful. It reminds me of..." and then he became quiet and still. One of those quiet moments that fills the space with its intensity.

I awkwardly heaved myself out of the couch cushions to stand next to him. To look at the quilt with him.

"I remember they always loved to climb that tree and play in its leaves. I remember they would make the biggest leaf pile in the entire neighborhood and all the kids were envious. They would play in it for hours. I wanted to make you something to tell you how truly sorry I am that you lost them in the war."

Mr. Thompson stood there quietly for a few moments. We both did. I then noticed that his shoulders started to gently shake as he quietly wept. I reached out and gently grabbed his hand to give it a squeeze. He turned to me and kissed my knuckles before giving me a lopsided, watery grin. The saddest grin I'd ever seen.

"I'm so sorry." I squeaked out before feeling my own tears fall. The next thing I knew, Mr. Thompson enveloped me in a hug. I never really grieved for my lost neighbors. I hadn't been very close to them but when they died, one right after the other, I felt numb from everything going on. From the war itself. I remembered mom

Falling

though crying for days because of those sweet boys and that poor, poor man.

Mr. Thompson patted my back and then took a step backwards. His eyes looked red and tired as he took his glasses off to dry his eyes before putting them back on.

"Thank you for this. For this beautiful gift and for your visit. My boys were the very best and I couldn't be prouder of them." Mr. Thompson paused and then looked towards their pictures displayed proudly next to each flag. "Sometimes when I sit outside on a beautiful day, I swear I can still hear them laughing and playing like they did when they were young boys. It always makes me happy, not sad. This quilt makes me feel the same way. So again, thank you."

Wiping away my own tears, I smiled at him. I was so glad that the quilt made him happy. I now realized that it could have been a gift that made him sad instead. A reminder of all that he lost. Although I imagine every day is as much a reminder as it is a gift. Waking up every day you get to feel the sun on your skin, hear your favorite song, and feel the wind tickle your hair. But you also wake every day knowing that you don't get to share that day with your loved one. There is no greater sorrow in this world for a parent. I had the fortune of creating a new life, experiencing new joy and happiness. I'm not sure how much of a gift life would feel if I were in Mr. Thompson's shoes.

"I'd like to give you something as well, Margaret. Let me go find it and I'll be right back." said Mr. Thompson as he started walking towards his hallway.

"It's alright, you don't have to give me a gift in return." I said as he kept walking.

"No, no, I want to. It's for your baby." His voice sounded muffled from the back room. "Aw, here it is!" I heard him say before seeing him walk back down the hallway towards me.

He handed me a worn book, a poetry book by Robert Frost. One corner looked as if it had been chewed on. It also carried with it a smell, the type you get when you walk into a library.

Ellie Lynn

"I used to read it to Charles when he was little. Phillip could barely sit long enough for a nursery rhyme, but Charles could sit for hours listening to me read poetry if I let him. This one used to be his favorite. While grading papers in my study he would run in with this book saying, 'Pop Pop, read to me.' Mr. Thompson chuckled at the memory.

"Anyway, I thought you may enjoy reading it to your new one."

"I will. I'm honored that you want me to have it." I held the book against my chest. "I should probably go now. I'm supposed to help mom and Aunt Evie bake today."

"Of course, of course. You are a busy young woman. Thank you again. Oh, and before I forget, please tell your mom that I'll be over later today. She has a squeaky door that needs to be fixed." Mr. Thompson said as he walked me to the door.

"I will, Mr. Thompson, and thank you again for the book." I said as I walked out into the bright sunshine.

Stepping out the house I shivered at the chill of the slight breeze despite the bright sun shining. I continued my way down his walkway and past the tree standing tall in his yard. Today it looked bare and empty, with not a single leaf left. On a beautiful summer day though, it would have bright green leaves carrying with it heavy shade to cool anyone who stood underneath it. The sun would glint off the leaves with its golden brilliance, putting on a show. Looking naked and stark as it did now, I never appreciated the beauty of it in that way. It looked strong and protective. I guess I hadn't taken the time to notice that before.

Chapter Eighteen

Maggie
January 4, 1948

Nature's first green is gold,
Her hardest hue to hold.
Her early leaf's a flower;
But only so an hour.
Then Leaf subsides to leaf.
So Eden sank to grief,
So dawn goes down to day.
Nothing gold can stay. - Robert Frost

I have always wondered if those who fought in battle would still do so if they knew they were going to die. Not knowing that you could, but that you absolutely would. Giving your life freely for the good of your country. All your hopes and dreams right along with it. Most young men signing their life away knew it held a good possibility that was exactly what they were doing. Literally giving their life away. I always wondered about those courageous people. The one who runs towards the bullets. The one covering the grenade so that their friend can live. The men who found the inner courage to keep going no matter how hard things got. The friend beside you who would do anything to protect you, and the parents who watched their sons depart, knowing they may never see them again.

If the war taught me one thing, it's the world is filled with these types of people and they are all around us. People who will sacrifice all for what is right. For the sake of our humanity and for the greater good. Their courage hiding just below the surface and waiting for the opportunity to show itself. After all, we all die someday. It's how we lived that truly matters. As for the rest of us left behind, well, we better make sure that we live the rest of our lives in a way that is worthy of their sacrifice.

I opened the door to mom's house and walked into the warmth. The smell of baking a welcome as my tummy rumbled from hunger.

Ellie Lynn

The delightful, sweet smell also a warning that mom and Aunt Evie decided not to wait for me to bake. I sighed in relief for that. I felt tired physically and mentally and preferred to relax and visit.

"Margaret! How did it go?" Mom yelled out the moment she saw me. Her face was lit up in anticipation. I showed her the almost done quilt a week ago, and she loved it.

"It went well. I think Mr. Thompson loved it." I could feel a lump form in my throat. My eyes burned a little as I held back the tears burning the back of my eyes. Trying to swallow the lump, I continued. "It was a little emotional, but it went well. He gave me this." I said as I held the book out to hand to mom.

She flipped through the pages. "Oh, Robert Frost. Such beautiful poetry. Why did he give you this?" she asked.

"Well, it's a book that Mr. Thompson used to read to Charles as a child. He thought I would like it for the baby." I said, sort of sheepish.

"Poetry, ugh. I've never liked poetry. If you're going to say something, just get on with it already. Speaking of that, Maggie, you have gotten huge!" Aunt Evie spoke up after taking a big gulp of milk and then wiping her mouth on the edge of her apron.

"Uh, thanks Aunt Evie. I guess. Is huge a compliment?"

"It is when you are carrying a baby." Aunt Evie pointed out.

"She's right, you know. Huge is good." Mom said as if she had the final say.

"Well, I definitely feel huge."

I took a seat at the kitchen table. Mom got out of her seat and poured out boiling water into a cup for tea. The swirling steam from the pot looked mesmerizing. There was something about the process of making hot tea that I found comforting. Even more so in my childhood home. I carried with me so many memories of mom making me tea. It seemed to be her cure for almost everything. Skinned knee, a bandage and tea. Scratchy throat, hot tea with honey in it. The schoolboy I liked who didn't know I existed, tea and a shoulder to cry on.

Setting the cup of tea down in front of me, she leaned down and

Falling

kissed the top of my head. She always did this, so often I rarely noticed. Today I did. Reaching out, I grabbed mom's hand before she sat down next to me.

"Love you mom." I said as I squeezed her hand. She looked at me, a little surprised.

"Love you too Mags." She said quietly. It was her special nickname for me. She preferred to use my full name, Margaret, never used the nickname Maggie that Uncle Liam gave me, and on rare special occasions called me Mags.

"Maggie, you remind me so much of your grandma. I remember when she was carrying your mom, she was huge too." Aunt Evie said. Back to me being huge.

After a moment of sitting there, letting Aunt Evie's words sink in, we all started laughing. One of those out of the blue laughs where you aren't even sure what exactly you're laughing about. We needed it, though. Just as the laughter died down, and I had wiped the tears that had formed in my eyes, mom's front door opened, and we could hear Aunt Harry call out.

"Sorry I'm late. I accidentally burned Liam's shirt as I was ironing it. I walked away for one moment and it left a brown imprint of the iron right on the front. Can you believe that? He was running late to court, so I had to quickly iron another one." After walking into the kitchen, she continued, "You'd be happy to know that I did not burn the second shirt." Harry stood there in a bright purple sweater with big buttons along the pointed collar. Her bright red hair was up in a lopsided bun and her dark blue skirt swam about her calves as she walked straight from the door to the teapot to make herself a cup of tea. Sitting down next to Aunt Evie, she sighed and took a hesitant sip.

"What were you all laughing about, anyway?" She asked, eyeing us all suspiciously.

"Apparently I'm huge." I responded simply.

"Well, stand up."

I stood up to parade my enlarged belly in front of her.

Ellie Lynn

Yes, you are." She said, "but you also look beautiful my dear."

"You're sweet." I said as I sat back down with a shy smile and a hand on my belly.

"So, what did you two bake today? It smells amazing." Harry asked.

"Cinnamon rolls." Aunt Evie answered before mom could. "Aileen wanted to make banana bread, but I didn't want to on the count of it giving me gas. I don't know what happened. One day I just couldn't eat it anymore."

"I think it's called 'old age'." Mom said under her breath.

"Bite your tongue about being old my dear, you're getting up in age too." Aunt Evie retorted. "Just you wait and see."

"Anything new going on with your son, Evie?" Harry asked, trying to change the subject as she continued to sip at her tea.

"With Alroy? No, nothing new. He's working hard trying to please that jezebel of a wife of his. Aileen drove me home the other day to see Alroy and check on the house. Half of my houseplants are dead, and the other half needed serious care. They promised me they would take care of them. I don't think Martha knows how to take care of anything besides herself. She certainly isn't good at housekeeping either. It's not like she shouldn't know how to do these things. She's thirty for Pete's sake. When I move back in, I will have to deep clean the entire house." Aunt Evie puffed out a long breath of air.

"When do they plan on getting their own place again?" Harry asked.

"Well, according to Alroy, it will be soon. I don't think so though. They can't afford to rub two pennies together let alone have enough to get their own place. If only he hadn't married her. She's ruining his life and mine." Aunt Evie said quietly as if she hadn't meant to say it at all, at least out loud.

"Aunt Evie, if you miss being in your own home, why don't you move back in?" I asked.

"Move back in? With her? Are you crazy, girl? I'm not living in that house with them, and they can't afford to live on their own so

Falling

here I am and here I'll stay. Well as long as I'm welcome, I guess." Aunt Evie said looking over at mom.

"Of course, you can stay here as long as you want. I enjoy your company." Mom said, patting Aunt Evie's thin veined hand. The room fell quiet again as everyone sipped their tea. We all jumped a little when the kitchen timer buzzed. Mom hopped right out of her seat and headed to the oven to open it, a visible wave of heat washed over her, and the room filled with the delicious smell of freshly baked cinnamon rolls. I took in a deep breath of it in anticipation. I could almost taste the sweetness on my tongue from that one breath. The baby in my womb seemed to stretch in anticipation as well. There stood a good argument to be made that this was the reason I'm huge.

"These need to sit and cool a little, then I'll dish us out each one." Mom said as she spread the thick icing over them.

"Hmm, hmm, those smell good. I can't wait." Aunt Evie exclaimed as she rubbed her hands together in anticipation.

Aunt Harry and I looked at each other and smiled, one of those knowing smiles. Aunt Evie would devour one quickly and then spend the next ten minutes letting everyone know how they could have been better. How the cinnamon rolls could have used more butter, baked longer, more sugar, less cinnamon, or any other imperfection she could taste. It became a habit that annoyed grandma Faye while she was alive. alive. Thinking of her, I felt a pang in my chest. It always stunned me how thinking of her could still cause that deep and never-ending feeling of missing someone.

"Did you all hear about what happened to Mr. Westerly a couple of nights ago?" Harry said in a low, conspirator voice as if she was divulging a deep secret. George was right. We ladies gathered as much to gossip as we did to bake and sew. It's what women did for centuries.

"Who is this Mr. Westerly fellow?" Aunt Evie asked.

"I heard about it from Sandra Beasley." Mom chided in as she sat back down in her seat after she finished spreading the icing. "Mr. Westerly wasn't a very nice man. I know I shouldn't talk bad about the dead, but he really wasn't. A drunk, he treated his family terribly, and well, to put it bluntly he was a drain on our society." Then turning to Aunt Evie to further explaine, "He was the husband of that woman I told you about. The one who has many male acquaintances."

"Well, what happened to him?" Aunt Evie asked, a little louder, sounding annoyed.

"Someone shot him to death!" Mom said dramatically. I may have imagined it, but I thought I saw a glint in her eye. A true murder mystery in our hometown. I wanted to remind her that this wasn't an Agatha Christie crime novel.

"Maggie, do you know any inside scoop about what happened? I mean, your husband is a police officer. He's had to have told you something." Aunt Evie pressed.

"I don't have any further information than what mom said. George said little to me about it."

"It is interesting." Aunt Harry started off, almost as if she were speaking to herself as she contemplated. "It's interesting that the Westerly family has had two major tragedies this close together. I mean, what are the odds of that happening? First someone attacked and raped Harmony and then someone murders her father."

"Are you saying you think there is a relation?" Mom asked, her voice pitching in her excitement. Mom loved a mystery despite the tragic nature of this one.

"Not necessarily. It makes you wonder is all I'm saying." Harry said, a bit defensively. Harry loved to sit and gossip as much as any of us, but she wouldn't be caught dead spreading unverified rumors, especially something as serious as this.

"I bet it was the wife." Aunt Evie said with conviction after we all sat for a few minutes in silence. After everyone stared at her blankly for a moment, she continued. "Oh, seriously Aileen, you've called that woman twenty different names since I've been staying here. Harlot being your favorite. She is the common thread. Someone assaults her daughter.

Falling

Three months later, her husband is killed. The pieces fit. She probably found out that it was the husband that did it and so in a drunken rage, she shot him!" Aunt Evie's eyes seemed to bulge out a bit with her wide stare and her confident revelation, as if Miss Marple had nothing on her.

Everyone continued to stare at Aunt Evie in disbelief as she looked satisfied with herself for her keen observations and sharp intellect. Mom even sat with her mouth ajar as if she were about to catch flies. Her accusation felt quite presumptive, of course, and probably not true, but I couldn't help but think that there was some logic to what Aunt Evie said. There were never any charges filed in Harmony's assault because Harmony claimed she couldn't remember who violated her. I had got the feeling from George that he hadn't believed her.

"It's possible I guess." Aunt Harry said, looking like she needed to judge her words carefully. "It's hard to believe that a father would do that... I mean, his own daughter. I don't know." The entire conversation felt uncomfortable.

"Unless she isn't really his daughter, and he knew it. That woman gets around town, you know what I mean." Mom said emphasizing her last words.

It felt dramatic, even for mom. I could feel a small chill go down my back at the thought of all this. It was too horrible to think about because it wasn't just a book with fictional characters. These were real people and Harmony a real girl who could be scarred for life. For the first time, the gossiping and speculation bothered me. If Aunt Evie voiced her thoughts around anyone in town, it would spread like wildfire. It could prove devastating if it wasn't true just as much as if it were.

"Please say nothing." I said before thinking or gathering my thoughts better. Looking right at Aunt Evie; obviously addressing her. Instead of retorting with a sharp comeback, Aunt Evie simply patted my hand and smiled warmly.

"I would never, Maggie." She whispered. "I know I say a lot, but I

Ellie Lynn

would never intentionally hurt someone." Then on second thought, "Unless it was Martha."

At this we all chuckled. The tension seemed to ease out of the room like a heavy mist as the subject seemed to be changed. Mom got up and dished out the cinnamon rolls, which paired perfectly with a second cup of Earl Grey. We did not discuss the topic again, even though it probably lingered in the back of everyone's mind. I know it did mine.

A couple of hours later, I was back home putting a pot of water on the stove to boil. Minutes before I put a whole chicken in the oven to roast, and I planned to make some buttery mashed potatoes to go with it. Mom sent home with me a couple of large cinnamon rolls for dessert. George would be excited about this, as they were his favorite. He always told me that his favorite thing about my mom was the way she made her cinnamon rolls. Considering how much she annoyed him, this was saying a lot.

As I continued to prepare supper, I couldn't help but think of the conversation earlier that day. It all gave me a sick feeling. There had been too much death and suffering over the last few years that this tragedy, so close to home, felt incredibly wrong. I wondered how Mrs. Westerly would support her young children now. They did little to support them before. I wondered if Aunt Evie was possibly correct, and she pulled the trigger ending her husband's life. And poor Harmony. How could a mother like that possibly support her through what would probably be a lengthy healing process? Then again, if Aunt Evie was correct, then maybe Mrs. Westerly was a better mother than I gave her credit for. If anyone ever hurt my child, I'm certain I could pull the trigger as well.

"Okay, so that is the third sigh I've heard you make since I've been standing here, what's wrong? Is it the baby?" George walked up behind me, looking worried and disheveled as if he had gotten little sleep.

It wouldn't surprise me if this were true, as he rarely slept well. His arms encircled my waist, and he placed a brief kiss on my cheek

Falling

in greeting. I could only turn my head to him and smile as he took a seat. I began mashing the potatoes with the thick slab of butter and some fresh milk, so I couldn't turn around and embrace him as I wished I could.

"Everything is fine. I gave Mr. Thompson the quilt. He loved it. We both cried a bit and then he gave me a book of poems for our baby. It was sweet." I said, feeling that darn lump rise in my throat again.

"I am proud of you for doing that. I know I said nothing before, but I am. I'm sure it meant a lot to Mr. Thompson that you made it for him." George said quietly with sincerity as he walked over to the table to sit down.

I felt a small tear fall down my cheek. I wiped the tear away with my shoulder, then turned to George to give him another smile. This one as a thanks. I didn't dare speak yet, I couldn't. He seemed to understand as he smiled back and then rolled out a cigarette.

After mashing the potatoes, I left them in the pot and proceeded to pull out the chicken. The entire kitchen filled with the succulent smell, causing us both to sigh in anticipation. This caused me to smile with happiness. This is what I dreamt of my entire life. To be a wife. To share a home with the man I loved and to take care of him. To start a family.

Grabbing a carving knife, I carved off two chunks of breast for George and a single one for me. Then I dished out the mashed potatoes. I noticed as I carried the plates to the table that my mound of mashed potatoes seemed to be twice the size of George's. I felt a little embarrassed about that until I reasoned with myself that I ate for two. There would be plenty of time to worry about that type of stuff after I birthed this baby. Being huge while pregnant was okay. Being huge afterwards, maybe not so much. It would be something to work on then. For now, I'd enjoy my mashed potatoes.

George took one last drag of his cigarette before putting it out in the ashtray on the table. He rubbed his hands together in anticipation before grabbing his fork and knife to cut off chunks of the chicken.

Ellie Lynn

Putting a piece in his mouth, he chewed slowly, as if he was savoring the flavor. This, of course, made me puff up a bit in pride.

"Is it good George?" I asked.

"Hmm, hmm. It's perfect." George said with his mouth full.

"Well, wait until dessert. Mom and Aunt Evie made cinnamon rolls today and sent some home with me." I said before putting a spoonful of potatoes in my mouth. They were delightful. Just the right amount of texture and creaminess.

"Sounds delicious. So how did your visit go today?"

"It was good." I replied simply, although I could feel a slight anxiety run through me.

"Just good? Usually, you jump to tell me all about the gossip you women share." George said as he wiped his mouth with his napkin and looked straight at me. There was no getting around it.

"Well, we talked about a lot of things. About Alroy and his wife, the baby coming, Mr. Thompson, and... the Westerly's." I whispered the name as if it were forbidden.

"What about them?" He said shortly.

"What do you mean, what about them? There has been a lot about them lately." I started off a little annoyed. "You know how Aunt Evie is. Let's just say she has some theories on what happened."

"Oh, I can imagine. So, tell me, what are these theories she has."

"Well, first off she thinks Mrs. Westerly shot him."

"Really? And why would she do that? What would be the motive?" George said in a mocking tone as he leaned slightly towards me. He seemed entertained by the conversation.

"Well, her theory is that Mr. Westerly is the one who actually attacked Harmony. That he's not even her real father, and Mrs. Westerly found out about it and shot him." I said, realizing after saying it all out loud how completely ridiculous it sounded. I then waited for him to respond, which took a minute. He even leaned back in his chair and took a drink of his water first.

"Wow, she has some imagination. None of the facts add up to that though. There is no proof or suggestion that Harmony isn't his

Falling

daughter, and furthermore Mrs. Westerly has a rock-solid alibi. She was with company at the time and on the other side of town. Mr. Westerly's body was found not too far from his property. There is no possible way she did it."

"But don't you think it's awfully coincidental that someone attacked Harmony and then not long after, her father is murdered?" I asked, not sure why I tried to perpetuate the baseless theory.

"It's unusual, but strange things sometimes happen. I think you four should stick to your mystery books. Believe me, we are investigating every possibility." George said dismissively. "Now how about those cinnamon rolls?"

I got up, gathered both of our empty plates to put in the sink, and dished out two cinnamon rolls. I planned on warming them first but decided to serve them as they were knowing. They would still be good. Walking back to the table, I placed both plates down and sat back in my chair all the while trying to decide if I wanted to continue the conversation or not. The one thing that George proved exceptionally good at doing was changing a subject when he didn't want to talk about it anymore. I found it to be annoying, him always being in control of our conversations.

"So, who do you think did it?" I asked.

Looking at me sharply with surprise, I could my question didn't make George happy. "What do you mean, who do I think did it? It's an ongoing investigation. I can't talk about that with you. You know that. The last thing I plan on doing is giving you information on this to gossip about."

"I never would, you know that, George. Couples talk about things. That's what marriage is about. You should be able to talk to me about what's going on. With your work, with your past, your thoughts, your nightmares; all of it." Throwing my hands up in the air in exasperation, I didn't know if I was being unreasonable or not. I also didn't know if he really couldn't talk to me about the case, but I felt tired of him closing himself off to me.

"We do talk, Maggie. What else would you like me to say? Do

Ellie Lynn

you really want to know what I saw in the war? Do you want to know what keeps me from sleeping well? Or about the things I see at work? I share the things that are good because you are my wife. My job is to protect you and our baby from the horrors of this world, not to share all of that with you. As far as this Westerly business, I want you to stay out of it. There is no good in speculating about this with your mother and Aunt Evie. Harry should know better. You know how presumptions and half-truths grow. Sometimes they get out of control and you have much more important things to focus on right now anyway." Then he stood up and started to walk straight out of the kitchen. Then on a second thought, he came back to grab his cinnamon roll and left.

I sat there a little stunned for a few minutes. The evening started out so nicely but turned south quickly. We didn't have many arguments, but when we did, they always made me feel dreadful but strangely I also felt that for the first time since our marriage, his wall that he built around himself made sense. It wasn't a wall around him but a protective wall around me.

After finishing my cinnamon roll and cleaning supper dishes, I made my way upstairs to see George. He already bathed and put on his uniform. He looked so handsome. As I walked in, he looked up to see me. I said nothing to him as I walked over and put my arms around him in as close of a hug as my protruding belly would allow. His arms slowly circled around me as well, and he kissed the top of my head.

"I love you, George. I love you so much and I never thought of you just wanting to protect me, it has always felt like you were shutting me out." I said as the tears welled up in my eyes.

"I'm sorry. That's not what my intentions are. I love you too." He said, all the while rubbing his chin and cheek on the top of my head, trying to comfort me. Pulling away, he rubbed the tears off my cheeks with the pads of his thumbs. "I need to leave for my shift. Will you be alright?"

"Yes, I'm fine." I replied simply and with a small, watery grin. He

Falling

stood there and looked at me for a moment before planting a small kiss on my lips then walked out of the room. I walked over and sat on the bed as I listened to him leave. I heard the click of the door locking as he left the house. Everything suddenly sounded so silent and I felt the gripping feeling of being completely alone.

I made my way downstairs again to do the rest of the clean-up and to make sure I locked everything up. After that, I started walking back upstairs. I planned on lying in bed and getting lost in a book for at least an hour before succumbing to sleep. On the second to last stair, I stopped as I felt a sharp tightening in my abdomen that seemed to radiate from my lower back. I stood there for a moment, taking in a few deep breaths and holding onto the handrail until the pain stopped before continuing on. I felt a few of these before, although they hadn't been as strong as this one.

After the pain eased, I continued my way into my bedroom to change into my nightgown. I chose a thick cotton full-length gown with small purple flowers on it. It was one of the few nightgowns that fit me still. After brushing my teeth and hair, I settled in bed and pulled out *A Tree Grows in Brooklyn*. I wasn't that far into it but hadn't decided yet if I liked it or not. Aunt Harry suggested it and loaned me her copy. She insisted it was a brilliant book that she enjoyed. I promised her I'd give an effort to try it out and to venture a little away from the typical genre that I usually read.

About fifteen minutes later, I felt another strong contraction. This was strong enough to make me put the book down to breathe through it until it eased. I also noticed a general cramping pain similar to what I experienced during my menstruation. Ten to fifteen minutes later, I felt another contraction. This time, I also felt a warm liquid spill between my legs. It suddenly hit me with a cold reality that I was indeed going into labor. I never felt contractions quite like this before. I experienced periods of tightening in my belly over the last several weeks, but they were not painful, and they were inconsistent.

I couldn't help but feel a slight panic being alone and going into

Ellie Lynn

labor. Lifting myself gently out of bed, I walked to my dresser to pull out a clean sweater and skirt before walking downstairs to the kitchen to ring mom to drive me to the hospital. I paused on two other occasions to breathe through the pain and tightness. I then put a call into the police department to leave a message for George. I wasn't sure when he would get the message, but I hoped it would be soon.

At the hospital I felt the pains becoming stronger and much more frequent. I heard the nurse tell mom I was in active labor and this brought on a feeling of panic. The last time I felt some of these pains and pressure, my entire world crashed around me. I was all too aware of how things could go so terribly wrong and all I could do was pray that this baby would be born healthy.

Chapter Nineteen

George
June 23, 1944

The night sky stood dark and quiet as I sat outside, up against a tent pole, smoking a cigarette. The first one in a long time. It burned my throat and my hand shook while holding it. More importantly though, I sat in the peace of the night sky free to do so. I experienced tastes of freedom since being captured, but they were like drops of water to a man dying of thirst. I escaped twice, only to be captured shortly after. The temporary reprieve never felt like true freedom since I couldn't sit and just breathe. The fear and unknown still imprisoned me. How I escaped being shot instantly after found is a mystery to me. Especially after the second time. They instead put me on the German's execution list to be carried out the next day. This never came though as I died of some ailing disease or starvation shortly after. At least the corpse of the poor man wearing my identification tags did.

Emmett Somerville was the kindest man I ever met. He managed to maintain that aspect of him throughout all the surrounding misery. His very instinct was to help who he could. He even gave up one of his socks to a prisoner once who wore none. It seemed like a lost cause to me as the prisoner's toes were already turning black and socks could be a life-or-death commodity. He still gave up one of his own. He prayed over the sick even as he shook from chills himself. At night when we all laid in our cots, shivering and hungry while trying to fight off the overwhelming feeling of hopelessness, Emmett told stories of hope and inspiration. His voice became the balm to our insanity. A twenty-two-year-old kid from Iowa with a slight build, pale body, and hollow cheeks was the strongest man I ever met.

I prepared to die the next morning by firing squad. I sat on the cold ground next to Emmett's cot while listening to the death rattle in his chest. It felt as if everyone in the room could feel his life slipping away. We all waited for it to end just to hear the next breath shakier than the last. My head hung between my knees and I hugged myself to keep warm when I felt a light touch on my shoulder. Looking over, I saw Emmett with a tired, dazed look about him. His dried and cracked lips moved, but no sound came out. Then I looked at his

Ellie Lynn

hand that reached out to me. He had his tags dangling from his bony white fingers. By the time I looked back up at his face, he was gone. Even in his last breath, Emmett thought of another. He saved my life. I quickly switched our tags, putting his around my neck. The weight of his felt heavy with his sacrifice. They felt heavy and cold as I once again hugged my knees to my chest to retain some warmth.

Now, sitting here thinking about everything, my chest feels full as I breathe in the thick cigarette smoke. So congested with emotion that I'm shocked the smoke can even fill my lungs. My throat feels like I swallowed a fist full of dirt, and my body and spirit seem to be limp with exhaustion. It was as if the terror of what I endured suddenly showed itself. I tucked it away neatly so I could think, plan, and survive. Now it wants out. It drapes across me like a black fog. Soon my hand holding my cigarette began to shake and the tears rolled down my face. It's only true freedom when you can not only walk where you would like, sit, smoke, sleep; but when you can feel. I could accomplish everything else on an autopilot with a deep sense of numbness. But instinctively knowing that you are now allowed to feel; to cry, to laugh... now that is what true freedom is.

Chapter Twenty

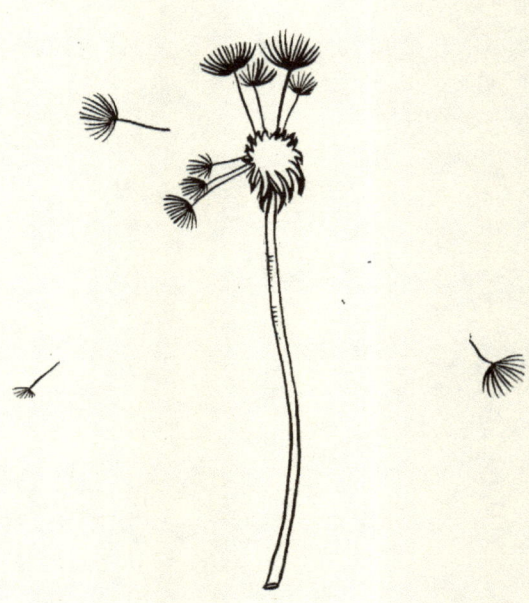

Maggie

January 5, 1948

As unfair as this all feels, this dying young, dying at the hands of another; I'm strangely overcome by a sense of fullness. A realization that my life was one to be admired. In it's shortness there was so much love.

The baby came quick, at least that is what the nurse tending to me said. Nothing about it felt quick. The minutes felt like hours, and it was painful and terrifying, but it also became so incredibly worth it once the nurse placed my long-awaited baby in my arms. At shortly after midnight, my sweet baby boy was born. The immense sense of relief I felt when I heard him cry overwhelmed me. I couldn't help the tears rolling down my cheeks as well.

The only thing missing was George waiting down the hallway for me. I wished he sat by my side right now and I craved his soft kiss on my cheek as he told me what a good job I did bringing his son into the world. I knew he would come as soon as he could.

For now, this was my special time to cradle my newborn and take in every little part of him. Mom sat next to me, and she seemed to be in as much wonderment as I. She stayed next to my side the whole time, much to the doctor's annoyance. She coached, cried, laughed, and when the tiny baby took his first breath, she clasped her hands over her mouth and became silent in her complete awe. She was now a grandmother, and I a mom.

He now laid quietly in my arms. The nurse swaddled him up in a white miniature hospital blanket and a blue hat. My baby's face a pink hue and one of his eyes kept peeking open and then sleepily closing shut again as he made small sucking noises with his lips. His little chest rose up and down with each little breath. Such a simple thing that probably too many mothers simply take for granted. Shivers ran through my body with relief, excitement, and pure love. I could feel life throughout his entire body, and I absolutely marveled at how perfectly tiny every part of him was. I leaned down and placed my cheek next to his, and I closed my eyes, and breathed in his

Ellie Lynn

very essence. The rest of the world seemed to melt away as if we were the only two people on earth.

A few minutes later, George walked into the room. He looked worried and anxious and when he saw me lying there holding our son, he stopped in his tracks and took the sight in. Everything became quiet and still in that moment as his eyes searched mine. He then broke out in a huge grin and hurried over to my side.

"Are you okay, is the baby okay?" George quickly said as he kissed my cheek.

"Yes George, we are both fine. We have a son." I said excitedly and proudly. I envisioned another daughter but felt completely in love already with the little boy cradled in my arms.

"I'm so happy for you two. I'm going to step out so you can have your privacy." Mom said in a raspy voice while wiping away a small tear at the corner of her eye.

"Thanks Aileen. And thanks for being here for Maggie." George said sheepishly as he smiled up at her.

"Of course." Mom replied before making her way out into the hallway and quietly shutting the door.

It was now the three of us, my little family. I felt my chest tighten with so much pride that I felt I could pop from it. George leaned forward and placed a light kiss on my forehead before doing the same with the baby. He then chuckled at the enormous yawn and scrunched-up face of our newborn. At this one moment, everything was completely perfect.

"What should we call him?" I asked, while lightly stroking the pad of my thumb across the baby's soft cheek. We narrowed it down to two boys' names, Christopher, and Patrick. We hadn't been able to settle on one or the other yet, deciding instead to pick one if the baby was born a boy.

"I'd like to call him Emmett." George said with some thought. He looked at me with pleading eyes for me to agree. He never mentioned the name before, and I was confused about the sudden change. Nevertheless, it seemed important to him. Looking down at the now

Falling

sleeping baby cradled in my arms, I leaned down and softly muzzled his cheek once again before whispering his name, Emmett.

A few days later we were on our way home from the hospital. Pulling up to the house, my idea of spending some quiet time napping with Emmett were quickly dashed. Mom came rushing out the door to fuss over me climbing out of the vehicle with the baby. Next, Uncle Liam walked out of the house while Harry held open the door.

"Congratulations, sweet niece." Uncle Liam said as he placed a kiss on my cheek and gazed upon Emmett snuggled up next to my chest.

"Thank you, I'm so happy." I said with a smile before continuing to walk towards the porch and front door.

As I walked in, Harry whispered in my ear, "I'm so sorry, they all insisted on welcoming you home."

"It's alright, I understand. And thank you." I replied, and as much as I wished for the quiet time, I did understand. This was the first baby. The first grandchild and the first great nephew. After all the loss, everyone needed this joy.

"Welcome home!" yelled Aunt Evie as we walked through the doorway. She stood underneath a big homemade welcome sign that was hung from the ceiling. The smell of food and freshly baked bread met us as we walked in. It was unexpected, but also completely perfect.

"Thank you everyone, this is so kind and, well, wonderful. Plus, I'm famished." I chuckled a little.

"Let's get you fed then." Mom said behind me.

I walked over to the sofa and sat down carefully. I was still a little sore and the couple of stitches that were placed, pulled. Emmett was a big baby and weighed just over nine pounds. George beamed with pride when the nurse told him. He was proud of his healthy and hearty son, but I couldn't help but think he also felt pride in me for having birthed him.

The family passed Emmett around and kissed him more times

Ellie Lynn

than I could count as I ate my lunch of roast beef, pasta salad, and rolls. He didn't know it yet but was a very lucky boy indeed to have so many people who loved him so much. The feelings this invoked were almost overwhelming. That and I started to feel quite tired. After my second yawn, I decided I should go upstairs for a quiet nap after all and despite the visitors. Emmett started making his adorable suckling noises letting me know he also needed to be fed.

George carried Emmett and followed me upstairs to the bedroom. I loved having the family here supporting us and loving on little Emmett, but I could also feel myself crave the peace and quiet as we walked into the bedroom. The sun beamed through the partly undraped window, highlighting the dancing specks of dust in the air. The voices downstairs were a distant hum, and the bedding looked crisp and clean. There was also a small crib sitting next to the bed, ready for Emmett to sleep in.

"Your mom came here early getting things ready for you two to come home." George said as he waved his free hand at the room and cradled the baby with the other. "She offered to stay here for a couple of days to help as well. I told her it would be up to you."

"That's kind of her, but I think I want it to be just us three. I'm sure I can manage." I said, covering another yawn.

"You mean we can manage. You're not in this alone, Maggie. I'll even learn how to change his diapers if I must. I want to take care of you both." George said as he helped me get settled in bed, propped against some pillows, and ready to take Emmett who started to fuss at this point.

"Thank you, George." I said quietly as I adjusted my clothing to pull out a breast for Emmett to nurse on. I couldn't help but feel a little shy and clumsy with the process. Breastfeeding, one of the most natural things a mother can do, and yet I felt terribly awkward with it. Emmett let out a loud squeal of frustration as he tried to latch onto the nipple. His face turned red, and his hands were fisted up by his face. I tried calming him with soothing noises before trying again. This time he latched on hungrily and nursed.

Falling

"You're a natural mother, Maggie." George said as he looked at us lovingly. I forced a smile. I wouldn't dare tell him that my nipple felt raw and abused and that I sat with an overwhelming feeling of wanting to cry for no reason at all. They didn't show this in the perfect magazine pictures of motherhood. The truth is, I wasn't sure if what I was doing was right or if I could trust my instincts and not fail him. I pretended to know what I was doing, but deep down I wasn't sure. I felt the weight of the world in this small nine-pound package, who completely depended on me. It felt overwhelming, wonderful, and scary, and I felt all these emotions swirl within me. But I wouldn't tell George all of this, I couldn't. And so, I just smiled.

As Emmett nursed, George and I quietly talked. We talked of the family downstairs, the food, the nosy roommate I had been stuck with at the hospital, and of course how perfectly adorable Emmett looked. All small talk, nothing important or heavy. I looked down at Emmett, sound asleep, with my nipple still partly in his mouth. I lifted him up and was getting ready to lay him up on my shoulder when George offered to burp him instead. He grabbed up a burping cloth, laid it on his shoulder, and then gently lifted Emmett.

"How hard do I pat him?" George asked as he sat in bed next to me with Emmett propped up on his shoulder, this being his first time trying.

"Gently but firmly... yes, like that George." I said, thankful that he could figure it out before I tried to explain it. After a couple of minutes of sitting peacefully, hearing the gentle patting on Emmett's back, I felt my entire body relax and the swirling emotions within me settle.

"I once knew another Emmett." George started off quietly and as if he carefully planned every word. "We were prisoners together, and he saved my life. In actuality, I believe he saved more lives than mine. More so, though, he reminded us that life was worth saving. That humanity could prevail amongst all the evils of war. He never made it out of the prison alive." George was silent for a bit, continuing to lightly pat Emmett's back even though it wasn't necessary anymore. I didn't try to speak or ask questions. I knew he would tell me more if he wanted to.

George turned to look at me as he stopped patting Emmett's back and grabbed my hand. "Thank you for our strong, beautiful son, and thank you for letting me name him."

"Of course, George, I rather like the name Emmett, and even more so now that I know why you chose it. Emmett is a new beginning. We will raise him to be kind and strong and I hope that when he is older, your friend will look down upon him and be proud that he is his namesake."

George didn't respond with words, but simply smiled. His eyes were a little glossy, and he seemed tired. Much more tired than I realized.

"Do you think your parents will come? I have yet to even meet them, and I imagine they would at least want to meet their grandson."

"I don't think so." George shook his head tiredly. "Honestly Maggie, I don't want them to come. I prefer to have as little to do with them as possible. I know that it's inevitable that one day you and Emmett will meet them. Just not now, not when everything is so perfect."

"Okay, I can't say I fully understand but I trust you. Why don't you lay Emmett down in his crib while we take a nap together? No one would mind downstairs. You look tired. Maybe you should get some sleep as well." I asked.

"And leave your whole family downstairs left to their own devices? I think not." George said with a chuckle as he carefully rose out of bed to place Emmett in the crib next to me. Covering him with a small blanket, he kissed his cheek, and then mine. "You two get some rest, I'll be downstairs."

"We will. Thank you and I love you." I said as my eyes began to feel heavy.

"I Love you too." George quietly closed the door.

Chapter Twenty-One

Maggie

April 12, 1948

The next few weeks passed quickly. Before having Emmett, I imagined those first few weeks as a time that I would soak in every moment, every cuddle, every kiss, every new facial expression. What I hadn't imagined is how busy it would be and how tired I would feel. The first week, pure wonderment fueled me. Everything was new, beautiful, and scary. I barely slept in case I missed something, or in case Emmett needed me. The times I slept, George was there to hold and sooth Emmett.

Then we developed a routine. The changing and washing of diapers and clothes. The rocking, soothing, burping, and bathing all became things I could practically do in my sleep. I somehow cleaned a little and cooked when Emmett would nap so that George could come home from work to a clean home and a warm meal. He did his best to help me, much more than most husbands did, or so I heard.

The 3:00am wakeups were my favorite, as absurd as it sounded. When in the quiet of the early morning, the house enclosed in darkness besides a single lamp, it was only Emmett and me, and I would sit in my rocker and nurse him. I felt most at peace in those moments. It was at that time that I marveled at his eyelashes and toes. The only time that it felt like just the two of us in the world, and I cherished it.

It seemed like a blink of an eye, but before I knew it spring arrived. It was still cold most of the time and muddy from melted snow, but sometimes the sun would poke through the clouds, and I could feel its warmth. There were buds of fresh growth forming, and a subtle anticipation in the air of rebirth of the land.

Emmett changed every day, it seemed, as well. Smiles were more frequent and seemed more deliberate. He moved around more and cooed every time his beautiful brown eyes saw me. His eyes would especially light up when George came home. George held him and talked to him like an old buddy, and Emmett seemed to hang on to his every word. It was the cutest thing.

On this cool morning, after buttoning up the last button on Emmett's sweater and making sure his hat was on tight, we left the house to head to the store to pick up some fresh mushrooms. I

Ellie Lynn

planned to make stroganoff for supper that night since Anna Beth was in town and going to be visiting us along with the twins. Her husband wouldn't be able to come, as he had patients to see. She'd yet to meet Emmett, and I could burst with excitement to show him off to her. Plus, I was eager to see her little ones as well.

After pulling into a parking spot next to Pete's Grocery, I grabbed Emmett from his seat next to me and we walked into the store. I walked in proudly with my son, talking to him as if he understood why we were there and what we were going to purchase. He seemed to listen, although I'm pretty sure he was only curious about all the new things to look at. Stopping at the produce, I gathered a few pale mushrooms into a bag, using my one free hand.

"Here, let me help you." A voice startled me from behind.

"Taylor, hello it's nice to see you." I said, a little breathless from the surprise.

"You as well Mrs. Harkins. And 'hello' I've heard all about you little one." Taylor said in a high-pitched voice to Emmett. "It's harder to shop when you are holding a baby. The wife and I have two of our own. Do you need any help?"

"Thank you, but no. I only came for these mushrooms. I appreciate your offer though. Hope you have a good day." I smiled and then turned away to walk towards the register.

"Mrs. Harkins, if you wouldn't mind, do you have a few minutes to spare? I could buy you a coffee?"

"I, uh, probably shouldn't. I need to get back to start on supper soon. We have company coming over." I said, thinking of the only excuse I could on the spot. Not thinking, of course, about the fact that it was only eleven in the morning and needing to get supper ready didn't make a great excuse.

"It won't take much of your time. One cup of coffee, then you will have plenty of time to start on... *supper*." He said with a knowing smile.

"Of course, then." I said with an embarrassed smile. I couldn't help but also feel a little annoyed as I didn't want to have a cup of

Falling

coffee with him. Yet he left me with little room to get out of it without sounding like a ninny. If George knew, it would upset him. And yet, I couldn't help but feel a little curious why Taylor wished to speak with me. I only met him the one time and never met his wife. George made it clear that they weren't friends. I would not even think of the fact that I had an entirely inappropriate dream about him, which only added to my feeling uncomfortable.

I paid for my mushrooms, placed them on the front seat of my vehicle, and then walked with Taylor to the diner, Emmett in my arms. I couldn't help but think of the walk to the diner with George a few years back that changed my whole life. In truth, it hadn't been that long ago. And yet it seemed in a way like a lifetime.

Walking into the diner, we sat at a small table off to the side. Within a few minutes, our coffee sat in front of us. I cradled Emmett in my lap with heavy lids and on his way to taking a nap.

"It's the unfamiliar sounds and sights. It always made my little ones sleepy too." Taylor said with a knowing smile as he watched Emmett lose his battle to stay awake. "I can make up your coffee if you would like? Do you take cream? Sugar?"

"Both please, thank you." I said quietly, feeling shy while I simply sat there watching him carefully pour the cream, add the sugar cubes, and stir. He then repeated it with his own coffee.

"I'm sure you are wondering what I want to talk with you about." Taylor said right before blowing on his coffee and then gingerly taking a sip. "There are a couple of questions swirling around in my head that I'm trying to find some answers for."

"What questions?" I asked cautiously.

"Questions about your husband and what happened to Mr. Westerly. There are a couple of things I want to clear up. I haven't gotten a straightforward answer from George. I'm not sure if he mentioned anything to you or not, but I'm the investigator working on the case. It's nothing to worry your pretty little head about though too much, just a couple of questions."

Then he smiled. He smiled in that way that would make most

Ellie Lynn

girls' knees go weak, although this time it made my skin crawl. He wasn't rude in the way he spoke, but the look on his face made it very apparent who was in charge of the conversation.

What a condescending ass, I thought to myself before I replied sweetly. "Alright, I'll try to answer your questions, although I'm not sure I know anything that would be helpful."

"Fair enough. On January 7th, what time did George come home that morning?" Taylor asked, his eyes never leaving mine.

"I'm not sure. That was a few months ago. George worked nights then, and I was usually sleeping still when he got home." I replied, trying to remind him of what he should already know.

"But you don't remember specifically that day? He left his shift early that morning. He said you weren't feeling well, and he needed to be home with you. It's also the early morning Mr. Westerly was killed. I called the house that day to inform George of the incident. Do you remember that?" Taylor fired back with a small lift of his left eyebrow.

"I, uh, I remember the phone call of course. But I don't remember for sure if George came home early that morning or not, but if that's what George said, then it's true." Even saying this to him, I knew it wasn't true. And worst of all, I could tell he knew it. I had never been good at lying. There wasn't a single time I ever asked George to come home early or take off a shift of work in our entire marriage. If I felt sick, I managed on my own.

"Alright. What do you know about Mr. Westerly and how he died?" Taylor asked after a pause and another sip of his coffee.

"I know that someone killed him. That he was shot. I don't know anything else, really. George doesn't talk to me about stuff from work." I said, knowing I sounded defensive. I couldn't help it as I could feel the hairs standing up on the back of my neck with this questioning.

"I'm sure you have heard rumors around town. Anything you think I should know?" He said with a sly type of smile. All I could

Falling

think about at that moment was Aunt Evie and her little theories. My stomach felt a little sick.

"No, I put little stock in rumors. I feel rumors hold little truth and can cause a lot of trouble. Besides, I thought police investigations were more about facts than rumors, anyway?" I said, a bit shocked that what I said came out strong and steady, despite what I was feeling inside. I had him there, and he knew it if his annoyed look was any sign. Being the niece of a prosecutor, and I wasn't entirely ignorant about how things worked.

"Of course, you're right. Although in my experience rumors can hold a layer of truth. If you can think of anything else about January 7th that would be helpful, please let me know." Taylor replied with a thoughtful and dismissing look.

"Yes, of course, Mr. Bird." I said, emphasizing the Mister part. Calling him Taylor seemed a little too friendly at this point. I stood up to leave without having taken a single sip of my coffee.

"Oh, I forgot. One other quick question. Did George ever mention wanting to kill Mr. Westerly to you or anyone else that you know of? Well, besides me, of course?" And then he smiled. I wanted to slap him.

"Of course not! What you are suggesting is wrong." I said in a slightly higher-pitched voice than I had intended. He had gotten to me, and it showed. It was obvious that's what he wanted. After giving Taylor a quick nod, I turned around and left the cafe.

I hugged Emmett tight the whole walk to the truck and only realized I was shaking after putting Emmett gently in his seat. What happened? I sat in the driver's seat as the blood seemed to rush through my head. I couldn't think, and everything seemed to echo. Looking down towards the cafe, I saw Taylor walking out, looking right at me. He tipped his hat, smiled, and then walked away as if he hadn't a care in the world.

Taylor believed George had something to do with Mr. Westerly's death. I couldn't possibly imagine why that was. George also being a

Ellie Lynn

man of the law. He believed in law and order. He believed in the justice system. Didn't he?

Taking a deep breath, I turned the engine on. I needed to get home so I could think. I had to tell George about my conversation with Taylor. That meant I'd have to tell him I sat with him for coffee, something I felt uncomfortable. George had shown before how jealous he could be, especially when it involved Taylor. He warned me about him. Now I understood why.

He wasn't just a pretty face who liked to flirt and there suddenly seemed something dangerous about him. I needed to have this conversation with George, and he needed to tell me what was going on. Why Taylor and he were not friends and why I was asked these questions. I wanted to know why he lied and what else he was lying about.

"Jesus, when?" I said to myself, ignoring my blasphemy since I was the only one that heard it. Mom wouldn't have ignored it. Anna Beth and the twins were coming over in a few hours and George wouldn't be home until afterwards. I had to sit with this all night and pretend that everything was okay.

After getting home, I quickly changed and fed Emmett before putting him down for a more restful nap. I then put my coat back on to go out to the barn because I wanted to look through some old newspapers. I knew we had a few months' worth sitting in there, and I hoped there would be some article or something about Mr. Westerly's death. I needed some details because I would not talk to George about this blindly.

It took about twenty minutes, much longer than I wanted to be away from Emmett, but I finally found the papers I wanted to look through. Surprisingly, we hadn't burned them in the fireplace yet. I grabbed December 28th all the way to yesterday's paper to be safe. Walking back to the house with my arms heavily piled up with newspaper, I could only pray that there was something useful.

After depositing them on the kitchen table, I first went to check on Emmett sleeping in a bassinet that was placed in the family room.

Falling

Afterwards, I walked to the sink to wash my hands before making myself a tuna sandwich. Seeing a drop of grape jelly on the counter next to the sink, I then wiped it off with the dishrag. It was then that I remembered the smear of blood on the sink. It had been inconsequential at the time, and it surprised me now that I remembered it.

It somehow seemed important to my frantic and suspicious mind. When was that? When was that? I thought repeatedly to myself. Then I remembered, January 7th. It was right before going through baby clothes that Anna Beth sent me. I remembered it clearly because that was also the day Taylor called to talk to George. Closing my eyes and taking a deep breath, I told myself that it was probably a coincidence. This was all a misunderstanding, and I felt certain that George could easily explain it all. I needed to talk to him.

After drying my hands and making the sandwich, I finally sat down at the table to skim through the papers. I had about three hours before Anna Beth would arrive and I also needed to make sure I had time to brown the beef and make the creamy mushroom sauce by 4:30. I took a deep breath and picked up the Okmulgee Daily Times dated January 8, 1948. I figured that the day after Mr. Westerly died would be the best place to start.

"At around 10:00a.m. yesterday morning, the police received a call that Mr. Frank Westerly was dead outside his home because of an apparent gunshot wound. Mr. Westerly's wife discovered the body of her husband. It is believed that Mr. Westerly died in the early morning of the 7th. Mrs. Westerly was not home during that time, but their four daughters were. Police have ruled suicide out and there are no suspects at this time. The police say they are conducting a thorough investigation into this. They are asking for anyone who knows any information to please come forward."

Right underneath the small article was a grainy black-and-white photo of the crime scene. Mr. Westerly was lying on his stomach with his arms at his sides. It showed no details, but I couldn't

Ellie Lynn

help but stare at it for a few minutes. How could Taylor even think that George could do something like this? Something so horrific and ugly.

I quickly scanned through some more papers, looking for any other articles that mentioned Mr. Westerly. I found one from the 11th when they buried him. It said Mrs. Westerly was accompanied by her four children and a couple of friends from town for the service. I remember Harry went to that funeral to offer support from her church. Harry and some other ladies brought Mrs. Westerly some food and other donations.

I couldn't help but wonder how Mrs. Westerly would get by now. I didn't know how they earned their meager living before, but I was sure Mr. Westerly's death caused a bigger hardship now. Those poor little girls. Thinking about it now, I was so thankful that there were people like Harry in this world. She was there to help anyone, no matter what or who they were. The next article I found was from February 7th. It blended in as a small black and white block, amongst other stories.

> "It's been a full month since someone shot Mr. Westerly dead in the dense wooded growth behind his home. According to the police, they have no suspects currently. When talking to Mrs. Westerly, she stated that the police department used to harass Mr. Westerly unfairly, and she doubted they were truly working to find his killer. When asked about these accusations, Detective Bird vehemently denied them."

That was it. Browsing through the other newspapers, I didn't come across another single article. Okmulgee wasn't a very large place, unlike other cities in Oklahoma. It seemed like there should have been more published in the newspaper than what was. Murder wasn't a very common occurrence here. I couldn't help but wonder if it was because of who he was.

Hearing Emmett begin to fuss I looked at the clock on the kitchen

Falling

wall and I realized it was already two in the afternoon. He would need to be changed and fed again before I could pick up the newspapers and put them back in the barn. I felt disappointed. I don't know what I thought I'd find, but I didn't learn anything new.

Putting my plate in the sink, I again washed my hands when I saw smeared newspaper ink on the pads of my fingers. I didn't want to get any of it on Emmett. About twenty minutes later, after leaving Emmett fed, changed, and laying in his wooden playpen, I crept back out to the barn to put back the stack of papers. I don't know why this whole thing made me feel like I was snooping around, since it's my barn too.

Walking back inside, I busied myself with cleaning up the house. I dusted, swept, and mopped until the house smelt of pine oil. Before I knew it, I heard a vehicle pull up our gravel driveway. I quickly took off my apron, patted my hair, and walked to open the door. Anna Beth was getting out of her car to walk around to the passenger side to grab the twins. Once she saw me, her face broke out into an enormous smile, and she gave a little wave. I ambled down the porch steps to help her carry one of the girls.

"This one is Alice." Anna Beth said as she handed me one beautiful blond haired little girl. At almost a year old, she felt heavy compared to my Emmett. Right after handing her to me, she grabbed Freya and then turned to give me a one-armed hug. I couldn't help but giggle with the two babies between us. Plus, being around Anna Beth always made me feel happy.

"I can't believe how big they have gotten!" I told her as we walked up to the front door.

"I know, and they are such a handful now that they are moving all over the place. They certainly keep me on my toes, especially now that they are almost walking." Anna Beth said, sounding a bit tired.

"Emmett keeps me busy enough, I can't imagine the work being double."

Earlier I laid out a blanket on the floor rug that I sometimes laid Emmett on. I would usually sit with him on it and hold his rattles.

Ellie Lynn

Anna Beth walked over to it and sat Freya down before walking over to the playpen to see Emmett.

"Oh my goodness, he's beautiful Maggie-Pie!" Reaching in, she picked Emmett right up and snuggled him close. He waved his fists and chatted away as if we understood his single vowel words. Although truth be told, I think I was starting to. He would talk and move for a while, smile a bit, but soon would be hungry again and need a change.

"Thank you, he's truly the sweetest little guy." I said as I walked over to where Freya was sitting, to put down Alice next to her. Then I pulled out a couple of Emmett's rattles and a stuffed bear for them to play with. "I can't believe how much Alice and Freya look alike. I truly can't tell them apart."

"Most people can't, but Alice has this adorable dimple in her cheek that Freya doesn't, and Freya has a slightly darker shade of blonde hair. Alice also is much shorter tempered than Freya is. If one is screaming for something, it's usually Alice."

I couldn't help but chuckle at this. Anna Beth had always been very strong willed, and it did not surprise me that at least one of her daughters would be the same way. Anna Beth sat on the sofa to bounce Emmett on her lap as she talked to him and nuzzled his neck. I sat on the rug next to Freya and Alice to play with them. It was funny, now that we were both parents, the days of lying side by side on a bed giggling and talking were over. Things were so different now, but not in a bad way. We just added three new members to our club that were once just the two of us. We were also different. I had a whole new respect for Anna Beth now as a mother, instead of only as a friend.

"So how is George adjusting to being a father?" Anna Beth said as she picked up Emmett to face level and sniffed. "Oh, I think this little one needs a change."

Standing to pick up Emmett, I couldn't help but be grateful that he needed to be changed. I didn't trust myself talking about George

Falling

yet, especially to Anna Beth. If anyone could sense something was wrong, it would be her.

"I'll go change him really quick, then I'll be back. Make yourself at home. I have a hot kettle in the kitchen for tea if you would like. Plus, I made some peanut butter cookies that the girls may enjoy." I said with a knowing smile. Peanut butter cookies were Anna Beth's favorite.

"I just may do that." Anna Beth said with a chuckle.

I took Emmett upstairs to change him. I didn't want the entire room to smell. A few minutes later I walked back into the living room to see Anna Beth sipping on hot tea with a napkin that had a couple of cookies sitting on it ready to be eaten. Both girls were gnawing on their cookies with their tiny little baby teeth that had come in. Alice kept saying a mumbled "yummmm yummmm yummmm" as she chewed.

"I guess they take after their mom with those." I joked.

"Hey, I have never eaten one of these quite like that!" she said in a mock serious manner while pointing her own cookie at Freya, who seemed to be wearing most of the cookie.

"Okay, you have me there. Emmett is hungry as well." Emmett let out a small fuss as he stuck his fist in his mouth. I then sat next to Anna Beth and shyly adjusted my blouse in order to nurse him. It still wasn't the most comfortable thing to do in front of others. Even Anna Beth. As soon as Emmett latched on, I covered us both with a burping cloth for some privacy.

Anna Beth took a couple of sips of her tea, giggled at the girls who had crawled around the rug before looking over at me. "I can already tell that you are doing great at this mother thing. I knew you would, you're a natural at it. How is George doing with the whole father thing?"

Leave it to Anna Beth to get right to the point and not forget what she had asked me before. I felt my lips thin slightly as just the mention of George right now brought a rush of anxiety. "He's doing wonderful with it. He is a great father." I said, knowing I was telling the truth. He was a wonderful dad. George seemed to be enamored of Emmett and Emmett of him. I noticed that George started having fewer nightmares than what he used to. Everything was working out perfectly. Well, until today that is.

"You have always been more like a sister to me than a friend. When we were younger, I could always tell when something was wrong. When you were stressed about a test or a boy or one of the mean girls at school. Even when you wouldn't say anything to me about it, I always knew. You see, you have this sort of sparkle in your eyes. When you are excited or happy, your eyes seem to shine even more. The gold and green specks stand out. I've always thought your eyes were beautiful. They are so full of life. When something is wrong; when you're sad or upset or whatever, they lose some of that sparkle. I will not force you, but I'm here. If you want to talk to me about what is bothering you, I'll listen."

I wasn't sure what to do. I wanted to talk to her so badly, but I also wanted to cry. I didn't do either, though. Instead, I reached for her hand and gave it a squeeze. I gave her a smile and a nod of my head. I wanted to lay my burdens at her feet and feel the reassurance that she always gave, but I couldn't. How could I tell her that there was a suspicion of George being involved in a murder? I wouldn't blame her if she packed up the twins and left immediately. The only person I needed to talk to right now was George.

"You are the best friend a girl could ever have. I... I can't talk about what is bugging me right now, but I will when I can. I have to figure some things out first." I said hesitantly before letting her hand go.

"I understand." Anna Beth said simply.

She then walked over to the girls who pulled themselves up to a standing position while hanging onto the coffee table. Alice had the little lamb's head rattle in her hand and banged it against the table while talking loudly, "ma ma ma ma." Freya stood patting her little chubby hand against the table, which seemed in rhythm with her sister.

Falling

"Alice, no no." Anna Beth said as she pried the toy from Alice's hand, which caused Alice to let out an ear-splitting screech. This in turn startled Emmet from his milk drowsy state on my shoulder as I lightly patting his back. He began to cry as well. Freya looked around with her bright blue eyes and, seeing the other two babies crying, decided that she would fall back from the coffee table onto her bum and start crying as well.

Anna Beth and I both looked at each other and started laughing. The whole situation seemed comical for some reason. Things had definitely changed for us. As I laughed, I soothed Emmett's back, and he calmed down. The girls stopped crying the moment we started laughing and now looked at their mother as if she was crazy. It wasn't the reaction from her they had been seeking. I suddenly had this feeling that everything was going to be okay, at least for a little while.

Chapter Twenty-Two

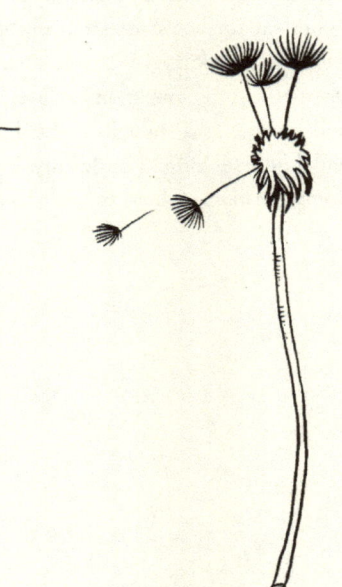

Maggie
April 12, 1948

Everything would be okay. Such an amazingly absurd thought, given the fact I'm falling to my death. Everything about it was certainly not okay; and yet I couldn't shake the sudden thought, as if it were whispered in my ear.

A few hours later, I hugged and kissed the twins and Anna Beth goodbye as George stood next to me. I stood waving from the open doorway as she started her car and drove away, leaving dust to billow out in the moonlight.

"That was certainly a pleasant visit, darling." George said next to me before kissing my cheek and walking back inside.

It had been pleasant. We laughed, ate supper, played with the twins, cuddled Emmett, and we talked about our lives. Anna Beth talked about the girls and about Hank's practice, and how busy he had become. George and I mostly talked about Emmett. How he managed to become the center of our lives.

"Yes, it was nice. I didn't realize how much I missed her." I said as if I just realized it at that moment. Then I closed the door and walked back into the house. George sat down and lit a cigarette. Emmett quietly slept in his bassinet that sat next to his playpen. My stomach felt queasy at the thought of the conversation I couldn't put off any longer.

"George, I need to talk to you about something." I started, then at his nonchalant nod, I emphasized. "Something important."

"Okay, shoot." He said in a joking manner as he pointed his finger like a gun at the wall next to me. The coincidental joke did not escape my notice, which did nothing to help calm my nerves. Sitting down next to him, I took a deep breath, trying to think of how to start this conversation. George's grin faded a bit as he recognized the tension.

"What is it, Maggie?" George asked as he patted my hand sitting on my knee.

"I took Emmett out to Pete's to buy some mushrooms for the

stroganoff today. I ran into Taylor while there, and he insisted on buying me a cup of coffee. He said he needed to ask some questions and became quite insistent. Emmett and I followed him to the cafe." I paused a moment to sort in my head how to continue. George started to say something, but I held up my hand and continued. "Please, let me finish. He asked me some very disturbing questions. He wanted to know what time you got home on the night that Mr. Westerly died. He said you clocked out early that morning to come home. I told him you did, but I think he could tell that I was lying because you didn't come home early. He's insinuating that you are responsible for Mr. Westerly's death."

The room became so quiet at that moment it was deafening. George took another drag of his cigarette, turned his head, and blew the smoke away from me before putting it out in the ashtray sitting on the lamp table next to him. Then he turned back towards me but still sat quietly, as if he tried to decide what to say. This wasn't a good sign. He didn't seem angry. He wasn't yelling or denying. He just sat there quietly.

"George, please tell me this isn't true. You have got to be honest with me. Did you have anything to do with Mr. Westerly's death? I saw a spot of blood in the kitchen sink that morning. Please tell me it was from a paper cut or a nosebleed or something else inconsequential." My voice at this point was high pitched and grated on even my own nerves.

"I think that it's unfortunate that Taylor questioned you at all. That he got you involved in all of this. I can't say as I'm surprised though as we haven't been friends since we were boys." Then at my surprised look, George continued, "Yes, we were once friends. The best of friends. Taylor and I always played together when I would come and stay with my aunt and uncle. We used to fish together, catch tadpoles, tease girls, all the things that friends do. When I lived back home with my parents, we would write to one another. He kept me updated on everything that was going on around town. He would even check in on my aunt and uncle once in a while for me. I loved

Falling

him like the brother I never had. I loved him like you love Anna Beth."

Then, with a deep sigh and a shake of his head, George continued. "Right after I turned sixteen, I started seeing a girl named Nora. She was from here. From Okmulgee. I fancied myself in love with her. We wrote to each other often and spent all our time together when I came here to visit. When I enlisted, I told her I would marry her as soon as I got back home. Taylor hadn't been able to enlist, even though he desperately wanted to. He has a heart condition which prevented him from it. Before I left, I asked for him to look after Nora for me as well as my aunt and uncle. What I didn't expect was that he would marry her while I was off fighting."

"Oh George, I'm so sorry. I can't believe I knew none of this." I said, a little shocked. It made me realize how little I really knew of my husband. How quickly we married without taking the time to know much of one another. Plus, it didn't escape my notice that George simply chose to not tell me any of this.

"Taylor wrote me a letter telling me about their marriage a couple of weeks before the Germans captured me. I was so angry. I felt so betrayed. So, I wrote him back to tell him he was dead to me. I said some terrible things to him. I told him he was a coward and weak for having not served his country. I'm ashamed to say that I spoke some awful things about Nora as well. I seethed with so much anger, but some things I said, well, I shouldn't have."

George shook his head slowly while lost in his thoughts before continuing. "Then, shortly after coming home, my aunt and uncle died in that car accident, and I inherited this place. Even with all the pain Taylor and Nora caused me, it was still better than living at home with my parents, so I moved here. I applied for the police officer's position before knowing that Taylor worked there after getting married. I dealt with it. We agreed to keep a professional working relationship. Although, I've always been able to tell that the past and everything that happened ate at him all that time. Where our friendship used to be, stood a black empty hole."

Ellie Lynn

George then put his head in his hands. I could feel his emotions vibrating off him. Not that he was crying, but I could feel his sadness, his regret over what happened. "George," I said as I laid my hand on his shoulder, "what happened with Mr. Westerly? Why is Taylor trying to blame you?"

George slowly sat upright and looked at me with pleading eyes. He was asking me in his quiet way to understand, to be patient. "Mrs. Westerly's name used to be Gwyneth Darnell. She was my aunt's niece, although my aunt and her never got along. She thought Gwen was a troublemaker and much too wild." At my wide-eyed expression, George hurried up and continued. "She's of no blood relation to me. Remember, my uncle was my mother's brother. Anyway, blood relation or not, I've always felt a soft spot for Gwen's kids. I even tried talking with her a few times about their living conditions and how her kids deserved better.

"She never wanted to listen. She would tell me it was none of my business, and my 'butting in' made Mr. Westerly angry. Anytime he would get drunk, which was most of the time, he tried to pick a fight with me. My position limited me to what I could do. Especially since chief was trying to improve the image of the department. So, I mostly ignored it, did my job, and bit my tongue. That is until Harmony. You see, Aunt Evie is partly correct. Harmony isn't Mr. Westerly's actual daughter. Gwen had been pregnant with her before they got married. Mr. Westerly found out only after a three month premature Harmony came out a healthy full term baby. After that, things seemed to go downhill. I remember my aunt talking about it, worrying about the baby.

"Harmony never said exactly what happened to her. She was too afraid and too traumatized. But I had my suspicions. On January 7th, I told the sergeant that I needed to leave early. I used you feeling sick as an excuse. I meant to go home. I felt so tired, and I needed some rest. Instead, I ended up driving to the Westerly home to check up on the girls. As soon as I pulled up, I heard yelling and crying, so I went in. I found Harmony in the middle of the dirty floor with Mr. West-

Falling

erly on top of her. He was pulling at his pants, and I could see the panic and fear in Harmony's eyes.

"I just saw red, and I literally shook with rage. I should have arrested him, but I pulled him up and off her and then hit him. He fell backwards and hit his head against a table. He wasn't moving, and I thought maybe I accidentally killed him. Everything suddenly seemed silent and as I walked over to him to check his pulse, I heard this little voice say, 'please don't let him hurt me again.' That's when I knew that something needed to be done."

Georg sat silently for a moment, as if thinking about how to continue. I could feel my shaky breath as I sat there, waiting for him. I didn't quite know what to think yet. I hadn't been able to think at all. Everything felt so surreal as we sat there in silence for a moment. Then he spoke again, deep, resonating, and yet assured in what he was said.

"I couldn't fail her, Maggie. This was my chance to stand up for her, for the little girl floating in Italy, for all the other children that were thrown away like garbage. I dragged him out of their little shack of a house and around to the back. I didn't think, I didn't have a plan in mind. I had to get him out of that house and away from Harmony. Once I dragged him a little way towards the trees and shrubbery in the back of the house, he woke up. He yelled at me to let him go. I did. I let go of his arms and he got up on his feet. He swayed back and forth as he tried to right himself on his prosthetic leg. I could smell the liquor mixed with the smell of his unwashed body surrounding him like a fog. It made me want to puke.

"Then he spoke. He told me he would go straight to the chief to tell him what I had done. He would claim that I tried to kill him just for disciplining his daughter. He said as her father he could discipline her any way he chose. It was none of my business." George paused again as his fist clenched.

"I told him to leave Harmony alone or he would spend the next few years in jail. I started to walk away; I even headed back towards the house. But then what he said next, changed everything. He said, 'the little whore isn't worth your time and job anyway' and then he laughed. I turned around, and saw he still faced away from me. I knew what would happen to Harmony if I left. He would hurt her even worse as punishment for my interference. And so, I did the only thing I could. I took my gun out of my holster and I shot him, once in the back of the head. I then went back into the house to make sure there wasn't any evidence that I left and to make sure Harmony was okay and knew not to say anything."

He stopped at this point, took a deep breath, and let his shoulders sag as if the weight of the world suddenly lifted from his shoulders. I sat there, feeling the hot tears roll down my cheeks. I felt so many emotions at this point that I didn't even know what to call them. Sad, anger, disgust, shame, disbelief... I couldn't put my finger on it. I understood, oh I did. I wasn't sure how I felt about it.

George then turned to me and brushed away the tears with his thumbs, as he always did when I cried. "I'm so sorry Maggie. I never wanted to hurt you; I know that this is a shock, but I have it all figured out. Everything is going to be okay."

"How do you know that, George? How do you know Harmony won't say anything, or one of the other girls? And then there is Taylor. He already thinks..."

"Taylor suspects, Maggie, but he knows nothing. He is fishing for information. He wants to rile me up as punishment is all he's doing. The truth is, he hated Westerly as much as I did, as much as everyone did. No one cares that he's dead Maggie, no one." George said calmly, as if he was talking to a child.

"I'm so scared George, I don't know what to think." I said, finally breaking down and crying as George pulled me into his embrace. I cried like a baby for George and the weight he had carried. For Harmony and everything she went through. For myself, as I felt like my husband was a stranger that I knew nothing about. After I finished crying, George held me for a while.

"Why don't you take Emmett upstairs and get some rest, I'll be

Falling

up soon." George said as he pulled away. Then he kissed me and told me he loved me.

I got up and gently picked Emmett out of his bassinet. Then we tiptoed up the stairs and into the bedroom, where I laid Emmett down in his crib. I then climbed into my bed, leaving our doors open so I could hear Emmett when he woke to be fed. I felt exhausted, all the emotions from the day completely drained me. Before I knew it, I was sound asleep.

Chapter Twenty-Three

Maggie
April 13, 1948

The next morning, I woke up feeling as though I hadn't slept at all. Emmett woke up twice to be fed, and I did so in a sort of sleep induced haze. I didn't take the usual time to look at his eyes flutter as he nursed. I didn't deeply breathe in his baby scent and marvel at the joy it brought. Feeling almost numb, I simply changed, fed, and burped him. Then I went back to bed.

When I woke up, I could feel my head pound and all I wanted was to bury my head with a blanket and go back to sleep. Emmett soon woke up and began to fuss wanting to eat as desperately as I wanted to sleep. His needs far outweigh my own.

After taking care of Emmett, I walked back into my room to change out of my dressing gown. I put on a cream and blue polka dot day dress that buttoned up the front. Then I put on my nylon stockings, sensible black flats, and a dark blue cardigan sweater. I pinched some color into my cheeks, put on some eyeliner, mascara, and a light pink lipstick.

Afterwards, I sat there at my dressing table and looked at my reflection in the mirror. I looked okay. I looked better than okay if I were to be honest. I would do for another day of baking with mom, Harry, and Aunt Evie. I desperately wanted to hide the turmoil that spiraled inside. Since I was a child, I always felt like I could talk with mom about anything, and the things I couldn't... well, I could always talk to Harry. This time I couldn't. I couldn't tell anyone what George told me last night. I could never reveal the fact that he murdered someone.

Just the thought of it sent a shiver down my spine. I understood why he did it. I could understand the reasoning, the desperation, and his need to protect. It was completely in George's nature to want to protect. But I couldn't quit playing the imagined scene in my head. I couldn't quit thinking of that article with the picture of Mr. Westerly lying dead. I felt an inner turmoil with what was right and wrong in this situation. I knew that Mr. Westerly was definitely wrong in his role, but did that mean he deserved to die for it? Was it right for George to make that decision?

Ellie Lynn

Shaking my head to clear my storming thoughts, I plastered a serene smile on my face and decided it would do. Although, to be honest, it looked forced. I then got up to get Emmett ready to leave. George was presumably at work. He hadn't come up to bed last night after his confession. I briefly remembered hearing the door close as he left that morning, and I couldn't help but feel relieved. I wasn't ready to face him yet, and couldn't be sure what I would see when looking at him. I desperately hoped he would still look like the same old George to me.

An hour later I sat at the table in mom's kitchen enjoying a nice hot cup of coffee. Aunt Evie was holding Emmett as he chewed on a ring of measuring spoons. Harry kept busy kneading the dough for the Babka that we were making. Mom wanted to make some basic wheat rolls, but a friend gave Harry an old recipe for Babka, and she insisted on making it.

The Jewish sweet bread sounded delicious and yet not too difficult to make for the first time. That didn't mean making something different in mom's kitchen didn't cause chaos. Quite the opposite. Mom felt she needed to be in complete control of every step. I could tell it annoyed Harry, but she kept kneading the dough and went along with the fussing about.

"How is the coffee, Margaret?" Mom asked. "You were a little pale when you walked in. I hope you're not catching anything."

"No, I'm fine mom. Just got little sleep last night. Emmett had me up a few times and I couldn't get back to sleep." I replied, only telling a small fraction of the truth. I should have known that mom would recognize something was wrong instantly. Thankfully, I had a small infant to blame it on.

"Is Emmett usually up through the night still?" Harry asked, turning towards me as she wiped her floured hands on her pink apron.

"Usually once, but then he settles down pretty quickly." I said, feeling a little guilty for putting the blame on Emmett.

"I bet it's the beginning of teething. Can you chop these walnuts

Falling

up for me?" Mom said as she brought over a bowl of walnuts, a cutting board, and a knife. "A dab of whiskey on the gums should help with that, you know." Mom said offhandedly as she continued her work.

"Yes, I'll have to try that." I said as I started chopping the walnuts, glad that I had a job to do to keep me busy. I also watched Aunt Evie try to baby talk to Emmett. He sat on the table facing her as she held his sides to support him. He was obviously enjoying the measuring spoons as they were clanking together as he gummed them, shook them, then gummed them some more.

"I wish my Alroy would have given me a grandbaby. Heck, I'm old enough to be a great grandmother. Not to say that I wish he would reproduce with that wife of his, the brat would come out with horns! But before, with sweet Marie..." Aunt Evie sounded almost regretful before her words faded off. Alroy dated Marie many years ago, but they never got married. It was surprising to hear Aunt Evie mention her.

I hadn't thought of it before. How cousin Alroy, having no children of his own, would bother Aunt Evie. She never mentioned it. "Aunt Evie, I've always considered you like a grandma to me. That would mean Emmett is like your great grandson." I said with a consoling smile.

"Don't be ridiculous, girl. I appreciate the sentiment but 'like' a grandchild is not quite the same as 'is' a grandchild, is it? It's probably for the best anyway as I wouldn't have wanted anyone calling me grandma, especially in public. I know I'm old, I just wouldn't want to be reminded of it all the time."

Just as quick as her sentimental and regretful moment came, it was gone. I couldn't help but chuckle a little. The Aunt Evie I knew and loved.

"Well for me, I don't mind being called grandma, it doesn't make me feel old at all." Mom cut in with a proud smile on her face before turning around to continue measuring out the brown sugar.

"Aileen, make sure you measure out enough for a fourth loaf. I

Ellie Lynn

want to take a loaf to Mrs. Westerly later today along with some extra pot roast that Mrs. Beverly made. We try to help out at least once a week." Harry explained.

"How is Mrs. Westerly doing?" I asked, sounding much more casual than I felt.

"She is doing very well, Maggie, her and the girls. Mrs. Beverly and I brought over some donated clothes for them and a few of us from church got together and helped get that place straightened up too. It smells and looks so much better now. Plus, the exciting news is that Mrs. Westerly interviewed yesterday to work at the diner in town. I hope she gets it so she can start making some money to help support those girls. She almost seems like a changed woman." Harry replied in her usual energetic way. I envied her desire to do as much charity work as she did. I couldn't imagine how she had the time and energy.

"Of course, she's a changed woman, that worthless husband of hers is dead." Aunt Evie pointed out in her usual blunt way.

"She probably feels relieved and like a weight has been lifted since she no longer has to worry about what trouble Mr. Westerly is up to." Mom added as she looked up from reading the recipe once again.

"Yeah, a dead weight." Aunt Evie added under her breath with a small chuckle. She smiled at me and at my disgusted look, she shrugged her shoulders as if she really could not care less. I saw mom from the corner of my eye cross herself and shake her head. She obviously heard the comment, too.

Emmett let out a small fuss, which was followed by a much louder one. This, of course, prompted Aunt Evie to hand him over to me across the table post haste.

"Your cute, little one, but Aunt Evie doesn't do fussy babies." She said matter-of-factly. Picking up Emmett, I snuggled him up onto my shoulder. I felt him rubbing his lips back and forth over my neck, telling me he was hungry.

"I'm going to get this little guy changed and fed. Aunt Evie, you

Falling

can finish the walnuts." I said as I turned to take care of Emmett in the family room.

After changing Emmett, I sat down with him on the sofa and adjusted my dress to feed him. The room was quiet and the sun shone dimly through the partly opened curtains. I always found it comfortable here. It was home. This is where I sat and listened to the radio as a kid and where I read books, colored, and dreamed of being an adult. Sitting here now, I suddenly felt like crying. Life became so complicated as an adult. As a child, things seemed so much easier.

As I let out a shaky breath, Aunt Harry walked in quietly. Looking up at her, she gave me a concerned smile before walking over to sit next to me.

"Do you mind if I join you for a few minutes? I love her, but your mother is driving me nuts." Harry said with an exaggerated smile as her dangle earrings danced about her ears.

"She has a tendency to do that, especially in the kitchen." I replied with sympathy.

"I have been working so much lately that I've hardly seen or talked with you since you had Emmett. How are you doing?" She asked simply.

"I'm good, truly, I am just tired and..." My voice trailed off as my throat suddenly felt dry.

"It's okay, everything doesn't have to always be good. There is so much pressure put on young mothers to act and feel a certain way. Lots of mothers feel overwhelmed, tired, sad, even depressed. It's completely normal." Harry said in her comforting way. I imagine Harry sat and listened to many young mothers complain of the early days of motherhood, not knowing how badly Harry wanted to be a mother herself.

"It's not that. I mean, I am tired and overwhelmed feeling at times, it's... I have something else weighing on my mind right now is all." I replied with what I hoped was a warm smile. I wanted so badly to tell her everything so that she could smile and tell me everything would be alright. She had a way of making me believe it.

Ellie Lynn

"Is it something you can tell me about, something I can help with?" Harry asked with sincerity.

"No, it's something I must figure out on my own. Why does life have to be so complicated, Aunt Harry?" I asked, knowing I sounded tired and upset.

"Sometimes life feels complicated, Maggie. But when you take a deep breath, block out all the noise and ask for God's help, He will answer. You will feel it, and everything becomes clearer. It does not mean we have to carry all of life's burdens on our own. Ask for God to carry some of that burden and if it's still too heavy, know that there are people who love you and can help you carry the weight of your troubles." Then she smiled in that knowing and confident way that only someone with true faith can.

"You always know what to say, how to put things in perspective. Thank you for that." I whispered as I pulled Emmett up to my shoulder to pat his back.

"You're welcome. Well, I better get back in the kitchen before your mom changes or adds something. Before it's not even a babka at all." Harry said with a warm smile. Her face as bright as ever with her red lipstick, shining eyes, and red hair pulled back in a loose braid.

Laughing a bit at this, I told her I would join them in a few minutes. Emmett slept softly now on my shoulder, and I took the few extra minutes to snuggle him close, to smell his scent and to feel his warmth. Before meaning to, I closed my eyes and prayed for understanding and strength. I prayed for George and the hidden demons he must bear, and I prayed for forgiveness of his sins.

I hadn't prayed in a long time, although I used to pray all the time during the war. I prayed for everything to go back to normal; for my neighbors to come back home safely. I prayed for all the people whose lives and homes the war destroyed, knowing I had it easy, that the bombs weren't at my doorstep. So, I did what I could; I prayed. I and so many others prayed every night. And yet, my neighbors never came home. Millions of people died, and everyone felt the wounds and tragedies of the war in so many ways. I hated to admit it, but I

Falling

lost some of my faith when it was all over. I had a hard time understanding how God could allow it all. How my prayers every night meant nothing.

Even praying now, I knew I did it halfheartedly. I felt too much anger bottled up to do it with my whole soul. The last time I did that, my bleeding continued, and my unborn daughter still died. No, I couldn't give myself over completely again. I couldn't deny the truth that there's a possibility that everything would not be alright. That George could be discovered and taken from us, no matter how good his intentions had been. He wasn't above the law. He killed someone, and no number of prayers could change that.

I laid Emmett down next to me, making sure that I propped a cushion next to him to keep him from rolling over if he should awaken. I would make sure to check on him every few minutes as well. Then I kissed him on his chubby cheek and walked back into the kitchen to lose my thoughts in baking and gossip.

Chapter Twenty-Four

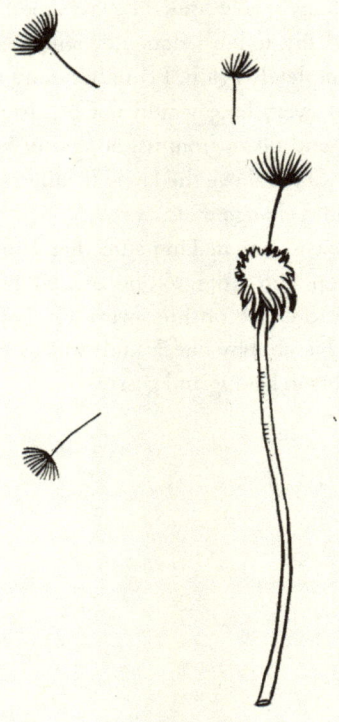

Maggie
June 14, 1948

They say that there is power in prayer. I have always misjudged this statement as an assertion of the existence of miracles. On the ability to heal, to keep someone safe, or to change one's fortune. Maybe, though, it is something much different. Maybe the power in prayer is one's knowledge and affirmation of their importance. Of their ability to feel connected and not so alone in this crazy life. To not change a destined outcome, but to feel supported through it. God didn't create the war, the concentration camps, the bombs, the bullets, the famine, and the suffering. But maybe, just maybe, He was there to comfort each one as they closed their eyes for the last time. Keeping some hope alive when all would otherwise be lost to despair. And maybe, just maybe, everything will be alright, and I will fall right into His arms as I leave this life.

"Why do we need to leave now to visit your parents? I don't understand this. You have avoided the topic of them since we first met. They have never bothered to come visit, then suddenly now you want to make the trip to see them." I yelled at George while packing mine and Emmett's bag.

"I think the trip will be good for us. My parents can finally meet you and Emmett, and it will give you a chance to understand where I come from. The visit will also give me a chance to talk with my father."

"Talk with him about what? Please don't tell me you plan on telling him about what is going on. *About Mr. Westerly?*" I still spoke the words Mr. Westerly in a whisper as if anyone could hear me in our own home and if they did would instantly *know*.

Walking over to me George placed his hands on my shoulders and looked at me pleadingly. "Please Maggie, I need this. I can't explain why I just do."

Turning away from him, still annoyed, I reluctantly agreed. The next morning, we left.

Ellie Lynn

The warm sun shined through the passenger window of the truck, heating my cheek and causing me to feel content and drowsy. Emmett sat in my lap, playing with a stuffed bunny that Aunt Harry spoiled him with a few days before. The bunny's ears were no longer soft and fluffy as they were used as a teething toy and now looked wet and matted. At five months old, he seemed to change on a weekly basis. He constantly seemed to be learning, making new noises, giggling, and moving around. Crawling would come any day now, despite being so young. For now, though, he pulls up on his hands and knees and rocks as if he's about to take flight.

George drove while smoking a cigarette and humming a song to himself. Looking calm and at peace, despite the nervousness I can read below the surface. On our way to New Mexico to visit George's parents and my stomach felt knotted since this would be the first time meeting them. George received a letter occasionally from his mother, but they were far and few in between and were usually short. Whenever I asked about his parents George would usually give short answers and then change the subject. At a point I quit asking.

Last week George suggested we go for the visit. The suggestion surprised me, but I agreed it would be a good thing to do. They could meet their grandson, I could meet them, and the road trip would be a perfect way for George and me to reconnect. I felt a distance slowly dividing us since George's confession. We hadn't made love since, and our conversations were becoming shorter and less important. I couldn't stop picturing George shooting Mr. Westerly. I even dreamed about it.

We had, of course, talked more about what happened. George had continued to reassure me that everything would be okay, that he talked to Taylor and expressed his anger at him trying to interrogate me. He tried to reassure me he cleared things up with Taylor so that there would be no more questions. I wasn't sure if this was truly the case or not, but I hadn't seen or heard from Taylor since the cafe. It

Falling

seemed as if everyone let the topic drop besides me. The last time I brought it up to George, he became angry and couldn't understand why I didn't just move on.

"Do you know how many other men I've killed, Maggie? I was in a war, for Christ's sake! What is the difference really?" He shouted, and maybe he was right. I hadn't thought about it that way. George of course killed before while fighting in the war and it shouldn't feel different, but somehow it did, at least to me. It obviously didn't to him. Although truth be told, I couldn't imagine in any way how it would feel to take a life during wartime or not, so was it right for me to judge?

I also noticed that there were no other articles written in the paper about Mr. Westerly's death. I scanned through the Okmulgee Daily Times every morning looking to see if there were any new articles, but there wasn't. As if the man everyone in town disliked was also someone no one missed.

The gossips in town even moved on to other topics. It was now back to who was dating who, what so and so said in church, and how Mrs. Alderson's baby had a suspiciously dark complexion. Even Aunt Evie, who'd been under the weather the past two weeks from a persistent cough, seemed to have forgotten about her theories in the Westerly case and moved her attention elsewhere. Mostly back to Elroy and his wife and how they would inherit everything when she died. She hated the thought of that jezebel getting the deed to her house, but in rare defeat insisted there was nothing she could do about it. According to Aunt Evie, Grandma Faye visited her in her sleep a few days ago. This convinced Aunt Evie that she was dying.

I thought it was probably just her usual dramatic and over exaggeration speaking, even though there was a nagging voice in the back of my head reminding me of her advancing age. It was something I didn't even want to think about. Either way, I appreciated that she lived with mom and that Aunt Harry could check in on her while she was unwell.

Putting my worries about Aunt Evie aside, I instead thought of my latest row with George a couple of days ago. I hinted at not wanting to be with him anymore. I also instantly regretted it, seeing the hurt look on George's face. I wasn't sure why I had said it at all except that I wanted him to listen to me. To understand that I wasn't okay with letting things go. That the entire thing bothered me to my very core and that I needed him to understand that. This trip would hopefully mend that hurt. We had this beautiful baby, who had fallen asleep with the tip of a bunny ear in his mouth, to raise.

Deep within my core I yearned for someone to talk to other than George who naturally becomes defensive. The problem was who? Mom or Aunt Harry would usually be my first choice, but there was no way I could ever tell them the true story of what happened to Mr. Westerly. As much as Aunt Harry thought of George, she would want to protect me more and we would find ourselves in a bigger mess. I felt confident that mom wouldn't say anything, but I feared she would never look at George the same again. That left Anna Beth.

I knew that talking with my dearest friend in the entire world would be so beneficial to my state of mind. She would probably reassure me that everything would be okay, that George wasn't a bad person, and that it was okay to forget and move on. We would hug, smile, then play with and giggle at our children. This was, of course, the best scenario, it could go a different way. Maybe she would never look at George and me the same way. That we would slowly drift apart until we were no longer friends. This was something I could never take the risk of happening.

The fact of it all was that I couldn't tell anyone, ever, about what George had told me. The mystery behind Mr. Westerly's death would have to forever remain a mystery. Unless it didn't. Unless Harmony or one of her young sisters spoke out about what happened that night. This possible reality could never be reassured away. Harmony and her three sisters were undoubtedly better off with Mr. Westerly dead. Mr. Westerly deserved to be shot where he stood for what he did. What worried me though, and kept me up some nights with anxiety, was the constant fear that one day the truth would

Falling

come out. I worried that one day what George did would catch up to him and he would spend the rest of his life in prison for it.

These are the fears that I have but can't share. They fill my brain and soul so much that I feel like bursting at times. It's beginning to make me feel resentful and angry. I wanted to talk about the what ifs and the possible outcomes. I wanted to plan for different scenarios and be prepared for what could happen. What I didn't need was continued reassurances from George. I needed reality. I planned on talking to George about all this when we returned. I wanted to visit George's parents and see where he grew up. I hoped that in doing so, I would have a better understanding of George and why he always felt the need to shield me. It was time he understood I was made of stronger stuff.

We planned to visit the Santa Fe National Forest while visiting George's parents. George frequently talked about how beautiful the place is, and I longed to see it for myself. This happened to be my first time visiting an unfamiliar state, and I felt like the change in scenery may be what I need. The excitement swirled alongside the nervousness in my stomach.

"We should be at my parent's home in a couple of hours." George said as he rubbed the pad of his thumb lightly over Emmett's cheek before continuing, "We may have to take more road trips, he's been a little trooper."

"He really has. And I'm so glad we will get there soon, I'm tired of sitting and I'm ready to get out and stretch my legs." I replied tiredly.

"Do you need me to stop sooner? I can at this next exit." George replied, as he glanced around to make the lane transfer, if needed.

"No, no, don't be silly. If we are almost there, I'd rather wait. George, do you think your parents are going to like me?" I asked, feeling a little shy about it. I hadn't really thought about if they would like me or not until this point. They always seemed so distant, as if I would never have to meet them. It was silly, really, thinking that we would never visit, or that they would never come visit us. I was sure

Ellie Lynn

that at some point they would want to meet their grandson, even if they hadn't exactly jumped at the chance to meet me.

George acted as if he really had to think about my question, dramatic sighs, scratching his head and all before finally answering, "You know, now that you ask about it, I'm not too sure they will. I mean, you're much too pretty, for one. You spoil me rotten, much more than I deserve anyway, and you're awfully opinionated."

"Oh, stop!" I said right before lightly punching him in the arm and laughing a bit, thankful that I didn't wake up Emmett from his nap.

"Maggie, they are going to love you almost as much as I do. This I can promise." George said in a more serious tone. He then reached over and patted my hand that was around Emmett, holding him while he slept. Then he continued, "I do love you, Maggie. I hope you know that. I know the last few months have been a little rough, but I promise it will get better."

"Yes, I agree it's been rough, and I do think this trip will be good for us. We can relax, have fun, and enjoy our little family. Then when we get back, we need to talk, George. Like seriously sit down and talk about everything. And... I love you too." My eyes teared up a bit as we connected at that moment. George smiled, nodded, then turned back to concentrating on the road. I leaned my head against the warm window again, adjusted Emmett since my arm had started to go numb from the weight of him and closed my eyes to take a small nap.

A few minutes later, just as I began to nod off to sleep, George spoke in a serious tone. "Maggie, we should probably talk a little about my parents before you meet them."

"That sounds ominous." I said dryly as I yawned and sat up straight, ready to listen.

"I know I've told you little about them before, just that we don't have a very close relationship. Let's just say they are *different*. I have always seen my mom as if she were a china doll and my dad her protector. She's quiet, proper, and reserved most of the time but also

Falling

has a tendency towards melodramatics. Everything has always been about her. How I made her feel as a mother and how dad made her feel as a wife was most important in the home while growing up. When I enlisted, my mother couldn't get over how I could do something like that to her. My dad was angry because I disobeyed him by enlisting and even more angry because I upset my mom. Dad...well Dad is a straightforward and serious person. I suspect he suffered greatly from World War One although he never really talked with me about it."

At my drawn in breath, George continued quickly. "I don't mean to imply that they were bad parents in any way, but they are different, and I had to be different with them."

"What do you mean you had to be different with them?" I asked.

"Well, I never felt like I could be myself around them, like I was always pretending to be someone else. Someone who they approved of. Someone as perfect as I could pretend to be. If I messed up, got bad grades, got into a fight, said something that was deemed inappropriate, mom would get upset, she would cry, and dad would discipline. I remember it being this way when I was very young before mom's breakdown. Afterwards though, it became much worse. It seemed that at times my very presence would cause mom to suffer extreme anxiety. She would cry, suffer from headaches, or become despondent. Dad would always assume I did something wrong to cause it."

I reached my free hand out to touch George's sleeve. I know I looked at him with eyes filled with sympathy which I knew he would hate if he looked back at me. I couldn't help it though, my heart ached for the little boy he had been.

"The first summer I stayed with my aunt and uncle, I finally learned who I was, and I was allowed to be that person. Allowed...it's not even the right word. Encouraged would be better. They truly loved me. Just me and not who they wanted me to be. It's funny how you don't even realize you've been holding your breath for years until you are able to finally release it." George choked on his last words as if the emotion they brought caught him off guard.

"It became harder to be who Mom and Dad expected me to be, the older I got. The more used to just being myself I became, the harder it was to be what they wanted. I think I convinced myself that enlisting in the military was strictly out of duty and patriotism when in fact there was a part of me that simply needed to escape. I hope I'm making sense and not just rambling." George chuckled uncomfortably.

"Why now George?" I asked after a few minutes of silence. "Why are we visiting your parents now?"

"I've been thinking about this exact question a lot. I'm older now, I have a family of my own, and I have my own expectations of who I want to be, as a father and husband. I think it's easy to copy what you know, what you've grown up with and I fear that I have done that exact thing. I fear that I've treated you as my father treated my mother for all those years. I love you Maggie and I don't want to do that to you. I don't want to protect you to the point of suffocation. I want to visit them, for them to see who I've become, to meet their grandson and my beautiful wife, and to remind myself that I am not like my dad and that I never will be."

A couple of hours later we pulled up to a small average looking house that seemed to glow a freshly painted light blue. Moments after parking along the street, a middle-aged couple walked out the front door.

"Looks like he finally painted the house." Stepping out of the truck George said, more to himself than anyone else.

I didn't respond but gathered up Emmett's things that were scattered about the seat and floorboard. Then I climbed out with Emmett on my hip to meet my in-laws. They walked down their driveway and around to meet us at the curb, making sure not to walk on the grass. I

Falling

found it interesting. I would have run to my son to grab him up in a big hug if I hadn't seen him in years.

They did each hug George but did it in a benign and almost unemotional way. It was as if they had seen him the week before. Turning to me, George made the introductions. George's mother Patty took a few steps and awkwardly hugged me before stepping back and smiling at Emmett who stared at them with an open mouth with drool running from it. I probably stared right back at Patty with open-mouthed awe as well. For an older lady, she looked quite stunning. She held herself with an almost fragile ethereal look about her, and she seemed much too young to be George's mother.

Next, George's father George Sr. held out his hand to shake mine as he looked Emmett and me up and down, as if he was judging on if he would approve or not. I wasn't too sure afterwards if he did.

"You can call me Sarge if you would like or George Sr., that way we're not both answering to George. Makes it easier." His father said straightforwardly.

"Of course, Sarge." I said with a smile and a quick salute, which I quickly regretted the moment my hand snapped back, and I saw the annoyed look on George Sr.'s face. My George also gave a slight groan.

"You could also just call the younger George, Georgie. It's what I've always called him." Patty added, to which I simply gave an embarrassed smile as a response.

The entire exchange seemed awkward, even more so since George Sr. looked like an older version of my George. Their likeness was almost uncanny, as they shared the same hairline, jaw, nose, and dark brown eyes. George's eyes were his most handsome aspect, I always thought. They were always so full of life, lighting up when he was happy or excited about something. George Sr's eyes were the same deep brown color except for the difference being they seemed to lack any real depth. His dark hair streaked with gray, and his build looked a little slimmer. Was this my George in another thirty years? I understood now why George insisted on not naming Emmett the third George. Emmett also shared George's brown eyes, and I wondered now if he would also look so similar.

George's parents invited us in to have sandwiches for a late lunch. We followed Patty and George Sr. through the front door and to the table where bologna and cheese sandwiches were cut diagonally on little matching plates. There were five of them. I wondered at how they thought a five-month-old would eat a whole sandwich. Before sitting down, I asked if it would be alright if I laid Emmett down on the floor to stretch and play.

Patty had already sat down, but quickly jumped back up to grab a crochet blanket off of the arm of the flower printed couch and spread it over the gray shag carpet. She then patted it for me to lay him there.

"In case he spits up." She blurted.

"Thank you." I mumbled as I laid Emmett on his back, smiling as he immediately rolled over to be on his tummy. He then started cooing and talking as he wiggled and stretched out his arms and legs. I placed his bunny in front of him, kissed the top of his head, and walked back to the table to sit down in front of the sandwich. Patty sat next to Emmett on the blanket and watched him. She seemed mesmerized about him, as if this was the first time she had ever been around a baby.

"I'm glad you guys finally brought your mother the baby to see. She's been bugging me about it these last few months. Telling everyone she's a grandma now. It's been a little embarrassing that she couldn't tell anyone what he even looked like." George Sr. remarked while motioning to Patty and Emmett.

"Well pa, I've been busy. It was hard enough getting time off work to come now." George replied, not sounding particularly offended.

While they continued to talk back and forth in their strange sarcastic way, I picked up a triangle of sandwich and took a small bite of the corner, feeling the mayonnaise ooze out of the sides a little and fill my mouth. I chewed slowly, then swallowed. I couldn't help but wash the overwhelming mayonnaise taste with a drink of water. I

Falling

repeated this until I ate the full sandwich. I didn't want to be rude, and mom always taught me to mind my manners when eating in someone else's home, so despite wanting to spit it out, I ate it.

George picked up his sandwich, squeezed the excess mayonnaise out, and ate it in two bites. I guess he knew that's how his mother would make them, and I wish he would have warned me. Having already eaten my sandwich, all I could really do was sit there, listen to George and his father catching up in their half arguing sort of way, and watch Patty as she continued to sit next to Emmett as he played. She whispered to him, smiled, and truly seemed happy sitting there with him. I instinctively knew that this wasn't always the case with her, being happy.

As strange and surreal it was, I felt like an outsider watching them all. It was Emmett that my in-laws wanted to meet, not me. That much was apparent. I couldn't help but feel slightly hurt about it while at the same time grateful they were so happy to meet their grandson. The longer I sat and watched and listened, the more I understood why George loved his time visiting his aunt and uncle, who were wonderful and caring people. I became more understanding about why he didn't talk about his parents much and why it took so long for us to come visit. There was something a little off about them.

George Sr. seemed to have a coldness hidden behind the surface. He smiled a few times as George talked. He seemed argumentative but not angry, not mean... just cold. It was the opposite with my George. I could feel his love for me with a single look. When he looked at his infant son, his love for him seemed to radiate off him. So much so that a blind person would know. George and his father may certainly look alike, but that was where the similarities seemed to end.

Looking over at Patty and Emmett, I saw her hand lightly caressing Emmett's back as he rocked back and forth on his hands and knees. Patty's light blonde hair, cut in a bob just above her shoulders, seemed almost like a halo. Her face looked to have very few

Ellie Lynn

wrinkles and her blue eyes were bright. I couldn't help but feel less than her in looks. She was slim, where I still carried some of the weight from being pregnant. Her hair laid perfectly around her flawless face, whereas mine curled up in awkward areas and my cheeks were speckled with freckles. I wasn't jealous by any means, but it certainly added to my uncomfortable feeling. Patty was quite beautiful, even if there seemed to be a sadness that loomed about her.

A picture of George as a bright and happy boy appeared in my mind. A boy so full of life despite living in a home with parents like these. Parents who sent him away for long periods of time so that his mother could have a break from him. What a blessing those breaks must have been. To go from a cold, sad home to a loving and caring one. It made me appreciate my family that much more.

"So, George here told me you want to go up into the mountains?" George Sr. asked, and at my nod continued, "We can go tomorrow if you would like. I know a suitable spot where we can park and have a picnic and look about the cliffs."

"Sounds good, pa." George replied between chewing. He picked up the last half of the sandwich intended for Emmett.

"Yes, that sounds wonderful, I've never been up in the mountains and I'm looking forward to it." I said, deciding to call him by Senior instead of Sarge given how awkward that mistake turned out. I then stood as Emmett started to cry.

Patty looked surprised and worried, as if she did not know what was wrong or what to do.

"He's probably hungry and needs a change. I have some wheat cereal for him if you wouldn't mind me making some real quick?" I asked Patty as I picked up Emmett and carried him over to his father, who welcomed him with a big smile.

"Of course, I'll help you." Patty said as she stood up and started making her way towards an open doorway.

"George, would you mind changing him while I make his cereal?" I asked as I deposited the wiggling baby in George's lap. Then, not waiting for an answer, I fished the can of cereal from my bag and

Falling

started following Patty to the kitchen. George never minded helping change Emmett's diapers. When he was home, we shared responsibilities of taking care of Emmett. George even seemed to enjoy helping.

"Got you doing women's work, eh?" I heard George Sr. remark as I walked through the doorway into the kitchen. The remark wouldn't have normally bothered me but coming from him it did. I couldn't help but feel sorry for Patty.

In the kitchen, Patty got out a small pot to boil the water for the Gerber's baby cereal. I walked over and poured some water into it as Patty lit the stove. I didn't need to measure anymore, having made it so many times I seemed to be able to tell the measurements by sight at this point.

"He sure is cute, my grandson. I really am thankful that you brought him here to visit. It's real nice seeing Georgie too. It's been a while since we've had a visit from him, only once since the war ended and that was when he first got back. Oh, I get letters and calls occasionally but it's nice to see him in person, you know?" Patty tried making conversation, which sounded more like a guilt trip in the making, as she watched me work.

"It is an awfully long drive and George works so much, but I'm glad that we could come visit. It's so nice to finally meet you and for you to get to meet Emmett." I said, hating that I was reminding her they were meeting me for the first time as well. Hadn't they been at least curious who their son married?

"Yes, it is nice. Georgie wanted us to come to the wedding but his father..." Patty said, a bit hesitant and yet still left her thought unfinished.

"His father what?" I encouraged.

"Well, his father was still a little angry at him for having joined the war to begin with. He forbad it you know. But my stubborn son went and enlisted anyway. He was lucky that he survived it at all. Deep down, I didn't think he would. That was very hard for me, you know. Anyway, after he finally came home, Georgie picked a fight with his father and told everyone he would never come back. That's

Ellie Lynn

when he moved to Oklahoma. You better hope your son doesn't grow up to be as stubborn as his father." Patty said matter-of-factly as she nodded her head at me pointedly.

"I think that George wanted to start his life anew after the war. Moving into his aunt and uncle's farm was a fresh start, that's all. I'm sure it had nothing to do with you two." I tried assuring her, although I knew his moving away had everything to do with getting away from his parents.

"Well maybe, I'm sure most of the things he said was his anger talking. I think he probably would have moved back home. A boy needs his parents, you know. But then you and he married and well... that was that." Patty looked up from staring at her hands to look sheepishly at me, as if she didn't mean to imply exactly what she had.

I didn't respond. How could I really? Their less than warm welcome suddenly made perfect sense. Of course, they blamed me for George staying away. For taking him from them. They couldn't possibly see that it was them he avoided.

"Could I use a small bowl please?" I asked before pouring the small amount of warm cereal into the bowl, cleaned up my mess quickly, and walked out of the kitchen.

Patty sat quietly watching me the entire time before following me out. Sitting at the table next to George, I pulled out a bib, a baby spoon, and a jar of pureed peaches to mix in with the cereal. Emmett loved his cereal this way and couldn't get enough of the little cans of peach baby food. It always made me smile because George loved peaches as well. However, now, I found it difficult to enjoy Emmett's excitement. Patty took a seat at the table next to her husband and they both watched as I fed Emmett small messy bites of food as George held him.

"Well, isn't this cute." George Sr. said sarcastically, obviously annoyed that George was once again helping with the baby, with the women's work. I didn't know if I wanted to cry or throw the rest of the cereal in his face, but I literally swallowed down the rage that I started feeling at that moment. My heartrate went up and my fingers

Falling

tingled. I did not know how I would make it for three days here if I felt this way after a couple hours. I knew I would have to bite my tongue and try.

George looked at me, and I could tell that what his dad said annoyed him, too. He rolled his eyes, and I couldn't help but cover a knowing smile. At least we would be in misery together, I thought.

After feeding Emmett, cleaning off his messy face, and washing and putting everything away, Patty showed me where we would sleep the next three nights. I knew that we were in George's old bedroom the moment I walked in. There were a couple of running trophies and a picture of his aunt and uncle on the desk. I noticed how clean the unused bedroom was. Not a speck of dust anywhere and the full-size bed looked freshly made with a gray patterned quilt. Thankfully, Patty had been thoughtful enough to have placed a small crib in the room. Obviously brand new, she bought it for just this occasion. Blankets and stuffed animals already sat inside it. Looking up from the crib, Patty walked over towards it to tweak a couple of the stuffed animals inside.

"George let me buy it from Sears. I admit I went a little crazy with the shopping. I was so excited. I hope he likes it all." She said, looking at me as if I would know.

"Of course, he will and it's very thoughtful of you to think of it." I replied with a smile.

"Well, I must admit, I hope it will help to encourage you both to bring him for more visits. A child should know his grandparents. Well, you make yourself at home. You can unpack if you want. The dresser is empty, as is the closet." Patty said as she walked out the door, leaving me standing in the room by myself.

I walked over to the bed to sit on it as I took a long, shuddering breath. Moments later, George walked into the room and closed the door behind him.

"Where is Emmett?" I asked.

"Don't worry, he's being held by my father." He responded nonchalantly. Then at my panicked look, "It's okay, he will not eat him up for a snack. My parents are... different, but they aren't bad people. I hoped for a little warmer reception, but honestly, I'm not too surprised. I didn't leave on the best of terms with them." George said as he sat on the bed next to me. Then he grabbed my hand and kissed it. "I wanted to make sure you were okay. I should have probably warned you better on how they could be. I can tell they have you upset."

"Well, when you said that you thought they would love me, I'm thinking you might have been mistaken." I said with a crooked grin. I couldn't possibly blame him for his parents. I felt sorry for him for having to have grown up with them.

"They will learn to love you. Besides, we are only staying a few days and who knows when we will visit again... or if we will, depending on how things go. Try to relax and enjoy yourself. I promise we will have fun tomorrow."

"I'm holding you to that, Georgie!" I said jokingly, before planting a kiss on his lips. Just as I pulled back, George pressed me closer and deepened the kiss. Soon his mouth was on my cheek and neck as his hands ran up and down my back.

"I'm holding you, Maggie. Tonight." George said breathlessly next to my ear, and I felt a familiar tingle run down my spine. It had been a while since I felt it. Since I wanted him to hold me.

We sat for a moment, holding onto one another, our foreheads touching, our eyes closed. It was the first time in months that we felt this close. It didn't last long though, as we could hear a loud squeal from Emmett coming from the family room, followed by some mumbled laughing, and talking. We both stood up then. I smoothed down my hair, and we walked out of the room.

Emmett sat on George Sr.'s lap as he gently bounced him up and down. Patty sat right next to them, watching Emmett's every move. It was such a normal grandparent scene that I couldn't help but relax a bit and smile. Maybe I rushed to judgement. Maybe I hadn't given them much of a chance yet. Admittedly I'm much more sensitive and protective since having Emmett and hearing of George's secret.

Falling

Looking over at George, he looked pleased as well. He wore a smile and a happy gleam in his eyes. I imagine, with all the difficulties with his folks, seeing them happy and enjoying Emmett was special. Maybe it would be this small, messy, drooling, adorable little boy that could mend their relationship. Our joy in him was slowly helping us to mend ours.

A couple of hours later, Emmett slept soundly in the new crib that Patty had bought him. I left him in the room with the door cracked so that I could hear him if he should awaken. Patty had pulled out some scrap books to show me as George and his father drove to the local hardware store to purchase some new pickets for a section of fence that had come down. George, when hearing about it, immediately offered to help fix it.

It seemed to make George happy his father was finally fixing up the place, painting the house, removing the rotted-out parts of the fence, and trimming the hedges and bushes. George always took pride in making sure our little house was well taken care of, remarking occasionally he felt it irresponsible to let your home fall into disrepair.

While George and his father were at the store, I sat next to Patty as she slowly flipped through a book filled with newspaper clippings, ribbons, and a few pictures. I had never seen a baby picture of George, so I practically tingled with excitement to see the slightly blurred picture of a chubby-cheeked, brown eyed little boy looking back at me from the scrapbook. Next to it a clipping of his dark brown hair, with the words underneath reading *Georgie's first haircut*.

I oohed and awed at the fourth-place ribbon in track and field and his second-place ribbon from his third-grade spelling bee. There were a few birthday cards, Christmas cards, and a thank-you card for Patty's help at the vet's club. I saw obituaries from relatives who passed and wedding announcements from those relatives who were just starting their lives. There was a picture of a ten-year-old George on the front porch of our home in Oklahoma. He stood next to his

Ellie Lynn

aunt and uncle Clemmons and wore the biggest, happiest smile ever. Patty passed over that one quickly.

"As I'm sure you know, Georgie used to stay with my brother and his wife. My nerves were not suitable for a rambunctious boy running about. Little Georgie acted quite the handful, much more than most children, I'm sure." Patty said as an explanation for what I already knew. George told me she suffered a mental breakdown and was never quite the same afterwards.

"Yes, I'm sure he was. Being a mother can be quite challenging I'm learning." I said to help make her feel more comfortable about the topic.

"Oh, your little one is an angel. They are always so cute and sweet when they are that age. But just you wait, he'll get older, then you will see." Patty then smiled with a knowing and smug look. I swallowed my reply down like spoiled milk. I would never say it out loud, as I'm sure it would only cause problems. I would never tell her it was her and her husband who were the problem, not George. Instead, I smiled and gritted my teeth.

The next page, an old newspaper clipping with a picture of a young George Sr. wearing the uniform from the first World War. He looked young and handsome in it with his hat slanted just so, his boots a little muddy, a cigarette held between his fingers, his sergeant stripes standing out boldly, and a deeply haunted look in his eyes.

"That's my George." Patty said as she gently traced the outline of the picture. "He was such a brave soldier, you know. The only one to come home from his group of friends that also enlisted. They all died in this one particularly nasty battle. He missed them terribly after that, but like all good soldiers do, he moved on with his life after the war. He never complained or suffered any shell shock or other nonsense like that. He got to work on taking care of his family. It's always best to put the past right behind you. There is always a brighter future ahead."

It surprised me at how cheerful and optimistic Patty sounded when talking about something so tragic. She sounded like an ad in a

Falling

woman's magazine on how to be an excellent housewife. I sincerely doubted, given my experience, that George Sr. could put the war behind him and move on as she implied.

"Is that why George's father became unhappy with him for enlisting?" I ventured to ask, a little nervous at what her reply would be.

"It upset George Sr. that Georgie enlisted because he forbade it. He didn't think the boy knew what he was getting into. Georgie should have listened to his father. Always so stubborn, though, never listening and always getting into trouble. This was why George Sr. treated him so harshly. Georgie needed to learn to be a good boy. Now, how about a cup of hot tea? I'll go put on a pot of water." Patty said before standing up to put tea on.

Everything started making more sense now. This is what George talked with me about in the car ride, not wanting to treat me like his dad treated his mom. It became clear why George wouldn't talk about the war and why he tried to shield me from anything bad. This is what his father always did for Patty. He kept her safe and ignorant to protect her sense of how things should be. He protected her from knowing how much he must have hurt inside. What the war and losing all his friends costed him. He kept her from having to deal with the anxieties and tribulations of parenthood, and he kept her bitter and hurt over George's betrayal of enlisting rather than the reality of him fighting in a war. I couldn't imagine how they treated George after coming home from being a POW. Was he expected to move on with no real chance at healing? Was he looked at with eyes that only said I told you so?

I realized at that moment that I too judged George based on my own beliefs. Our whole marriage, I tried to get him to talk to me about how he felt, what he experienced, and what kept him up at night. Was needing to know everything, about *him*? Or was it more about me and what I needed. Did it only fulfill my preconceived notions of what a good marriage would be? That I was the one who could heal him if only he would talk to me, to give me the chance?

The fact of the matter is that it wasn't about me. At all. It wasn't

Ellie Lynn

about George Sr., or Patty. It was about George doing what he needed to do for himself. If that meant talking about it, trying to put everything behind him, asking for help, not asking, sharing with me, or shielding me... George needed to do what he felt best for him to heal. My job as his wife was to support him, encourage him, trust him, and love him. That meant loving him despite his faults, despite mistakes that he may make. Despite the challenges that we may continue to face.

George took care of me and Emmett. He worked hard. He tried desperately to move on, and that included protecting me from the demons terrorizing him. My body and mind felt heavy with exhaustion. Our marriage had thus far been filled with so many obstacles, stresses, and heartaches. What kept us going was that we also filled it with a deep sense of commitment and love. I loved George with everything in me, and I suddenly realized that I needed him to know that. To know that I would be there for him, no matter what obstacles were thrown at us.

I also realized at that moment that despite looking so much alike, George was nothing like his father. Where surviving the war turned George Sr. into a cold and controlling man, my George was loving and protective, even if that meant at times distancing himself. He tried to be worthy of others' sacrifice.

Standing up and walking into the kitchen, I found Patty standing next to the sink with a teapot sitting on the counter next to her. She looked dazed and jumped a little in surprise when I walked in.

"I thought I'd see if you needed any help. Here I'll make the tea, you go ahead and rest." I said as I started taking over making the tea. The pot sat on the counter empty, so I filled it and lit the stove.

"Thank you." Patty mumbled as she serenely walked to the small table sitting next to the back wall that was next to the kitchen door. The wallpaper in the room was a print of bright yellow flowers that had taken on a sort of dingy look from years of cigarette smoke. Sitting down, she pulled out a cigarette from the pack laying on the table and lit it.

Falling

Even the way Patty smoked her cigarette looked dainty and very feminine. Holding it between her painted fingertips and blowing the smoke between her gently parted matching pink lips, the smoke gently billowed upwards. She could be sitting in a cocktail lounge or on Hollywood Blvd. Yet she sat in this little house in New Mexico with faded, dingy wallpaper. At that moment, a small bubble of laughter threatened to escape as I thought about what Aunt Evie would say if she was here.

I smiled then because it would probably be something terribly inappropriate. Mom would roll her eyes and shake her head, and Aunt Harry would laugh out loud. I suddenly craved to be home baking bread with them. Feeling their love, listening to their gossip, knowing that I was always welcome.

Before I knew it, the water in the teapot rumbled and I pulled it off the heat before it could whistle. After preparing the two cups of tea, I brought them over to the table, set them down, then grabbed the small sugar dish and spoon from the counter. I sat down and smiled at her as she put the rest of her cigarette out. She grabbed her cup, putting no sugar in it, and sipped it. I heaped two spoonsful of sugar in my cup, stirred, and sipped, thoroughly enjoying the sweetness of it. We sat in silence for a few moments before I spoke up.

"George has, of course, talked to me about spending time with his aunt and uncle as a child. I hope you don't mind me asking, but I was curious about the... the breakdown that you suffered. If it's something you still struggle with?" My voice shook a little as I spoke. I debated on even trying to bring it up, being a sensitive topic for sure, but one I felt I needed to ask.

"You are direct, aren't you?" Patty responded as she lit another cigarette and pierced me with her gaze for a moment. "I feel anxious, maybe a little down, but nothing more than most people, I'm sure. My anxiety made me feel trapped when Georgie was little. I needed some breaks and he liked to visit them. That's all."

"Yes, he did." I said with an understanding smile. Although deep down I didn't understand. I hadn't been a mother for even a year yet, and I couldn't imagine having Emmett away for long periods of time. I would miss him way too much. I tried not to judge though, as I never dealt with mental health issues. Aunt Harry told me once that some new mothers did. I let the issue rest, deciding I probably pried enough hoping she could have explained more. I would have been sympathetic, and we could have bonded a little, but that wasn't to be.

"I hope you like pork chops as I plan on frying some for supper tonight. Maybe you could help make the salad to go with it?" Patty asked.

"Of course. If there is anything else, you want help with, I'd be more than happy to." I offered, remembering the bologna sandwiches we ate for lunch and hoping the pork chops would be better.

"Just the salad." Patty said as she flicked the ashes from her cigarette into the ashtray sitting in front of us.

Crying from the other room, Emmett thankfully saved me from having to converse with her more. I told her I needed to attend to him and left. He would need to be changed and would probably want to be fed.

Later that evening, the four of us sat around the dining room table for supper. The fried pork chops were a little tough, but they tasted good. The salad crisp and fresh, and the baked mac and cheese tasted surprisingly delicious. My stomach embarrassingly growled at the sight of it but it didn't bother me. Even when Patty looked disapprovingly at me as I spooned another helping of the mac and cheese on my plate.

"My baked mac and cheese was Georgie's favorite when he was a boy. I'm glad you like it." Patty said, overly sweetly. My full mouth smiled back.

I never experienced a more uncomfortable meal. Patty's disapproval was something I could handle, and which only managed to annoy me. George Sr. barely spoke to me and yet kept sending dark looks my way as if he was angry at me. I couldn't possibly understand what I did to have earned it. My George even seemed to be a little on edge.

Falling

A couple of hours later we thankfully retired to George's childhood bedroom for an early bedtime so that we could wake up early to go for our picnic and hike the next day. At this point I wanted it to all be over with. I fully decided that George's parents were unhappy and thoroughly unpleasant people who I would be grateful to not visit again.

After feeding and settling down Emmett, I climbed into bed next to George. He immediately pulled me into his arms and nuzzled my ear and neck.

"George, what was wrong with your father tonight? He seemed angry at me." I asked as I pulled away to look at his face still quite visible in the darkening room. The sun hadn't quite dropped all the way down, leaving everything in shadows.

"He's not angry, he... uh... can't we talk about this in the morning? I hoped for some you and I time." George said as he tried to pull me back in his arms.

"I'd rather you just told me now, that way I can relax for our "you and I time" otherwise, I'm going to be thinking about your dad..."

"We definitely don't want that!" George said with a chuckle that quickly went serious. "Okay, so I told pa everything. Everything about what happened with Westerly." At my groan, he quickly continued. "My father can be a mean son of a bitch, but he's as loyal as they come. He's my father and I trust him to keep my confidence. I just... I needed to hear his thoughts on the matter. Any advice that he may have. I hope you understand."

Understand? I didn't know how I felt about it. I certainly didn't trust George Sr. and it felt risky for George to have told him. "I'm not sure how I feel about it to tell you the truth, but why did he look like he wanted to murder me throughout supper?"

"He asked me how you reacted to the news, how you felt about everything, and how loyal you are. Of course, I told him how hard this is on you, but also that you would stand by me. I'm not sure how convinced he was. I plan on having another conversation with him again on the subject. I'll make him understand that you and Emmett

Ellie Lynn

are my everything. That everything would all be fine. I probably shouldn't have said anything to him about it at all. I'm sorry that I did." George said as he closed his eyes and rubbed his brow in that way that he does when he is stressed out about something.

"Okay, did he at least give you any advice or say anything helpful?" I asked, as I scooted closer into his arms.

"He said he thought it did not differ from what he or I have done before at war. It's just one is legal while the other isn't. He said he would have done the exact same thing and that if we lock it away and not speak of it again, everything will be fine. I knew this of course; I've told you as much. I guess it just helped to hear it from him, I'm not sure why, but I still feel the need for his approval. It's silly I know." George said quietly acting a little embarrassed about his confession of needing his father's approval.

"I don't think it's silly at all. I think most boys and even men need to hear of their father's approval. Especially when they spent most of their childhood never hearing it." I replied as I rubbed his cheek with the pad of my thumb. George seemed vulnerable at this moment, and I couldn't love him more for it. So, I kissed him. I kissed him with everything I felt at that moment and for everything we had been through in our marriage. I kissed him as a promise of tomorrow and all the days we had left together.

Chapter Twenty-Five

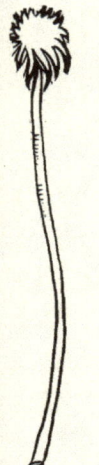

Maggie
June 15, 1948

I hadn't realized it wouldn't be long. It's astonishing how fleeting life is. If we truly lived each day as our final one, wouldn't our embraces linger a little longer? Our laughter resonate a little louder? Wouldn't we memorize each speck of color as we gazed into our children's eyes? Life could be richer, more profound, and brim with more significance, sensation, and purpose. Why do we squander this potential? Perhaps because these are the questions you ask and reflections that surface only when the hourglass nears its end – when it's already too late.

Despite my doubts about being able to have fun on our little outing, I couldn't help but enjoy myself. The day felt almost perfect. The sky was blue and clear, and the sun warmed my neck without being stifling. The mountains were truly beautiful, and they had a surprising way of making you feel almost small and insignificant amongst such vastness of mother nature's beauty. I only considered it almost perfect because it wasn't just George, Emmett, and me on the mountain. Patty and George Sr. were of course with us as well. Although I had to admit, they seemed to also be enjoying themselves, which was refreshing and a little unexpected.

After parking on a gravel parking area, we walked a short distance on a clearly visible hiking path. I breathed in deeply the fresh mountain air and awed at its beauty. Even Emmett seemed to wonder at the place. He giggled and kicked his feet while watching birds flying above and at the chipmunks scurrying about. Besides that, he wore an expression of wonderment on his face with his mouth slightly open, surrounded by pink chubby cheeks. His dark brown eyes were wide and sparkly, and he truly looked happy, which of course, made me happy as well.

After a leisurely stroll, we arrived at a picturesque open meadow, adorned with sporadic trees and enchanting clusters of purple and white wildflowers. Stretching beyond the meadow's expanse lay a breathtaking vista from a precipitous cliff, a sight that held me spellbound. In the distance sat a couple, clearly devoted to one another

Ellie Lynn

reclining languidly on a blanket. Patty suggested a nice, shaded area under a tree to lay our blanket on while George Sr. sat down the picnic basket.

"It's a beautiful view. I'm so glad that you brought us up here for a picnic. Thank you." I excitedly told my in-laws as I sat Emmett down on the blanket. He immediately grabbed onto the basket and pulled himself up on his knees, all while talking excitedly with squeals.

"You're welcome. It sure looks like Emmett there is enjoying himself. Fresh mountain air is good for a baby." Patty said with a sincere smile before sitting down as well and pulling out a cigarette. George Sr. Pulled one out as well, lit it, then leaned down and lit Patty's. "Want a cigarette, Georgie?" Patty asked as her perfectly bobbed hair glowed in the sun.

Looking over at George, I could tell he looked a little annoyed as he shook his head no. Then quickly changed his mind and pulled out one of his own and lit it. He then sat next to me, grabbed Emmett up in his arms, and snuggled him in close as Emmett squirmed. He then tossed him gently into the air a few inches before catching him. Emmett squealed with delight. I couldn't help but laugh a little as I burned the image of George playing with his son, with his cigarette dangling between his lips in my mind. It would be something I could tell Emmett about when he grew older; how much his father loves him.

"Don't do that, Georgie, you're going to drop him!" Patty exclaimed nervously.

"He's fine Patty, he's playing with his son. You don't want him raising no sissy boy, anyway. He needs to make sure he's tough." George Sr. told Patty as he looked on proudly. Patty pursed her lips together, obviously unhappy with the scolding.

"I got him, don't worry. I wouldn't drop him." George tried to reassure his mother before handing Emmett over to me. I pulled out a jar of baby food so I could feed Emmett while everyone else ate, then

Falling

George could take care of Emmett while I did. It had become routine on how we worked together with him.

"I don't know why you use that store bought baby food. I used to only use natural, homemade baby food for my Georgie. If I fed him peas, then I would mash them up myself. It was cheaper and I'm certain healthier for him. You should really think of trying it."

"I feed him soft food from our home as well, Patty, but the canned baby food is easier when traveling. Plus, it's healthy and natural as well. My friend even feeds her twins canned baby food, and her husband is a doctor." I said, trying not to let her barb sting me too much. Plus, I figured she wasn't one to give me advice when she made a bologna sandwich for Emmett when we arrived. He only had two teeth.

"Well, it's something I wouldn't do, that's all." Patty mumbled as she unpacked the picnic basket. She pulled out some cold fried chicken, along with a handful of grapes and a chunk of cheese. My mouth watered at the sight of the food, making me realize I was hungrier than I realized.

In between messy bites of food for Emmett, I stole a grape here and there and thoroughly enjoyed the sweet crisp juice as they popped into my mouth. Soon Emmett wouldn't take another bite, so I cleaned off his messy face with a burping rag and sat him down next to me with his bunny. It had become quite the little buddy for him, and Emmett wouldn't leave a room without it. He seemed perfectly content chewing on the poor thing's ears. I wasn't sure how much more the little stuffed bunny could take of being chewed on by two sharp little teeth before it completely fell apart.

Finally, I could eat. I tore into the fried chicken as if I had nothing for breakfast a few hours prior. Emmett quickly grew bored with chewing on the bunny's ears, so he tried to crawl around, crawling on laps, and trying to grab food left on plates. Patty stood up and offered to carry Emmett around to show him the flowers. George Sr. offered to join her. A brilliant plan, as far as I was concerned as it gave me time to finish eating. George and I could then lay back and

Ellie Lynn

watch the clouds while Emmett got to spend some time with his grandparents.

"Do you see that cloud right there? I think it looks like a bird flying." George whispered in my ear a few minutes later after I finished eating and laid down next to him.

"Yeah, do you mean the one with the really large beak that's almost as big as the body?" I asked jokingly.

"Yes, that's the one." He laughed next to me as he intertwined our hands. It felt like we were the only two on this giant mountain at that moment. It brought back memories of one of our date under the stars. Oh, how I loved this man.

The only sign that we weren't alone was the faint talking and laughing of George Sr. and Patty, and of the other couple in the meadow getting up to leave. I turned my head towards George, who was still trying to identify objects in the clouds. I looked at him. For some reason, at that moment, it became very important to me; to notice the sprinkling of freckles around his hairline. Which made me notice a couple of gray hairs that started to show. I never noticed them before.

His nose held a very slight bend, and his eyelashes were incredibly long. He must have felt me staring as he turned his head towards mine and we just gazed into each other's eyes for a few moments. His eyes were a dark brown, but I noticed that there were small flecks of an amber color there as well. I felt my chest swell with pride, knowing that this man lying next to me was mine. I also felt a slight tremor of sadness roll through me. It left so quick that I barely detected it, but it had been there, nonetheless.

"Is everything okay?" George asked, as he must have noticed it. It surprised me, as *I* had barely noticed it. Nodding my head yes, he continued, "You know you can tell me anything, right?"

"Of course." I said before leaning forward and lightly placing a kiss on his lips. Then I sat up, wanting to see Emmett. He was sitting on the ground grabbing at flowers. Patty and George Sr. seemed to be glowing with pride watching him.

Falling

"Well, I'm glad to see they will be better grandparents than they were as parents." George remarked dryly as he sat up as well and packed away the picnic. I sat for a moment longer watching them. I watched the light breeze gently blow against Emmett's baby soft hair. For a moment I sat mesmerized. Then I got up to pack away the plates and toss the chicken bones.

While Emmett played with his grandparents, George and I linked arms and walked around the picnic area. I occasional stopped to pick a wildflower to add to a growing bouquet. If mom were here, she would insist that they were simple weeds and then sneeze. I laughed to myself at this thought.

"What's so funny?" George asked as he smiled and looked at me.

"Oh, nothing really. I was thinking of how mom would hate these wildflowers, that's all. Is it weird that I miss them, and it's only been a few days?"

"No, we miss the ones we love." George replied simply. "Let's walk over there and look at the view."

We walked to the edge of the cliff. I felt a slight shimmer run through me at the thrill of being so high up from the ground below. I didn't dare look straight down. The view up ahead was so magnificent that it made me forget my usual fear of heights for the moment. I wasn't sure if I ever saw a landscape so beautiful in my life.

"Careful Maggie, that's a long way down there." George said cautiously as I must have leaned forward for a better view. I was thankful that our arms were still linked, and he stood solid next to me.

"I'll be careful. Plus, I know you will never let anything bad happen to me." I said as I smiled into his eyes while inching backwards and away from the edge a bit.

"Georgie, come sit with me and Emmett." Patty yelled out to us.

"Alright ma, be right there." George yelled back to her before turning to look at me.

"You go ahead George. I'm going to look at the view for a few minutes more." I said, then at his worried look, "I'll be careful, I promise. And George... I love you."

Ellie Lynn

"I love you too." George said before he unlinked his arm with mine and left to go sit with his mother and our son.

I felt a slight breeze pick up and ruffle my hair as I watched the tall grass in the meadow began to sway around me. It gave me an idea to drop wildflowers off the cliff one by one and watch them being swept up by the wind as though they are dancing in their descent to the rocky ground below. Smiling, the scene reminds me of blowing on a dandelion as a child and watching the seeds fall. I always remembered to make a wish.

Standing so close to the edge felt a little dangerous yet exhilarating as well. A few steps forward or backwards can literally mean life or death. There are few moments in life when you are fully aware of the tightrope we all walk daily. Most of the time we choose to ignore it. Who would truly live if they were constantly afraid of dying?

The sun glared before me and I had a drowsy feeling from the food, sun, and at my pondering. I heard footsteps come up behind me, so I turned around with a big smile, expecting to see George standing there. I anticipated in that split second of wrapping myself into his arms to feel safe and protected. To feel loved. Instead, my eyes fell upon his father who stood before me. The other George with the almost same brown eyes. Eyes that did not look at me lovingly.

"Maggie, might I have a word with you?" George Sr. asked in his straightforward type of way.

I looked behind him to see that Patty and George were sitting with each other, playing with Emmett, and focused on their conversation.

"Of course, what would you like to talk about?" I asked, trying to plaster a friendly smile back on my face. The first one had surely faded.

"George told me about what happened with that Westerly fellow. Good riddance in my opinion, but he mentioned you were struggling with it. That you even threatened to leave him." George Sr. said,

Falling

emphasizing the word *leave* as if it were unthinkable. Embarrassingly, I too believed it to be so.

"Yes, I may have said that in the heat of the moment, but I have no actual intentions of leaving. I love George and I love Emmett... but I also try to think about the situation logically. Like what would I do if they found George out and sent him to prison? It's complicated. It's not a black or white issue and I'm doing my best." I tried to reassure George Sr. while also knowing I sounded doubtful and unsure. Maybe even a little defensive. The topic caught me off guard and I felt ambushed. Honestly, it was the last thing I wanted to talk about. Especially here and now on such a beautiful outing.

"It isn't that complicated. Either you love him and are a loyal wife, or you're not. It's that simple." He said firmly. "You must understand, George needs you right now more than ever. Fighting in a war...fighting in a war does something to you. It leaves a scar that never goes away. Believe me, I know, and it was the last thing in the world that I wanted for my son. If he only listened to me..." George Sr.'s voice trailed off in his anger. I saw him close his eyes, regain control, and then continue.

"Patty has always understood what it means to be a good wife. She supported me through my difficult days and lifted me up to be the strong supporter and man that I'm meant to be. You need to allow George to be the man that he is meant to be as well. To be your supporter, your protector, and your son's father. That is done through strength, not weakness. Not *talking* about things and letting him know you doubt him, and certainly not turning him into a weakling."

The way George over emphasized the word *talking* felt like he was mocking me. I could feel the anger of the last couple of days build up and my face began to burn. These people looked at me like an outsider, had chastised me, ignored me, and now wanted to paint me as an unloyal and bad wife. Even being compared to Patty felt insulting.

"I do love and support George. He and Emmett are my everyth..." I tried saying before being cut off.

Ellie Lynn

"Do you really Maggie? I don't know about that. I'm just not so sure you are what is best for them."

I couldn't hold my thoughts in any longer. I felt the blood rush to my brain, clouding any self-control, and I felt instantly tired of feeling like I had to bite my tongue so as not to say something wrong 'or unpolite. Growing up I quietly hide as my father abused my mother. No one spoke of it. She became so good at biting her tongue and staying silent, that she still wouldn't speak of the pain years after he died. I learned to tip toe around touchy subjects so as not to cause any problems. Aunt Evie never did, and I no longer wanted to either. The pent-up anger in me finally reached a boiling point. I could no longer contain it.

"I find it quite hypocritical of you to dare lecture me about loyalty and staying with family when you and your wife sent your son away months out of the year because you two couldn't deal with him. You talk about love and yet you were so quick to abandon him. I would never do that to my son. Emmett is my entire world. As for my husband, well that is between him and me. If I choose to leave him, that would be my decision and not yours. If George and I want to talk things through like normal couples do, then that will be our business. I certainly would not want him to turn into a cold and hard man like you." Before I knew it or could even really think about it, the words were out. The words that Aunt Evie would be proud of.

"You don't know who you are talking to missy. How dare you! I would do anything for my son. Anything. He didn't fight in that blasted war to get married to a harpy like you. You've tried to turn him against us, you've taken him from us, and now you mention leaving him? Of taking his son from him. That will not happen." George Sr. spoke in a quiet and firm voice that seemed to resonate through my entire body. He was wrong though; I would never do it. I would never leave. I love George. The unspoken words stuck in my throat, feeling as if it were choking me.

Thinking about it, I shouldn't have said what I did, and at the very least, I should have stepped away. Instead, my back faced the

Falling

open nothingness of space and all I could do was stare into his dark brown cold eyes as I began my descent backwards. I hadn't even felt his hand lightly push against my chest while he made his last point. There wasn't much force required. I didn't see his hand reach out. I hadn't felt fear, and I certainly hadn't expected it. It was as if I missed a step on the stairs. I felt that catch in my breath, and that quickening of my heart. I was falling to my death and the man standing above me stood there and watched coldly. I didn't even know if I screamed. If George heard me, if Emmett felt my anguish of being pushed away from him.

I simply fell into nothingness. There was nothing to catch onto or to break my fall. Nothing I could do or any way that I could change it. Time slowed, and I felt like I spent a lifetime in suspension. Not really moving but acknowledging the wind at my back all the same. As I fell further and further away and as he continued to stare down at me, his face eventually turned to disbelief and then anguish. I felt time speed up again as my body fell faster and faster until it didn't anymore. My body hit the ground.

I see it happen. It doesn't bring fear, anger, or disgust. It's simply what it is. It is my body. My soul is no longer attached, and I feel the most wonderful sense of peace I have ever felt before. It's as if a thousand souls who feel nothing but love for me all embraced me at once. I recognize my grandma Faye, who I have missed so very much. I recognize my father, who has a pure love for me that is no longer clouded by doubt and alcohol. I feel my sweet Annabelle.

Their presence stays with me as my soul lingers like a glimmer of light on water. I'm not ready to leave yet and there is an understanding of that. Is anyone ready for their life to suddenly be over? Is anyone ever ready to leave their loved ones? Like an exhale of breath, I feel myself push towards George and Emmett. They are the ones that matter most to me. I approach the top of the cliff just as George is running to the edge. Patty is still holding onto Emmette. I see my beloved husband drop to his knees and scream. I feel an overwhelming need to comfort him, to let him know I am

Ellie Lynn

okay, that I am no longer at the bottom of that cliff. I just don't know how.

I see George Sr. drop down next to his son to gather him up in his arms. George tries to push him away, but his father holds on. George Sr. begins to cry in anguish too, knowing what he has done. Understanding the unforgivable pain he caused in that single action. I was unsure if he meant to do it or not, but I realize while watching him, that I can't feel any anger towards him. I understand that this broken man acted on protecting his son.

My love now is too great to feel anything as basic as anger. Looking at my husband, I feel his anguish. He's in pain and although I know his journey will be difficult and at times seem impossible, he will get through it. I understand this. I seem to understand *everything* now. I push closer towards George to whisper in his ear, "I'll always be with you, and I will always love you."

I know he can't hear my words, but I sense that he can feel my presence, my love. So, I move on to Emmett. I want to see him, to hold him, to smell him one last time, even though deep within my soul, I know I can't. At least not in the way that I could before. Instead, I feel everything I possibly can at once and I give everything as well. With all the love and energy I can, I reach towards him as if I can embrace him. I truly feel who he is and who he will be, and I am, and always will be, so incredibly proud of him. Of my son!

I stay for as long as I can. I feel the breeze, smell the earth, and connect with the swaying blades of grass like I never could before. It's as if I'm a part of it all now. I'm that wind blowing across Emmett's cheek. I'm that scent reminding George of being in my arms. I'm the sun warming them from the cold.

I stay until George and Emmett begin to leave, Patty and George Sr. trailing behind. Suddenly I feel my companions carrying the very essence of me somewhere else, and I need to go with them. I can't stay here forever. As I start my journey, I can't help but look back. I must see George and Emmett one last time. My soul craves and calls out for them. It is so hard to leave.

Falling

"It's alright Maggie, you can let them go." I hear my grandma Faye say in her earthly voice that is instantly recognizable. I hadn't heard that voice in so long and feared that I had forgotten it. It sounded real, she was real, and this was all truly happening. As strange as it seems, I'm instantly aware that everything is going to be okay. George and Emmett are going to be okay. They will live beautiful lives.

I want to reach out and embrace them, to be with them one last time but I'm gently being pulled away, and finally, I'm ready to go. I know it won't be too long and I will truly be with them again. I will look out for them and shower them with as much love as I can possibly send in the meantime. I know that they will feel it. I will be there when Emmett takes his first steps, I will protect him when he falls, and I will be there waiting for him when his time on earth ends, just as Grandma Faye has for me.

I no longer feel pressure to leave. I feel understanding and patience and a solidarity of having been there before. I feel my soul quiver at the thought of going, of this being my end and my beginning at the same time. So, I linger a moment longer. I watch them for a second more, and then I leave.

The End

About the Author

Ellie Lynn is an author based in the picturesque state of Colorado, where she shares her home with not only three spirited teenagers but also three dogs, a cat, and a slow-moving tortoise named Cosmo.

Ellie's lifelong passion for books and storytelling has been a guiding force in her life. Her fascination with people, keen sense of observation, and talent for perceiving stories from unique perspectives have fueled her creative journey.

With a heart brimming with excitement, Ellie is thrilled to introduce her debut novel, "Falling," to the world. Through her words, readers can expect to embark on a captivating journey, exploring the intricacies of human emotions and relationships. Ellie's storytelling is a testament to her ability to weave narratives that resonate with the depths of the human experience.

But that's not all. Ellie Lynn is not one to rest on her laurels. As her readers turn the pages of "Falling," she is already hard at work on her next literary venture, a novel titled "My Friend Ray." With her unique perspective and storytelling prowess, it's sure to be another compelling addition to her growing body of work.

Join Ellie Lynn on this literary adventure, and let her words sweep you away into worlds both familiar and uncharted. Your feedback and support mean the world to her as she continues to craft stories that touch the heart and stimulate the imagination.

Made in United States
Troutdale, OR
01/24/2024

17109778R00170